Usually when  disaster with ...... for them to realize their danger. This is done for dramatic purposes, to get the audience all worked up about it. Will they go over the falls? Will they find some way to avoid it? Will this waterfall mean certain death and, thus, will they all die, even though that would make no sense at all since—if they do die—there's really nothing left save for the villain to say, "Mwwa-hahah!" and roll the final credits. What fun would that be for the audience?

Anyway: This is not a movie, and so things can, and do, happen a bit differently.

So it was that between the time that Mary stuck her upper body out the hatch and the time that the Argo hurtled over the edge of a Very High Waterfall was no time at all. There was no big build-up, there was no realization that the slow, lazy river had changed into speeding white water rapids, there was no sudden understanding of the peril before her. There wasn't even time for her to shout, "Waterfall!"

Basically the instant she came out of the ship to see what was happening and the instant the ship headed over the edge was the selfsame instant.

Crazy Eight Press is an imprint of Second Age, Inc.

Copyright © 2013 by Peter David
Cover illustration by J.K. Woodward
Design by Aaron Rosenberg
ISBN 978-0-9836877-4-0

All rights reserved. No part of this book may be used or reproduced in any manner whatsoever without written permission except in the case of brief quotations embodied in critical articles and reviews. For information address Crazy 8 Press at the official Crazy 8 website:
www.crazy8press.com

First edition

Fearless

A Story of a Runaway Imagination

By Peter David

And his daughter, Caroline

CRAZY 8 PRESS

Chapter 1

How Mary Nearly Became Fearful

Mary Dear was fearless.
    She had no idea why she was that way; she just always had been, ever since she was a baby. And there are few things more terrifying to parents than an utterly fearless baby.
    Anyone who has ever had to deal with a baby in their life for a long time (as opposed to those people just passing through who clap their hands over their ears and say angrily, "Will you *please* gain control of your child?" because they themselves were *never* crying babies and a bother to others, heavens no), will tell you that babies have different cries for different wants or needs. There's the hungry cry, the uncomfortable cry, the Pay-Attention-to-Me cry, the I-feel-sick cry (which is a really miserable one) just to name a few.
    But the one more we will mention—the most important for

our story—is the frightened cry. A close cousin to the Where-did-everybody-go cry, the frightened cry is what you hear when something really scary shows up: a bad dream; a large dog barking fiercely into the baby's face; a favorite aunt with way-too-big lips all puckered up right in the baby's face, about to plant a big slobbering kiss. You know the kind I mean.

Mary didn't have a frightened cry.

Instead, for the most part, she seemed to have a single cry that could most easily be described—to use a fancy word—as "peremptory," and to use a very unfancy word, "bossy." In that one cry she could put across many different meanings, but never once did she sound scared the way that typical babies did at night when they were calling for someone to help them.

You know how other babies get very scared when there aren't other people around? That's because they haven't yet figured out that when someone leaves the room, they're simply next door. Babies think that if they can't see someone, that person had just disappeared forever, like a melted snowflake. Another fancy way of saying it (adults have so many fancy ways) is "not having object permanence." The simple way is, "Where the heck did everybody go?" Which is why babies can sometimes get really scared when no one's around. They think they're alone in the world, maybe forever.

Mary didn't have any problems with that idea. If her family wasn't around, she simply summoned them. She was never the least bit concerned that they would not return. Maybe she was so confident as a baby that she simply thought that, if she really was abandoned, she'd just manage for herself somehow. We couldn't say for sure. What we can say is that she wasn't at all afraid of being abandoned or alone or, as near as her parents could tell, anything at all.

It was something that was noticed and commented upon by her parents, Patrick and Colleen, and her older brother, Paul. Patrick and Paul seemed more amused by it than anything, and even mildly impressed. Colleen, however, saw it—correctly, as it so happened—as something that might be a serious problem for her in the future.

It was natural for Colleen to think this because, of the two adults in the family, Colleen was serious. Very serious.

Her husband was very *not* serious. This was why he always liked telling stories of the fantastic and amazing, talking about them so excitedly that it was almost as if he was describing things he had seen first hand. It was like, to him, the differences between fact and fantasy didn't really matter all that much. "You," Colleen would say, "have far too much imagination," to which Patrick would say, half-kiddingly but half seriously, "Well you, my dear, have none, so someone has to make up for it." It's actually kind of amazing that the two of them were a couple, but fortunately, opposites attract, and that's what happened here.

As for Paul, her older brother, he decided to make himself his sister's guardian, determined to protect her from her inability to feel fear should that result in any unforeseen trouble. It was a worthy goal to have, but sadly not terribly realistic. He had school, he had his own life to deal with, and he could not be there for his sister every moment of every day. Which is what he would have had to be if he intended to keep his baby sister out of harm's way, especially when she began crawling and then, even worse, walking.

Mary didn't waste much time crawling; maybe she thought it was beneath her. She crawled for maybe a month, displaying at a young age a knack for finding the smallest nooks and crannies of the house to hide herself, so much so that her father swore the child was part leprechaun because she could disappear at will.

And then one day, Mary pulled herself to standing with the aid of a chair, glanced around the living room, thought about it for a moment as if she was working it all out in her head, and then walked with complete confidence from one end of the salon to the other. The way she did it, it was like she was remembering how to do it from a past life rather than learning it for the first time.

That might have been possible, since Mary was something of a mystery, even to her parents. She was clearly a bright child, in addition to being fearless, with eyes as dark as the bottomless sea and a sturdy body that was constantly tilted forward as if sprinting headlong toward mischief.

Curiously, she was also missing a hand; her right arm ended in a stump at the wrist. Do not sob tears of "poor child" for her because she had no memory of having a hand there rather than a nub of skin-covered bone. Indeed, the first time at a playground when a rather nasty boy tried to grab a bright rubber ball from her left hand, Mary whipped her right arm around and gave him a solid crack against the side of his little skull that sent him howling and stumbling to his mother. Mary looked at her stub of a forearm as if seeing it for the first time, and a slow smile crept like an arched caterpillar across her face.

At which point she said her first word: a very satisfied, "Good."

Being able to smack people around with her club-like arm only made her even more fearless. Because of that, Colleen had a difficult problem in front of her. Certainly it was nice having a brave daughter who wasn't afraid to stand up to bullies.

But Colleen felt that her daughter needed to have *some* sense of fear, because without it, her behavior could well lead her into total disaster. As Mary's mother, she felt it was her job to make sure her daughter understood that there were some things you should be afraid of. Colleen may not have had much of an imagination when it came to coming up with stories about elves and fairies, but any mother in the world can picture a daughter with no sense of fear standing on the edge of a roof (for instance) and trying to fly because she isn't the least bit afraid of falling. You see the problem.

And so, beginning shortly after Mary turned one year old, Colleen started doing everything she could with her daughter that was safe and yet terrifying.

Instead of taking her to films that were calming and happy and friendly, she looked for the most frightening and horrific movies that she could find. People in the audience scowled at her for taking a child to such scary films, but she ignored them.

At amusement parks, she skipped the boring kiddy rides and instead strapped Mary and herself into the most dizzying, vomit-inducing rides that she could find. Adults would scream in terror as rides would twist and turn, and Mary would be belted and wedged into her child seat, air blasting past her face, with screeches from the grown-ups ringing in her round little ears.

At bedtime, Colleen had used to read her daughter such stories as *A Little Princess,* or even science fiction books like *The Time Machine*—very grown-up stories, yes, but Mary was a very grown-up young lady, with a vocabulary that many adults would have envied. Now, though, Colleen set aside such friendlier adventures, not to mention airy tales of fairies and unicorns. Instead Mary was sent off to slumber with the tales of Edgar Allen Poe and other such scary writers. For (Colleen reasoned) how could any child hear a story before bedtime about a murderer being haunted by the heartbeat of a man he killed and not wake up screaming from bad dreams?

As hard as it may be for you to do so, we ask you to forgive her actions. It might seem like Colleen was abusing her daughter, treating her terribly by trying to scare the living daylights out of her. We can only assure you that she did not do these things lightly, or out of anger or meanness. She did it for the noble reason of trying to make sure that her little girl did not run headlong into danger and so bring her life to a tragic and early end.

Besides which, it didn't work anyway.

At the films, she would watch with fascination as the characters on screen tried to avoid getting killed. Her first spoken word, as mentioned, was "Good," but her first sentence was "Look out!" to provide warning to the heroes when danger threatened. On the other hand, if things went badly in the movie and one or more of the characters wound up dying, she would simply shrug and say, "Not fast enough" to explain to her mother just why it was that the characters had not been able to make it to the end of the movie.

She never showed fear.

At the amusement parks, while others shrieked either in entertainment or in genuine fear for their lives, Mary was so calm you'd think she was out for a ride in the country.

She never showed fear.

At bedtime, she asked for more tales by the same scary author. Seeing that things weren't working out the way she wanted them to, Colleen said no. Mary simply took this as a challenge and taught herself to read so that by age three she was hiding under the covers with a flashlight, reading stories about being cut in half by a giant, razor sharp pendulum or being buried alive.

She never showed fear.

Now some of you might think that maybe she really did know fear, but that she was simply really, really, really good at hiding it. We can tell you with complete confidence that that was not the case. She was simply impossible to frighten.

When she was four years old, however, this changed.

Almost. It almost changed. It wound up being the same, actually, but it came very close to changing. And had it changed, everything else that happened, including her running away from home at age eight, her long journey, and her repeatedly facing death in various horrible ways would never have happened and this book would be exactly one thousand, eight hundred and ninety eight words long.

Here is how Mary nearly came to be frightened.

Her mother had taken her shopping, and was standing at a street corner dealing with far more bags than she really should have been. Mary was belted into her stroller. She was getting rather large for it, for she was big for her age. Not big as in overweight, but big as in tall and getting taller, with wide shoulders and long legs and arms that were hurrying to keep up with the legs.

They were waiting for a traffic light to change and one of the shopping bags chose that moment to rip. Colleen had been shopping for clothes for Mary, who was growing so quickly that her mother had to go clothes shopping almost every single month. When the bag tore, Colleen let out an angry cry when she saw the clothing spill all over the street. She was now going to have to find a way to jam everything from three bags into two, and wasn't looking forward to the challenge.

Mary paid her no mind, for her attention was captured by something else entirely. The child leaned forward in her stroller, and she gasped in surprise and excitement.

There was an alleyway across the street, and pedestrians were walking past it without giving it a glance, for what kind of person stands around staring down alleyways?

As a result, no one noticed the lion cub hiding in the shadows.

Even if they had, they probably would have figured they were wrong, deciding that it was simply an overlarge alley cat. What, after all, would a lion cub be doing in the middle of the city? It made no sense, and usually things that made no sense simply didn't exist.

But Mary did not question the sense of a lion cub that she saw across the street. Instead she simply accepted it for what it was.

The lion cub and she locked eyes, and even though she had never seen the creature before, she felt instantly attached to it. Whether the lion cub felt likewise about her, we could not say, but it seemed no less interested in Mary than she was in it. Its fur was a deep, golden brown, and it lowered its head, its ears flattening, as if it were planning to hunt her. After a few moments, however—as if recognizing her from somewhere—the lion cub relaxed. It flopped onto its stomach, resting its head on its paws and continued to regard her with open curiosity.

Mary, understandably, was intrigued.

A normal child would have tried to call her mother's attention to what she was seeing. But Mary, seeing that her mother was busy trying to reorganize the shopping bags, decided not to interrupt her. Mother clearly had other things on her mind, and the lion cub was Mary's business anyway.

Mary might only have had one hand to work with, but the little fingers on it were very nimble. She was able to undo the belt that was keeping her in place with no trouble. Pushing the belt aside, Mary clambered out of her stroller. Colleen, busy with the bags, didn't notice.

Mary bolted into the street in order to get to the lion cub on the other side. She did so fearlessly.

The truck that was hurrying to get through the intersection as the light was turning to yellow did not see her.

Now if she'd been left to herself, Mary might well have made it across the street with no problem. Her mother, however, saw her daughter's danger too late to do anything about it except to let out an alarmed and horrified shriek.

In response, Mary froze in her tracks, her head snapping around to see what all the fuss was about. The scream alerted the driver, and he was still too high up to see exactly what the problem was. But the terrified shriek was more than enough to let him know that something was very wrong, and so he slammed his feet on the brakes.

It made no difference. He was moving too quickly, and had Mary remained where she was, all the scrubbing in the world would never have gotten all of her remains out of the truck's grillwork.

But she did not remain where she was. All she knew was that one moment she was standing in the street, and the next she was hurtling through the air. Someone had picked her up and flung her clear of the truck, throwing her as if she were a shot put. Her mother angled toward her, and didn't catch her so much as collide with her, stumbling backwards and falling onto the sidewalk with a bone-jarring thump.

Immediately Mary was on her feet, and yet again she ran away from her mother. Or at least she tried to, but Colleen snagged her by the ankle and pulled her back, and held her tightly. "Don't run away from me," she whispered fiercely into her daughter's ear, "don't ever run away from me." Then both of them looked upon the scene that was awaiting them in the street.

There was what appeared to be little more than a heap of clothing wearing a person lying out in the middle of the road, directly in front of the truck. The trucker had gotten out of the driver's seat and was crouched over the bundle, his hands moving in vague, random patterns, and he was saying, "I'm sorry, lady! I'm so sorry!" In the distance, remarkably, there was already the sound of ambulance sirens, as if they had known this was about to happen and had only been lying in wait. How they were going to get to the spot was something of a mystery, because cars had stopped moving in all directions thanks to the truck coming to a halt in the middle of the intersection.

It was obvious to all what had happened: The old woman, seeing Mary's danger, had run toward her and thrown her to safety, but had been unable to get clear of the truck herself.

Mary's mother was trembling. Mary herself was not. It wasn't that she didn't care about the woman's fate; she very much did. And it wasn't as if she didn't care that she herself had nearly died; she was very much aware of the closeness of her call.

But you know how sometimes people have tight escapes, and they come through them, and afterwards they start shaking uncontrollably when they realize just how near a thing it had been?

Mary wasn't like that. Her mother was. She was not.

"Is that lady going to go to heaven?" she asked her mother.

"I don't know, honey," said Colleen, and it was true, she didn't know, but she had her suspicions.

Mary thought about that for a moment and then said firmly, "I need to see her. Right now."

"Mary, that's not a good idea..."

But Mary looked at her in a way that made it clear that she didn't care whether it was a good idea or not. It was her idea, and she simply wasn't going to accept a "no."

So her mother nodded and, taking her firmly by her left hand, led Mary through the crowd. As she drew closer, Mary could see the bundle of clothing more clearly; a tatty gray coat with bare feet sticking out from one end and a head thick with gray-white hair and a broad-brimmed hat on the other end. How the hat was still on her head, Mary could not begin to guess.

The woman was rolled over onto her side and Mary was aware, as she approached, that people were whispering and pointing and saying, "That's her. That's the little girl."

And for the first time, it really began to dawn on her just what she had done. This woman was likely going to heaven, and it was her fault. If she hadn't gone running out into the street, this would not have happened.

She was hit, all of a sudden, with the realization that she could do things that made bad things happen to other people. It was a pretty scary idea, especially for a four-year old girl. And if the idea were allowed to take hold in her, blossom and grow like a flower, it would eventually bloom into full-blown fear.

The fear hadn't arrived yet, but she was most definitely filled with sorrow.

She knelt down in front of the woman, and tears began to dribble down her face, and over her mouth. "I'm so sorry," she whispered.

The old woman looked up at her through eyes that had seen far, far too much life. Then she asked the oddest question: "Is there still war?"

Mary blinked in confusion. "Yes. There are wars."

"Oh well. I tried." Then she studied the child as if trying to figure out what to make of her. "You're fearless," croaked the old woman.

"Yes," said Mary, which was still true for the moment. She fished for something to say, and then offered: "Sometimes I suck my thumb. I can't help myself."

The old woman reached up with surprising strength and grabbed Mary by the back of the head. Colleen gasped in alarm and reached for her, but it was not quick enough, and the old woman pulled Mary's face right to hers. Her breath was surprisingly sweet; surprising because old people tended to have an old people smell, and this woman didn't have it. Perhaps she was so old that all the smells in her body had already withered and died.

"*They* will try to make you afraid," the old woman said. "Because of this. And things to come. Mark me: *They* will try."

"Who's 'they?'"

"The great unseen *They*. The same *They* who does everything else that nobody likes, and people shake their heads over it and cluck and say, 'How could *They* let this happen?' *They* will want you..." She paused, steadying her voice. "*They* will want you to be afraid, because keeping people afraid is how *They* stay in charge. But you are fearless. To fight *Them*, you have to stay that way."

"I don't want to fight anyone," said Mary. Yet she knew this was not entirely true. There was something deep inside her, something that had no name, but in her mind's eye, it was like a great, winged animal of some sort, filled with a golden glow. It had first stirred that day on the playground when she had battered the bully with her club hand, and when she had said "Good," it had been partly from the wind caused by its wings rustling within her. Now, hearing of the possibility of a fight, the glowing animal had stirred to life once more, extending its head and rustling its wings, letting her know that it was prepared to do battle on her behalf.

The old woman ignored her words, as if she knew that they were simply something a little girl was supposed to say rather than what she truly wanted to say. "If you take one lesson away from this moment, it is this: To be fearless does not mean to be reckless. The reckless person jumps off the cliff without hesitation. To hesitate is not to be fearful; it is wisdom. Be fearless but be wise. If you do this, you can defeat *Them*. Do you understand?"

"Yes," said Mary, who did not.

"You do not," said the old woman, who apparently could smell a lie as others could smell stinkweed or the corpse of a rotting skunk. "But you will when you're older."

"How much older?"

The old woman's eyes seemed to dig deeply into Mary's own, as if digging for gold.

"Eight, I should think," she said, and then she lay her head down on her arm. Her hand released its grip on Mary, and Mary stepped back from her, watching her with fascination.

The ambulance had drawn as close as it could, and now the medics were shoving their way through the crowd, shouting for everyone to step aside. They were pushing a stretcher on wheels that was obviously for the victim. Colleen pulled Mary clear, and Mary did not fight against the tug of her mother even though she wanted to stay at the old woman's side because she felt there was a good deal more to learn from her.

Colleen picked her up and turned away to face one of the medics, who took one look at Mary's stumped right arm and gasped in horror. "Oh, you poor child! Morrie! We're looking for a little girl's hand! Find her hand!" he shouted. "Maybe we can still reattach it!" His companion, nodding like a bobble-head doll, immediately started looking around.

"She's not the patient! She's always been this way," Colleen said.

"There's no blood," Mary pointed out, holding the stump out for him to see more clearly. There was a touch of *You must be stupid* in her voice, but she was far too polite to say it aloud. "If I'd just lost a hand, there would be blood, yes?"

"Oh. Right," said the medic, looking a bit embarrassed that he had to have the obvious pointed out to him by a child.

"Over here!" the truck driver was shouting. One of the medics quickly tipped his hat to Colleen and Mary and they hastily sped the wheeled stretcher over to the scene of the accident and the actual person who required their talents.

Colleen set Mary down and dropped to one knee. "Are you all right, baby?" she said. "You scared Mommy so."

"I'm sorry," Mary said once more, and she truly was. She loved her mother more than just about anything in the world, save for her father and her brother and scary stories, frightening movies, and terrifying roller coasters, and she was upset that she had caused her mother such distress. "It's just that I wanted to go pet the lion cub."

"Lion cub?" Her mother stared at her, not understanding. "What...what lion cub—?"

Mary turned and pointed to the alleyway, but somehow she knew even before she did so that the lion cub was going to be gone. And so it was, without even so much as a few stray hairs from its fur to mark that it had been there at all.

At that moment, there was an outraged cry of annoyance from one of the medics: "Is this supposed to be some sort of joke?"

Mary pulled forward and this time her mother, curious, allowed herself to be dragged along. It was with some effort that they managed to make their way to the front, and there they discovered that both medics were exchanging angry words with the trucker, who was alternating between stammering in confusion and stuttering in anger.

"There are injured people who are genuinely in need of us!" one of the medics was saying. "And we should be off helping them instead of standing here taking care of a pile of old clothes!"

At which point he seemingly kicked the old woman, except there was not, in fact, an old woman there. A large gray coat, yes, and a hat. There was no sign of any body within.

The trucker looked as if he thought he was going out of his mind, and then his desperate gaze rested on Mary. Quickly he pointed and said, "The little girl! She had a whole conversation with her!"

Together, the medics turned to see where the trucker was pointing. They paled slightly when they saw who it was, because they still felt embarrassed having tried to find her hand when there was none to be had. Mary stared at them calmly and it was for Colleen to say, "She did. I saw it."

The larger of the two medics took a step forward and said challengingly, "Where did she go, little girl?" as if Mary had somehow managed to hide the old woman inside one of her socks, or perhaps the lining of her coat.

Mary replied, "She must have gone to heaven." Which, as far as Mary knew, was the truth.

It was, as it turned out, the best answer anyone could come up with, and so it was the one that everyone accepted. Everyone, that is, except for the medics, who simply wrote "false alarm" on their report sheets.

And Mary's path did eventually cross with the old woman's once again, but that would not be for a very long time.

Chapter 2

How Mary Was Wakened from a Sound Sleep One Night

Mary had never seen anyone in hysterics before. In case you never have either, it's kind of like a temper tantrum, but far scarier. A temper tantrum is a howl of frustration when you're not getting your way, or maybe an attempt to grab some attention, but that's all. Usually parents deal with it by just walking away from it until the child tossing the tantrum realizes that things are not going to work out as hoped for. At that point the tantrum just seems to be too much work and usually stops.

That is a tantrum.

Hysterics are something very different. People don't become hysterical because they're hoping to get something out of it. Hysteria happens because someone is driven to it much like a car heading off the edge of a road and down a steep drop. The hysterics are what you hear and see on the way down, and they don't stop until the person having them hits the bottom.

It can be a terribly frightening thing for anyone to see, much less a child.

Luckily, Mary didn't get frightened since she was fearless. It was doubly lucky, actually, because Anna was the person having the hysterics.

We know this means nothing to you. You're wondering, "Who's Anna?" It's a fair question. We haven't told you yet. So in order for you to understand why it was heartbreaking for Mary to see Anna thrashing about on her bed, sobbing piteously, howling "*It's gone, it's gone forever!*" over and over again, with the occasional, "*What am I going to do?!*" thrown in for good measure, we will tell you all about Anna.

"Anna" was short for Annabelle, and her parents sometimes called her "Belle" for some reason that meant something to them, but she preferred "Anna" as did her friends. Her full name was Annabelle Whitford-Brown, and she was a few months older, but many decades wiser, than Mary. At least it seemed that way to Mary, because as far as she was concerned, Anna could do no wrong and knew everything about everything. That might have been because Anna was one grade ahead of Mary since her birthday put her on the other side of the school year. A handful of months between adults mean nothing; between children, it can mean a great deal.

The girls had known each other since they were little, because their mothers had met each other as a result of one of those classes or things that mothers do together and children put up with because, well, it's expected.

The first time that Mary and Anna met, Mary was busy exploring the bottom of the ocean. She was doing this using her favorite means of getting around: a cardboard box. Mary adored cardboard boxes, the bigger the better. She liked them far better than the things that actually came in them, even when they were playthings. Her parents had learned this the year before, when they had bought her a little car that she could actually sit in and pedal up and down their driveway and from one end of the block to the other (but no further). They had been dismayed (although that dismay had been tinged with amusement) when Mary had crawled inside the large box that the car had come in and pretended to drive that. "Why in the world are you driving the box?" Colleen asked her, confused. "You can't go anywhere!"

"I can go everywhere," Mary corrected her ever so politely. "In the toy car, I can only go up and down the block. In this, I can go to every block in every city in the world, as fast as I want."

"You have quite an imagination," her father said.

This was very true. Most children have excellent imaginations, but Mary, being fearless, had one that was absolutely superb, because the main limit on imagination is a deep-seated fear of just how far it can go. This is something that's a bigger problem for adults than it is for children. Adults are very often afraid of imagining things, since imagining often requires change from The Way Things Are, and since adults are settled in their ways, change is a Very Scary Thing.

So Mary would on occasion ride in the actual car her parents had bought her so that they wouldn't feel too badly, but on rainy days or snow days or any other days or times of day where chugging along in her pedal car wasn't an option, Mary could be found happily seated in the cardboard box, driving down the streets of Paris or through Atlantis or across the African veldt or the Australian outback.

And on one of those days, when she was four years old and busy driving along the bottom of the ocean (because her box was serving as a submarine that day instead of a car), there came a knock at her bedroom door. Her mother always knocked before entering Mary's room, and that knock always called Mary back from wherever she happened to be. She could have ignored the knock and stayed in whatever far off land she happened to be visiting, but she was well behaved and so felt that when the knock was sounded, she should immediately return. Which she did.

"Yes?" she said.

The door opened and Mary saw that her mother was standing there with a little girl. Her purple dress crinkled when she walked, and her round face was surrounded with blonde curls that seemed to bounce around all by themselves as if they were alive and each curl had a mind of its own. She had a purple bow in her hair that sat cheerfully to one side.

Mary loved purple.

"Mary, this is Anna," said her mother. "Her mother and she came over to visit. We thought maybe you'd want to play together." This was adult talk for, *Please, please, please play together, so we don't have to worry about you.*

"Uh-kay," said Mary uncertainly. Mary tended to like things just so. She wasn't afraid of new things (of course) but she preferred to be in charge of when those new things were introduced.

Her mother stepped out, leaving Anna behind. Anna studied Mary seated in the box, one pale eyebrow raised in thought. The two girls looked each other up and down for a long moment.

"You're missing a hand," said Anna.

"I know."

"Let's find it, before your mother notices." She glanced around the room. "Where was the last place you saw it?"

"I never had it, actually. I was born this way."

"Oh." Anna frowned at that. "How do you applaud?"

"Like this." Mary thumped the stub of her wrist against her

open palm and it made a satisfying slapping sound. Then, wanting to talk about something other than her missing hand, she said, "I like your dress. And your bow."

"Thank you." Anna's voice was as airy as a spring breeze. "I like your submarine."

"You know it's a submarine?" Mary was surprised. Her parents could never tell what her cardboard box was from one day to the next. As she had gotten older, and even though the box became more battered from use, it nevertheless had expanded beyond simply being a car. It was a car, a boat, a submarine, a space rocket... whatever means of getting around that she needed. But no one except for her had ever been able to tell what it was simply by looking at it. "How do you know?"

"There's water dripping from it."

There wasn't really. It was imaginary water, and even Mary hadn't seen it at first. But of course it made sense, because if she'd been underwater just a minute or so earlier, naturally she would have water on the submarine.

"That's right," she said, and was officially Very Impressed by Anna.

"There's a place," and Anna's voice dropped in that way people do when they're saying something secret, "on the very bottom of the ocean called the Mary Anna's Trench."

"It's got both our names!" Mary said, her eyes widening in surprise.

"Uh huh." Anna's head bobbed up and down, and her curls bobbed up and down and sideways and this way and that way. "And you know what's at the very bottom of the Mary Anna's Trench?" Her voice dropped even lower and she glanced right and left to make sure no one was listening. "*Mermaids.*"

"*Excellent!*" This sounded absolutely marvelous to Mary. "Let's go!"

"Can I come?"

Mary was surprised that Anna even had to ask. "Sure!"

Anna squeezed into the box behind Mary. "Ready?" said Mary.

"Always," Anna said with that self-assurance that would mark their relationship from that point on.

The submarine promptly sank through the floor, through and past the living room where the mothers were chatting and paying no attention to the passing submarine, and it kept going until it hit the river that Mary had decided ran underneath their house. That river led directly to the ocean, and they followed it until it spilled them out into the Atlantic. It was a calm day and the ocean was flat and blue and stretched as far as the eye could see and beyond that, as flat as glass.

"Ready to submerge," said Mary with authority, which meant that she was ready to go under water.

"Aye aye, Captain," said Anna, who was polite enough to allow Mary to be in charge even though she was older and technically could have taken command, because that's just how it works.

The submarine promptly sank beneath the surface of the ocean and down and down, and Mary steered it to the Mary Anna's Trench, and there they ran into mermaids who were having all kinds of problems with the demands of their fathers, and there was a whole adventure that we really don't have to go into at this point other than to say that it was wonderfully amazing and it's a shame you couldn't have been along for the ride, but there simply wouldn't have been any more room in the cardboard box even if you'd happened to stop by.

And when they finally resurfaced in response to yet another knock from Mary's mother, they emerged as the best of friends.

Because really, when two people have to team up to get their submarine out of the clutches of a gigantic octosquid, how could they *not* wind up being best friends? (Told you it was exciting.)

Sometimes Anna would come to Mary's house, and sometimes Mary would go to Anna's, which was far grander than Mary's, but Anna never made a big deal about it or acted like she was better because of it. Or they would go someplace together, such as a playground, and scale to the top of the climbing structure which was actually about seven feet off the ground but to them was a tower that stretched miles into the air, from the top of which they could look out and see everywhere and anywhere, from the lowest depth to the tallest mountain.

Anna draped an arm around her friend's shoulders and said, "It never gets better than this." Mary wasn't entirely sure what Anna meant by that, but she said it with a very official sounding voice and so Mary figured it was true.

Through their years together, Anna told her many wise and wonderful things, secret things that adults didn't want kids to know, but about which Anna was a great expert. The girls could not have been closer if they had been sisters.

One day, when Mary was seven, something truly major happened. She and her mother were out and about and suddenly Mary gasped. This sound alone startled Colleen so greatly that she jumped slightly, for Mary rarely got worked up about anything. So if something got her to react in that way, it must have been rather impressive. To Mary, it most definitely was. To her mother, less so.

There, by the curbside outside someone's house, was the largest box that Mary had ever seen. It was easily big enough for her, Anna, and any number of children. And it was simply lying there on its side, forgotten, abandoned, alone.

Colleen stared at the box, trying to figure out just what it was that was getting such a reaction from her daughter. When she looked down to ask her, she found that Mary was no longer there. She was scared for a moment, because that day when Mary had run off and nearly been run over was never far from her thoughts, but then she realized that, no, Mary had not suddenly sprinted off into traffic once again or done some other dangerous thing. Instead Mary's voice echoed from inside the box as she called, "Isn't this the most magnificent thing in the world?"

"*That?*"

"Of course it is. It is a magical transportation device that can take you anywhere you need to go. And it changes to be whatever makes sense for it to be when you get there. Like, if you're going to the moon, it becomes the rocket ship, or if you're going to be on a highway, it becomes a car, or..."

"It's a refrigerator box," said her mother, still not understanding. "It's an empty refrigerator box that someone is throwing out."

"*Throwing out?*" Mary had never been that shocked in her entire life. How could people not see the endless possibilities of this amazing, stupendous, gargantuan box? Were adults *that* lacking in imagination? Never had Mary felt as sorry for adults as she had at that moment. "We can't just *leave* it." She could not have spoken with more determination if they had come upon a baby lying in a basket with a sign attached to it that read, *Please give this child a good home or feed it to passing hungry dogs, we really don't care either way.*

"We most certainly *can* leave it," Colleen informed her. "Now come out and let's go."

There was deathly silence from within the box for a time, and then slowly, on her hands and knees—not begging, but simply because that was the easiest way to come out of the box—Mary came forward and stuck her head out. There was no pleading on her face, because begging wasn't Mary's style. Instead she simply fixed her gaze upon her mother, and in her calmest, softest voice, she said, "Mommy...I've never asked you for anything."

This may sound ridiculous, but the truth is that Mary wasn't exaggerating. If you didn't count things like, when she was a baby, "demanding" to be fed, the fact was that Mary really *hadn't* ever asked her for anything. She had toys, yes, given her as gifts for which she was always careful to say, "Thank you." But Mary's parents or friends or relatives had always done the buying, always without asking her. And sometimes she eyed toys in windows or at stores. However, when she was asked, "Would you like that?" she always replied, "I'm just looking at it." This might have seemed like some sort of clever plan to get her parents to offer to buy whatever it was, but really, she was merely an undemanding child.

Even now, with this empty box that clearly meant the world to her, she couldn't bring herself to do anything other than let her mother know what she wanted and point out that she wasn't big on asking for things. What she didn't say, but could have—and what her mother heard in her own head—was this: *What kind of mother are you, that you would refuse to give something to your child when she's never asked for anything before, and it doesn't even cost any money?*

Colleen looked deeply into herself and didn't like the sort of person who would refuse her daughter's request under such circumstances.

So it was that the next day, when Anna came over to visit, Mary brought her into her bedroom and Anna stopped dead.

There was no longer any available space in the room. Every square inch that had previously been unoccupied was now filled up by the refrigerator box, lying on its side, with the end toward the door opened wide. The top was decorated with an assortment of pictures: Unicorns, fairies, rainbows, castles, and of course lions, because they were still Mary's favorite animals, particularly lion cubs. Ever since that long ago day, she continued to glance down alleyways or around corners, hoping to spot that elusive cub, but she had never seen it again. Her secret hope had been that it might come bouncing out of the box, because no container could be this spectacular and not have a special magic to it. But the lion cub had not cooperated, which didn't make the box any less fantastical.

In big, carefully stenciled lettering on the front were the words, *The Argo*. Mary had asked her parents for the name of a famous legendary ship, and her father had promptly suggested the name, which had been a ship sailed by a group of famous heroes with names like Jason and Hercules (yes, *the* Hercules.) Mary figured that if it was good enough for Hercules, it was certainly good enough for her. So the *Argo* was the chosen name.

Anna's breath was literally taken away. Fortunately it quickly came back and she said, "It's the most magnificent thing in the world."

"That's what I said."

"Well, you were right."

They climbed into the box and seconds later were heading to the moon. They traveled there, and to planets beyond, for well over two hours until the knock of Mary's mother at the door summoned her back. As always, Mary answered the knock and instantly released the rocket from the grip of her boundless imagination. It was not the cleanest of landings, though, because Mary and Anna had been so deep into their imaginary world that the knocking startled them, like waking someone from a deep sleep by slamming a pair of cymbals together in their ear. Because of that, the box thumped loudly on the floor as it returned to the boring, ordinary world, with the shag carpeting barely absorbing the impact.

"Mary?" came Colleen's concerned voice, and without waiting for Mary's permission, she opened the door and entered. She looked in confusion at her daughter and Anna, who were peering out from within the box. "Is everything all right? I thought I heard a thud..."

"Rough landing," Mary said.

"Oh. All right," said Colleen. Then, with a patient look on her face, she went on to ask, "Are you sure you still want this box? There's no room for anything else in here."

"There's nothing else I need," said Mary, and Anna bobbed her head in agreement. Who could possibly need anything else when this magnificent crate was here?

Colleen shrugged in that way that mothers do when their children aren't doing anything they can take action against, but aren't make a terrible amount of sense. She figured that eventually Mary would tire of having the thing in her room and ask for it to be removed.

A year later, there were even more decorations on the box, and it was still nestled in the room. Colleen had long ago made peace with having the thing in her daughter's room, lifting the box up and vacuuming under it, and maneuvering around it to make Mary's bed. She was still convinced that the box was not a permanent addition, but wasn't holding her breath that Mary's love for it was going to run its course anytime soon.

To Mary's delight, and Colleen's mild annoyance, Patrick seemed to enjoy the box being there as much as the girls did. For instance: Occasionally Mary would have Anna over for a sleepover, and the two girls would lie on their bellies inside the refrigerator box, their heads propped on their hands, and Patrick would tell them ghost stories. When Mary's brother, Paul, had been young, he had preferred stories of adventure and leprechauns and other fantastical tales, but thanks to Colleen's early influence, Mary loved stories that were bizarre and spooky.

Patrick particularly liked telling the stories to both Mary and Anna, because Anna would at various times gasp or shudder or duck deep inside the sleeping bag when hearing some of the creepier tales. But Mary would take it all in, as if watching a tennis match, and occasionally interrupt with questions about the many aspects of ghosts, ghouls, and graveyards. She learned about poltergeists and specters, hungry ghosts, crossroad ghosts, psychopomps, and succubi, and many more besides.

It was one of those things where it seemed like it might be important someday.

She could not have been more right.

So...

You may remember how earlier we were talking about Mary having to deal with Anna being in hysterics. It has taken us a bit of a while to get around to it, but now at last we have arrived. We must warn you, though that it's not a happy moment in the lives of either girl. In fact, it's pretty upsetting. So brace yourself (if you must), because here is what happened.

Mary was used to her regular routine, particularly in the evening. She had family time until a certain hour, and then she was in her pajamas at a certain time, and in bed at a certain time, at which point her day was effectively over.

So it was very confusing to Mary that one evening, after she had gone to bed, after she had heard a goodnight story, been sung to, been tucked in, been kissed on the forehead and the proper "I love you's" said, when after all of that, the door to her room was opened and light flooded in from the hallway. Mary had just been falling asleep, and the first fingers of dream were just starting to tickle her under the chin, so she was momentarily confused and disoriented from having her evening going in a direction it ordinarily didn't.

"Mary," came her mother's voice, and it was filled with barely restrained concern. This was immediately enough to prompt Mary to think that something disastrous had occurred. That perhaps her father had suffered some manner of heart attack, or mother had suddenly realized they were out of syrup and thus there would be none available for pancakes tomorrow, or some similar disaster. "You need to get up."

"Is the house on fire?" She sniffed deeply to see if the air was clear of smoke. "Did I do something bad that I completely forgot to tell you about, because if so, I can promise you, I didn't do it."

"No, nothing like that," her mother assured her. "Just get dressed as quickly as you can. Here," and she already had clothes in her hand and was tossing them onto Mary's bed. "Put them on over your pajamas if it will take less time. We need to go."

"Are criminals after us?" Mary was doing as her mother instructed. She was wearing a nightgown and was busy pulling a sweater on over it. Her voice was briefly muffled by it as she yanked it over her head. "Are monsters rising from the grave and storming the city? Is an earthquake going to be swallowing the house?"

"Good lord, child," said Colleen, "where do you get these—?" Then she caught herself, and instead said, "Anna's mother called. Anna's in trouble and her mother thinks that you may be the only one who can help her."

Although Mary had not been moving slowly in getting dressed, neither had she been moving quickly. But those words from her mother slapped some speed into her, and within seconds she had finished with the sweater and was pulling a pair of sweat pants on underneath the nightgown. Then she stuffed the bottom of the nightgown into the top of the sweat pants and yanked on her shoes without bothering with socks. "Ready," she said briskly.

Another child might have asked for more details, wanting to know exactly what was wrong with her friend. Not Mary. As far as Mary was concerned, knowing that Anna needed her was all that mattered.

Patrick was waiting at the front door, the car keys in his hand. Without a word, he opened the door for them and they hurried out the door and into the family car.

On the way over, even though Mary wasn't asking, Colleen told her everything that she knew. Unfortunately, it wasn't all that much. Anna's mother (whose name, it should be noted, was Helen, just in the event that you were wondering) had called Colleen all in a panic. Anna had had some sort of attack, and was hysterical and weeping, and Helen was at her wit's end trying to calm her daughter down. She made it clear that she was not thrilled with the idea of dragging Mary into this, and she told Colleen that if she didn't want any part of it, she would fully understand. It was not, after all, her problem.

Colleen had replied that if it was Helen and Anna's problem, that automatically made it hers and Mary's problem as well. Nor was she worried about Mary's ability to handle just about anything that was tossed her way.

"You were right," Mary said with a nod.

Colleen smiled, although it was not a happy smile, but more the smile of a woman who was dealing with a bad situation the best she could.

In a short time, they arrived at Anna's house. Anna's father was at the front door, making Mary think that perhaps the entire purpose of fathers was to serve as the guardians of the front door (we would tell you the name of Anna's father, but it isn't important, and besides, we forget.) Even from the front hallways, they could hear Anna howling. Colleen couldn't help herself; she was rooted to the spot at the bottom of the stairs, paralyzed by the sound of a child in such agony. Mary, however, did not hesitate. She sprinted up the steps, taking them two at a time, trailing her left hand along the wall to balance herself.

She went straight up to Anna's room. Helen was inside, seated on the edge of Anna's bed, looking distressed. And Anna was lying in a heap on her bed, crying "*It's gone, it's gone forever!*" and "*What am I going to do?!*" She wasn't saying what exactly had disappeared, though. There was a man as well, standing nearby with a long, pointy beard and a black bag at his feet. He was holding what appeared to be a vial of pills in his hand. Obviously he was a doctor. He looked in confusion at Mary and said with deep, rumbling authority, "This is no place for children," in the kind of voice that was designed to scare any child out of the room.

Mary was not any child.

"This is a child's bedroom," she snapped off. "Obviously it is a place for children. You're an adult. Don't *you* have a bedroom?"

The doctor's beard seemed to stick out all on its own, quivering with its very own anger from having been talked to that way. But before he could bluster over her attitude or complain to Colleen that, if this was her daughter, she needed to do a better job of mothering her, Anna—through choked-back sobs—said, "Mary? Is that Mary?"

"It is, honey," Helen said to her daughter. "I asked her to come." She was talking quickly, obviously in order to keep Anna talking, because if she was talking, then she couldn't be howling. "I didn't know what else to do, and I hoped that—"

Anna's eyes were red-rimmed, and the more she spoke, the easier it was to hear how raspy her voice was. Screaming for lengthy periods of time will do that to you. "I want to talk to her," she said, sounding as if she had been gargling gravel.

"Well, she's standing right there," said Helen.

Colleen put her hand gently on Helen's shoulder and said, "I think she means alone."

"Oh. Of course," said Anna's mother. Understand that she was not a stupid woman; she was actually rather bright considering she was only a brain surgeon. But she was under a good deal of stress and so wasn't exactly thinking clearly. Otherwise she would have figured out what Anna meant. "Yes...let's leave them alone."

"I don't know if that's wise," said the doctor pompously, but then Mary gave him That Look. Unless you've actually met Mary, you haven't seen it directly from her, but you probably know the type of look, either from having given it to your parents or getting it from your child. All children have That Look in their toolbox, but Mary was extremely skilled with hers, and so it was enough to prompt the doctor to follow the mothers meekly out of the room. "At least she's stopped crying," said the doctor as if he were somehow personally responsible for it right before the door clicked shut behind them.

Mary drew near her, stepping around Anna's building set on one side and her purple rocking horse on the other, and sat on the edge of the bed. Facing her, Anna took Mary's left hand in her own right. She stared at Mary's stump for a moment. Then she reached over and placed her left hand atop Mary's handless right arm. Mary gasped in surprise. Anna had been her dearest friend in the world, but she had always been slightly uneasy about Mary's missing hand and she had never, ever touched it until now.

"Anna," she whispered, "what's wrong? What's all this about?"

It took Anna a long time to be able to get the words out, but her friend did nothing to hurry her. Finally she spoke:

"My imagination has run off."

Chapter 3

How Anna Discovered Her Imagination Had Run Away With Itself

An adult might have laughed, and even if they hadn't laughed on the outside, they would have been laughing on the inside. An adult would have made all the right, sympathetic noises, and assured her that everything was going to work out and certainly the imagination would come wandering back when it was of a mind to. Or if the adult was in a cranky mood, the adult might have told Anna not to be ridiculous. Imaginations didn't simply run off, like stray kittens or dogs. Things could be beyond your imagination, sure. And sometimes writers had something called "writer's block" when, no matter how much they tried, ideas simply wouldn't come to them. But no adult would accept the notion that an imagination was a separate thing that might decide to take off one day. It was as silly an idea as a shadow running away from the person casting it.

Yet such things do happen, as has been written about

elsewhere, and Mary was well aware of it. So she settled right down to business.

"Run off how?" she said. "Where?"

"*I don't know where!*" Anna's voice began to rise into the sort of wailing she'd been doing when Mary first arrived. Mary's left hand squeezed tightly onto Anna's hand, partly as a means of being reassuring and partly to bring her focus back. It worked; Anna's voice dropped down to its more normal level and she repeated, "I don't know where," but far more calmly.

Mary remembered that her father had once said that the main things one has to determine for a good story were who, what, when, where, why and how. She had the "what" pretty clearly: Anna's imagination had run off. "Where" it had gone was unknown.

"How did you notice it? And when?"

"I took a nap," said Anna, "and when I woke up, I started playing with my dolls. Or I tried to play with my dolls. But they wouldn't play. They were just...they were just plastic and cloth. They didn't look at me; they just had painted on eyes. So I...I tried putting on costume pieces and pretending I was a princess or a cowgirl, but all I could imagine was that I was...was..."

"What? You were a what?"

Barely above a whisper, she said, "An *insurance adjustor.*"

"No!" Mary was appalled at the notion. She had no idea what an insurance adjustor was, or what they did (truthfully, neither do we, and if you don't, we wouldn't worry about it if we were you), but Anna certainly sounded horrified, and that was more than enough for Mary. "Really?"

"And I tried, Mary, I really did. I tried as hard as I could to imagine things, but I couldn't come up with *anything*. It's like...like having a cloth bag pulled over your head, and there's a drawstring, and someone's pulling it tight so it's closing around your throat and you can't breathe and..." She put her hand to her throat, and Mary was immediately worried that Anna might get herself so worked up that she would stop breathing altogether. But then Anna's hand fell away from her throat and she looked embarrassed. "I was just trying to imagine what it was like, and I couldn't even do that. You see how bad it is?"

There was an obvious answer that occurred to Mary, and she almost hesitated to say it. But she wouldn't be doing her best friend in the world any good if she kept her opinions to herself. "Is it possible," she said carefully, not wanting to get Anna any more upset than she already was, "is it possible that you're growing up? That this is supposed to happen?"

She shook her head so furiously that it looked like it might become unscrewed. "No. That happens slowly, and as it happens, you don't care. This happened all at once. I told you, right after I woke up..."

Seeing something to explore there, Mary said, "Did you have any dreams? Anything unusual?"

"I dreamt of..." She hesitated and then started to tremble.

Mary reached over and took up Anna's hand once again, holding it between her left hand and her stump. "Calm down and tell me."

Her words worked as Anna got herself under control. "I dreamt of...a graveyard. A cemetery."

"Which one?"

"The one on the edge of town."

"What happened there?"

"I don't remember. I just have...like...it's like a photograph in my brain. I can see it and I remember being scared...so scared... and I can hear...that is, I heard...galloping."

"Like a horse's hooves?"

"Yes. Something was galloping away, every quickly."

"That could have been it. People's imaginations live inside them and they all have different shapes. Your imagination may be like a horse. That sound you heard could have been the sound of it running off."

"But why?"

That, of course, was one of the "w's" of the story that Mary had yet to learn. The other one remaining was "who," but she wasn't sure if "who" even applied here. Wasn't it obvious? The "who" was Anna...

Except...

What if it's not? Mary suddenly wondered. *What if there is a who involved at that? What if someone, or some thing, was responsible for this? What if Anna's imagination hadn't simply run off? What if someone had, in fact, stolen it? Or scared it away somehow?*

And what if Anna wasn't the only one this had happened to?

She realized then that Anna had kept talking while she had been thinking, and she had been nodding the entire time. She felt like a bad friend because she hadn't been listening, but then decided that perhaps it was more about Anna talking than her listening anyway.

"—what to do," Anna was saying, finishing the sentence that Mary hadn't been paying attention to. "And I just...I mean...we can't be friends anymore."

"We can't?"

"Think about it!" said Anna sadly. "Going into your refrigerator box and it's not a ship or a submarine or anything other than some old carton made of cardboard. All I would do is ruin your fun. It wouldn't be fair to you and it would make me feel..." Tears began to dribble down her cheeks. "I can't live like that. I don't want to live like that..."

Mary said firmly, "You won't have to. I'll find it for you."

"What?"

"Your imagination. I'll find it and bring it back, no matter how far it's run."

Anna had been slumped over, almost curled up into a ball of helplessness. But when Mary said that, she straightened up, and there was something new in her eyes: hope. "I can't ask you to—"

"You're not asking me," said Mary. "I'm telling you. I have to do this. I have to help. I can't not help."

"It could be dangerous."

"I don't care."

"I care. Mary," Anna said firmly, or at least as firmly as someone can when their voice is so hoarse that every word scrapes against the inside of their throat, "You have to promise me you won't. I need to hear you promise that."

Mary hesitated, and she looked deeply into Anna's eyes, and she read Anna's soul at that moment.

And she understood.

"I promise I will not do it."

Anna let out the sigh of someone who was utterly comforted. Her head slumped back onto the pillow, and her eyes closed, and she whispered, "Okay," and instantly fell asleep.

Mary continued to sit on the edge of the bed for as long as it took her to make sure that Anna was really, truly and deeply asleep. Then she went to the door and opened it. The adults were all clustered around the door, leaning forward, and they looked a bit startled when it opened to reveal Mary standing there. "She's going to be fine," she said, and pointed to her sleeping friend.

Helen was practically sobbing in gratitude, and the doctor was making noises about how children are prone to hysteria and the best thing to have been done was simply to ignore her completely rather than dragging professionals such as him out into the night when he was clearly not truly needed, and Colleen nodded in approval over the excellent way that Mary had handled the emergency.

In the car drive home, Mary told her mother everything that had happened. She saw no reason not to; Anna had not sworn her to secrecy, and besides, if this was some sort of wider problem—if imaginations were going missing everywhere—then certainly her parents deserved to know.

"And you promised her that you would find her imagination?" Colleen was smiling patiently in that way she had. That way that said, *I know everything you're saying is nonsense, but you are my child and therefore it's nonsense that I love.*

"Actually, no. I promised her I wouldn't. And then she went to sleep."

"Ah," her father spoke up from the driver's seat. "All right...well done you, then. She fell asleep because you promised you wouldn't put yourself in danger on some mission to find her imagination."

"No," said Mary, her hand resting flat on her lap. "She fell asleep because she knew I was going to go out and find it. She knew that I would solve the problem for her."

Colleen, who was sitting forward in the passenger seat, turned around to look at her daughter in confusion. "I don't understand. You said you promised that you wouldn't..."

"Right. Because that's what she needed to hear. But she knew, deep down, that I was just saying that. I lied to her so that she could tell herself that I wouldn't be in any danger, but she was aware that I was lying to her and that I would find her imagination."

Colleen cast a worried glance toward Patrick, who merely shrugged in return. This annoyed Colleen slightly, because Patrick was the one with the greater imagination than she, who had never had one even when one was supposed to have a good deal of it. If even Patrick was unable to explain what Mary was talking about, she was at a loss as to how she was supposed to understand it. "Mary, you're making this all sound very complicated."

"It's not, really," Mary said, and to her it wasn't. "I'm going to find her imagination."

"And put yourself in danger?"

"Only imaginary danger."

"Oh, good," said Colleen, which was naturally what she needed to hear as well, because then it was all just a big game and nothing to concern oneself about. What she did not know, of course, was that Mary was doing for her what she had done for her best friend: Saying what she needed to hear.

The reality that Mary was dealing with was very different.

The reality was that the danger facing her was very real and she might well not return. But naturally that was not going to stop her. The least she could do, though, was to protect her parents from what she was going to be throwing herself into.

That's how it often turns out. Parents think they need to protect their children, except sooner or later, the children wind up needing to protect their parents. It was just that, in Mary's case, it was happening far sooner than usual.

Understand that Mary did not enjoy lying. Lying was what people did because they were afraid of being punished for doing things that they shouldn't have. Mary, as you've learned by now, was fearless. If she took actions that she knew could be a problem, she was not at all afraid of being held responsible for the results.

But she was not going to be reckless either, a lesson that was drilled into her for reasons that you already well know. And as far as she was concerned telling her parents what she intended to do would have been extraordinarily reckless, because it would have caused them all manner of worry. It was her hope to get the job done and return, all in one night, while her parents slept, thus never causing them so much as a moment of concern.

While we don't think it was okay that she hid her plans from her mother and father, we should note that at least she did it in order to spare them unnecessary pain. Unfortunately she completely failed to do so, as we will shortly witness.

As soon as they returned home, Mary went upstairs to her bedroom. Her older brother, Paul, was away on a school trip that evening, so he had not been involved in any of what had happened. Mary considered this regrettable, because Paul was rather clever for a boy and might have been a valuable ally on this excursion. She briefly considered waiting for him to return but then decided there was no time to wait around. Anna was sleeping and thus spared further pain because of her absent imagination, but by morning she was going to wake up. Mary could not stand to think of the nightmare that school would present for Anna if she didn't have her ability to imagine. For one thing, Anna's favorite and best subject was art, and she loved making pictures of creatures pulled from her deepest fantasies. Closed off from such things, Anna would be helpless and even humiliated by her inability to perform. It was Mary's greatest desire to spare her that if it was at all possible.

That meant she needed to get to work immediately.

She had no idea what she was going to require on her expedition, and so she decided to prepare for anything. Grabbing a knapsack, she looked around her room for things that she felt might be useful.

"I'm going to need weapons," she muttered.

She grabbed a pen from a desk drawer, having heard that pens were mightier than swords, and if she found herself in a sword fight, then obviously she wanted to be better prepared than her opponent.

She was going to need a stuffed toy; preferably an animal.

There was simply no question about it. One couldn't set out on a journey of this sort without having a companion, and as far as Mary was concerned, only one would do: A plush lion cub.

His name was Hunter. At least that was the name that she had given him, and it had stuck. She had acquired him at a zoo several weeks after the traffic incident that had nearly ended her young life. In a way, she had wanted it as a way to remember the old woman whose words she would never forget, and so Hunter had a great deal of meaning to her. For this kind of journey, no one but Hunter could come along.

When he had first come to live with her, though, she had stared at him for many hours, and something from deep within her kept whispering to her, whispering to her, about an addition that had to be made. Finally, with Hunter tucked firmly under her arm, she had marched with him straight to her mother, held him up to her, and said "Wings."

"I'm sorry?" Colleen had said. This was not the first time, nor would it be the last, when she would feel as if she had wandered into the middle of a conversation with her daughter without having the slightest idea what it was about.

"Hunter needs wings," Mary had said firmly.

"Honey...what kind of a lion has wings?"

"A winged lion does," which you couldn't really argue with.

And if you think this is proof that Mary did indeed ask for things, you would in fact be wrong. She wasn't asking for the wings for herself. She wanted them for Hunter. That is a totally different thing.

Realizing that Mary wasn't going to let go of the idea anytime soon, Colleen had fashioned a pair of wings out of cloth. They were rather impressive, actually. Instead of single pieces of cloth, she had created each wing out of two pieces, sewn together with an open end like a pillowcase. Then she had stuffed them, giving them weight, after which she had closed up the open end. Then she had used her nimble fingers to sew the wings firmly to his body so that they remained upright rather than flopping limply to either side.

Mary had watched every step of the operation, and when Colleen had finished, she had handed the lion to Mary who pressed it against her chest and looked as happy as Colleen had ever seen her. "Thank you, Mommy, you're the best mommy ever," said Mary, and Colleen instantly stopped caring about the fact that her fingertips were still in pain from all the sewing. She did not care about her fingers because she was the best mommy ever and that was more than enough for her.

Some time had passed since that successful operation, and Hunter was getting a bit raggedy around the edges, but he still had plenty of fluff and fight in him. She stuffed him in her knapsack and then decided that more would be needed.

She put her ear against her bedroom door and carefully listened, unmoving. She could have been mistaken for a statue. The door to her parents' room had closed, but there was always the chance they might come back out to go to the bathroom, or make certain the front door was locked, or something like that.

In order to pass the time, Mary counted to a thousand in her head. Once she reached that amazingly high number, she opened the door noiselessly and crept out into the hallway. Mary could be extremely sneaky when she was of a mind to be, and in this case she was most definitely of that mind.

Once sure that she would not be interrupted, she made her way down the hallway and then down the stairs. Minutes later she was standing in her father's workshop, with her knapsack clutched tightly. She looked around thoughtfully, trying to figure out what she could take with her that wouldn't be too heavy but might be of use.

A few minutes later she had a length of rope, a long, narrow piece of leather, a small box of lug nuts, a flashlight, a crowbar, and a monkey wrench. She had specific ideas how to use all the others, and was bringing the wrench along mostly because she had heard about people interfering with other people's plans by "throwing a monkey wrench" into them. She wasn't entirely sure exactly how that would work, but she figured that if she ran into some evil plan maker, the wrench might come in handy somehow.

She then went into the kitchen and hurriedly made herself some peanut butter and jelly sandwiches with the crusts cut off. It didn't take her long, and then she stuffed the sandwiches in a paper bag, adding that to the knapsack. Lastly she took her canteen, the one they used for picnics, out of the cupboard and filled it with water, after which she slung it around her neck. She then drew the knapsack onto her shoulders and tightened it. She flexed her shoulders to make sure that it fit properly. It felt a bit heavy and she decided that she was carrying just enough supplies.

She then ran back upstairs, the knapsack bouncing on her back, making more noise than she would have liked thanks to the contents banging around. As Mary ran past her parents' room, she thought she heard movement from within. That would be poor timing; it meant she had to get going as quickly as possible.

Entering her room, Mary locked the door behind herself. She couldn't remember the last time she had felt the need to lock it, but she couldn't have her mother or father bursting in on her. They wouldn't understand. Grown-ups usually didn't when it came to things like this.

She had already pulled on her shoes, deciding to keep the nightgown on under her clothing. It seemed a wise thing to do since she wasn't sure where she would wind up at the end of all this. If she went somewhere cold, the nightgown would add an extra layer of protection.

The refrigerator carton was standing upright at the far end of her room. She grabbed it and pulled it down. Hearing the door to her parents' bedroom opening, she knew she didn't have the time to be quiet anymore, so she made no attempt to cushion the box's fall. It thumped loudly to the floor and Mary scrambled into it.

Normally she liked to take her time with these things, because rushing your imagination could lead to problems. There was no room for sloppiness in the sort of thing she was going to try. What she should have done was imagine, piece by piece, in her mind's eye what the cemetery looked like. That way nothing would go wrong in making the trip.

But then she heard a knocking on the door, and an attempt to turn the knob that refused to move. "Mary!" came her mother's voice sharply. "What are you up to? Why is the door locked? Why are the lights on downstairs?"

She had forgotten to shut them off behind her. That had been unforgivably sloppy. But there was nothing she could do about it now.

"*Mary!*" and Colleen's voice was rising in alarm, and now her father could be heard banging on the door with far greater authority.

She was out of time.

"Cemetery," said Mary, ignoring her parents on the other side of the door, pretending that it was a million miles away. She bit her lip, for she was a good child and hated to disobey her parents or cause them difficulty, but Anna needed her and there was simply nothing else for it. "Right now."

She threw herself sideways, sending the refrigerator box toppling over the edge of reason.

Seconds later, the door burst open, the lock snapping loose with a sound like a rifle shot. Her father stumbled in, Colleen right behind him. The room was dark, and she flipped on the interior light so that she could see if Mary was hiding in there.

Mary was gone. So was the refrigerator box. All that remained to show that it had ever been there was a fast-fading imprint on the carpeting.

"Oh no," said Colleen with a moan, sagging against the doorframe. "Not *again.*"

Chapter 4

How Mary Came to the Cemetery

Mary paid dearly for the haste with which she launched the *Argo*. Instead of a smooth landing, she hit with a thud and a thump.

It was also very quiet. And pitch black.

She shrugged off the knapsack, unzipped it, and felt around until her fingers wrapped around the familiar handle of the flashlight. She flicked it on and the light illuminated the inside of her container.

She looked at the far end of the box and saw that it was closed off. It was closed at the other end as well. Experimentally, she reached up and rapped on the wall of the box directly above her. It was now wood. So were the sides and the bottom.

This puzzled her a bit. She was used to the box changing into various metals as it became a submarine or some other sort of vessel. But solid wood—pine, by the look of it—that was new. She shined the flashlight all along the interior, trying to get an idea of what her carton had decided to transform itself into, but she could not for the life of her figure what it was. A pine box? What kind of vehicle was that?

Then as she studied the top of the box, she realized that there was a crack running all around the top of it. The box wasn't solid; there was some sort of separation, as if a large lid was closing her in...

"Uh oh," said Mary.

"This isn't good," said Mary.

"I'm buried alive in a coffin," said Mary.

Now...there is something you have to understand: There are rules when it comes to imagination, adventures, and such. Anyone with a powerful imagination—and Mary had as powerful an imagination as any child you could hope to run into—is fully aware of that, and knows what they are. It's not as if there's a book that spells the rules out; it's just something you *know* without being certain of where you first learned it, like nursery rhymes or "Happy Birthday to you" or that boys are annoying (if you're a girl) or that girls are a mystery (if you're a boy.)

And the first rule of adventuring is "Play it where it lays." It's one of the same rules as you have in golf. In the case of that endlessly fascinating (and sometimes fascinatingly endless) game, it means that wherever the golf ball happens to land, that's where you have to hit it from. You can't move it to someplace that would make it easier to hit. Whatever challenge is dealt you, you must meet it head on rather than sidestep it.

Breaking the rules of adventuring is simply not done, for two reasons. First, it is extremely Bad Form. Second, the gods of adventuring frown upon such actions and tend to bring terrible punishment down upon the adventurer, up to and including a quest ending in total disaster.

Mary dared not allow for that possibility. For Anna's sake, the adventure had to, simply *had* to, end well.

What that meant was that Mary couldn't solve the problem by doing something obvious, like forcing the *Argo* to transform into some sort of mole-digging machine. In a coffin in a graveyard was she, and she simply was going to have to deal with it.

Setting the flashlight down, she started pushing against the lid as hard as possible, not knowing if it was going to do her the slightest bit of good. Since she didn't have two hands to use, she lay on her back and shoved upward with her feet. If she was truly buried under six feet of dirt, then she didn't have any chance of budging it. She tried to think of something that she could have brought with her that would have enabled her to deal with this, and short of a shovel, nothing was coming to mind. Even that wouldn't have done her any good if she couldn't get the lid open, which at the moment didn't seem to be happening. All the strength in her legs wasn't doing her any good.

She felt around in the knapsack and pulled out the crowbar. Picking a point at random, she jammed it under the lid and started pushing down with all her weight. It was fortunate that Mary was a solid child rather than a lightweight, and that she had a great deal of upper body strength for an eight year old. Anyone who was petite would not have had a prayer.

Mary was fully prepared for the possibility that the lid wasn't going to budge, in which case she would have to find some other way to get out. She didn't know what it would be, but these types of things had to be done in an organized way. Try one option after the next after the next, hoping that each one will work, and deciding what to do next only if an option failed to succeed. This was simply not one of those situations for which you could plan ahead.

Still, the truth was that she wasn't really expecting to be able to budge the lid, and was already trying to work on the next plan of action even as she gave the current plan everything she had. Imagine her astonishment, then, when the lid actually gave way a little, and then a little more.

Mary braced herself, waiting for dirt to fall in, but none came. Having pried open the lid somewhat, she now had enough room and leverage to get to her feet. She was bent deeply at the knees, like a coiled spring and, balancing the lid against her shoulders, Mary shoved upward. There was some resistance at first, but the lid started to creak open. She didn't dare relax her efforts because the lid was heavy and could have slammed back down, but she managed to keep it going until it thudded open and the cool night air filled her lungs.

She looked up and saw the smooth sides of a freshly dug grave all around her. There were tree roots sticking out here and there, and the full moon hung mockingly above her in the star-filled sky. A tree stood off to the side, but there was no way for her to reach it.

Obviously someone was going to be buried there the next day, and they had already created the grave. Which meant that if she simply waited around long enough, someone would eventually come to rescue her...

...and then what? They would make sure to bring her straight home.

She was going to have to take matters into her own hands...or hand, as the case may be.

Studying her surroundings, she noticed that one of the heavier branches of the tree was sticking out over the grave. This suggested possibilities to her. Pulling the length of rope from her knapsack, she tied off one end around the crowbar. Tying things were never an easy job for Mary since she lacked the two hands such a task normally requires, but she had had eight years to practice the simple act of tying knots, and had, through practice, gotten the knack of it pretty well. As soon as the rope was securely attached to the crowbar, she swung it back and forth a couple of times and then, taking aim, she flung it upward as hard as she could.

The first few times, she missed her mark, and had to scramble to get out of the way as the crowbar clattered back to earth, narrowly missing her. But she was nothing if not determined, and the seventh attempt, naturally, was the lucky one. The crowbar flew straight and true and then fell back down with the rope looped around the branch. The moment it landed, Mary attached it to the *Argo* and then, once she had slung her knapsack onto her back, started climbing, hand over stump, her feet placed firmly against the sides of the grave. The unevenness of the wall's surface gave her extra traction, enabling her to find footholds to make up for the fact that she only had one hand to grip the rope. She wrapped the coils of the rope around the stump of her right hand, which gave her some additional heft.

Even so, climbing a wall was a challenge for a person with even two hands. Yet all Mary could do was mentally scold herself for taking so long to manage what others might not have been able to do at all.

Eventually she reached the top and pulled herself over. Mary lay there for a moment, gasping deeply. Once she had recovered her breath, she got to her feet and looked around, waiting for her eyes to fully adjust to the murky surroundings.

Then she began looking around for hoofmarks.

It seemed like as good a place as any to start. Anna had spoken of dreaming about this graveyard and a horse, and Mary believed faithfully in the power and accuracy of dreams. Particularly when those dreams happened right around the same time as certain disasters.

She came up with nothing, however. She found no signs of hoofmarks anywhere. It meant that she was going to have to try something else. Don't worry: She had something in mind, but it wasn't going to be easy.

She knew the cemetery reasonably well, because both her grandparents were buried there and she and her family had come there on previous occasions to pay their respects. Because of this, she was aware that the cemetery had something that might enable her to get some answers, although she knew that there were some risks involved.

Be fearless, but not reckless.

The old woman's words were never far from her. Indeed, it might well be that by this point Mary was so far over the line of recklessness that that advice wasn't really going to do her much good anymore. But Mary didn't feel as if she had any choice at this point. *In for a penny, in for a pound,* her father always said. Well, she was in for about a thousand pounds by her reckoning and the bill was only going to increase.

""Nothing else for it, though," she said.

She followed the main path, having shut off her flashlight to save batteries since the full moon and stars were providing her with all the light she needed. The trees that dotted the landscape had no leaves, and their branches stretched toward her like skeletal fingers. Other children might have been scared or startled by them, but not Mary. She had other things to worry about.

Soon she reached her destination.

It was a crossroads.

She slowly circled the edge of the crossroads, making sure that it was going to be right for her purposes. As she did, she thought of all the stories that her father had told her about crossroads and their mythical roots and all of the power they had and, most important for the moment, the goddess who watched over them.

Picking up a branch fallen from a tree that was stretched overhead, she began to draw a series of lines in the ground and, within a few minutes, had etched a name and a five-pointed star in the dirt. She stepped into the middle of the star and drew a circle around the perimeter. Then, tossing the branch aside, she closed her eyes and spoke three times, because that was what you were supposed to do.

"Hekate," she said, pronouncing each syllable carefully, *HEH-kuh-tee*, and then "Hekate" again.

Now...

When calling things from the darkness, you have to have absolutely no doubt in your mind that it is going to work. If you think, even the slightest little bit, that what you're doing isn't going to work, then it won't. Because such things don't have a proper place in the real world, and the only thing that can bring them through is the absolute belief that they're going to show up. That's why when you play at trying to summon ghosts or demons, they never actually show up. It's because, deep down, it's all just a game to you rather than something real.

Mary had two things going for her, however, that you don't. First, her father had told her these stories, and if her father said them, then there was no question in her mind that they were true. And second, she was unafraid to fully commit herself to the notion that something would show up out of nothing.

Being able to do something like that might not seem like something involving bravery or fearlessness, but it really is. Think about it. As soon as you find out for sure that even just one creature of darkness actually exists, then you know that all those times that your parents tell you that there are no monsters hiding under your bed or inside your closet...that your parents are either lying or mistaken. Either way, it's not going to end up going well for you. In other words, as soon as you know personally, without the slightest doubt, that unnatural things really existed, then chances are you'll never get another good night's sleep again and spend the rest of your life jumping at shadows and looking nervously over your shoulder.

Mary did not fear the night or the secrets it hid. She was perfectly willing to kick over the rock and see the things squirming beneath it.

And so it was that without hesitation, for a third time did she say, "Hekate."

She wasn't entirely sure what to expect right after that; all her father had ever said was that Hekate, the goddess of dreams and crossroads, would appear when summoned, and that standing within the pentagram (the name for the star-shaped design she had created) would protect the summoner from any possible harm. He had not gone into detail as to exactly how Hekate would appear, and she realized now that she wished she had asked him for those details. How could she have known that she would need to apply the lessons herself?

She braced herself for some sort of burst of light, a blinding flash or a deafening explosion of sound, or perhaps the roar of a tornado.

She was not, however, expecting a pair of low and angry growls.

Slowly Mary turned and saw two ghostly dogs standing directly behind her. They were large mastiffs, and their translucent skin was a pale green, with red eyes burning in their lowered heads. Their lips were drawn back in snarls, and something thick and gelatinous was dripping from the edges of their mouths.

There was a woman standing between them. She was tall and elegant, and in the moonlight she cast three shadows all by herself. Her skin was pale, her black hair piled high on her head, and she was cloaked in a loose fitting toga that was as ebony as the night itself.

"You are Hekate?" said Mary, staring at her, wide-eyed.

As if she were a model standing at the end of a runway, Hekate spread her arms and turned slowly in place, so that Mary could see all of her. "I am she that is the natural mother of all things, mistress and governess of all the elements, the initial progeny of worlds, chief of powers divine, queen of heaven, the principal of the Gods celestial, the light of the goddesses. I am the supreme guardian between that which is and that which isn't. That which was and that which will never be. Some call me Juno, others Bellona of the Battles, and still others...Hekate."

By this time she had turned in a complete circle and was facing Mary once more. "You are the most beautiful woman I've ever seen," Mary said, "except for my mother."

"That is very kind of you." Her voice was so soft that Mary had to strain to hear it. "I cannot recall someone as young as you having the sheer nerve to summon me."

"It's important."

"Important enough to die for?"

"That's neither here nor there," said Mary, "since I have no intention of dying. Because if I did, then the quest would fail, and I can't allow that."

"Things happen whether you intend them or not."

Then Mary noticed that clouds of fog appeared to be rising from a number of graves. They were the same green as the dogs. At first they were vague and shapeless, but as they separated from the graves, they began to take on the shapes that they had in life. Mary would have thought that ghosts would float, but not these. Instead they moved forward, dragging their feet as if they had weight, and they left trails of slime behind them that writhed around on the ground like a thing alive.

"What is your name, child?" said the elegant woman.

Mary was about to reply, but then she hesitated. "Names have power," she said, "and perhaps it wouldn't be wise to tell you mine."

"Your mother should have done a better job of raising you," said Hekate. "It is very rude not to introduce oneself, especially when you know the name of the other person you're meeting. And *particularly* rude when you have the nerve to summon me as if I were a common spirit." Then her voice dropped to a friendly tone. "Certainly you cannot be afraid to tell me. After all, as long as you remain in the unbroken pentagram, there is nothing I can do to harm you."

Mary wanted to believe that her pride was not wounded by the suggestion that she was afraid, but it was. For all her bravery, she was still a young girl and could be hurt by something as empty as words. "My name is Mary," she said. "Mary Elizabeth Dear."

"Thank you, Mary Elizabeth Dear."

Then Hekate snapped her fingers. In response, one of the tree branches from overhead broke off and fell upon the star etched in the dirt that served as Mary's protection. It knocked some of the lines askew and created a break in one section of the outer circle.

"Not good," said Mary.

She started to move toward the line to fix it, but one of Hekate's dogs had appeared directly in front of it. It snarled at her, and snapped at her hand, and she pulled it back quickly before she wound up with two stumps. With an annoyed expression, she whirled to face Hekate. "That," she informed her, "was just cheating."

"On the contrary," said Hekate. "Cheating gives one person an unfair advantage over the other. All I've done is make things even."

"You have ghosts and ghost dogs backing you up. I'm just me. How is that even?"

"I suppose it's not," Hekate allowed, "but then again, you *did* bring this on yourself. No one forced you to come here and no one forced you to summon me. So it's a bit late to complain about the unfairness of it all. Now," she continued, "we can go back and forth about this a while and at some point I will tire of it, at which time I will instruct my pets to tear your soul right out of your body and eat it as they would a tasty treat..." One of the snarling mastiffs drew its tongue across its thick lips as if loving the very idea. "...or you can tell me what is so important that you have risked life and limb?"

Mary went for the second option and laid out in as quick and no-nonsense a way that she could the events that had wound up bringing her to this place.

"And since you are a goddess of both crossroads and dreams, I thought you would be the ideal person to ask," she said, concluding her tale.

Hekate considered all that Mary had said. She walked slowly around the perimeter of the emblem that had previously been Mary's source of protection, and as she did so she stroked her chin thoughtfully and never took her gaze from the little girl. "And what do you bring in exchange?"

"Exchange?"

"Information is a commodity, my child."

"It's a what?"

"It is an object of value. It has worth. Things of value are never given away, except by charities. Does this," and she gestured around herself, "look like a charitable organization to you?" She then went on without waiting for Mary to respond (although if she had waited Mary would most likely have agreed that it did not look like one. She had seen women from charitable organizations, typically around Christmas time standing around metal buckets and ringing bells while asking for donations. Hekate was doing none of those things and it seemed unlikely she would be doing so anytime in the near future.) "If you want my help, you must provide me something in return. In ancient times, a typical sacrifice was a goat."

"Well, first of all, I don't think I could slaughter an innocent animal, and second, I don't have any goats. So we have a problem."

"No, *you* have a problem. You have caused me some inconvenience, bringing me up like this and making demands of me just for your own selfish ends."

"It's not selfish! I'm trying to help my friend."

"She's *your* friend, so that makes it in *your* interest to help her. And I'm afraid that not only have I no reason to provide you help, but you're going to find that getting out of here is far harder than—"

And then another voice spoke up. It was soft and whispery, like wind whistling through a field of wheat, and it appeared to be coming from one of the smallest ghosts there. Mary couldn't tell how old he had been when he passed away, but whatever it was, he was very young indeed. And he said, "Tell us a story."

"A story?"

He nodded. "I had a big sister and she told me stories a long, long time ago, so far back I cannot remember when, but I remember they made me feel..."

"Feel what?" said Mary, not ungently, for she was moved by the wistfulness of the pathetic, glowing green spirit.

The ghost seemed to work for quite some time to come up with a good answer, but nothing seemed to come to him. "They made me feel," he finally concluded, without specifying what exactly he felt. "I would like to feel again, if only for a short time."

He was drifting without apparently paying attention to where he was going, and he bumped up against Hekate. Far from being annoyed by it, she looked down at him patiently and patted his head. It wobbled under her touch like lime gelatin. She looked at him thoughtfully and then turned to Mary. "Perhaps you have something of value after all. Entertain him...entertain them," she gestured to the others, "...entertain me...and you shall be allowed to live. Perhaps I shall give you help beyond that, and maybe even explain to you what your friend's dream meant. So tell a story that will appeal to all here...if you can."

The last three words had a challenging tone to them. The ghostly child wafted over toward Mary and hovered there, waiting. Other spirits drew closer as well, moths drawn to the flame of life that burned brightly within her. Hekate remained where she was, being far too dignified to approach Mary.

Mary said to the child spirit, "What is your name?"

"Can't remember," he said.

"It's on your gravestone."

"Can't read. That's why my sister read me stories."

"You don't remember your name, but you remember your sister?"

"She was more important to me than my name."

Mary thought that was a very sweet thing of him to say. Even were so much not at stake, up to and including her own life—and she wasn't certain what it would be like to have her very soul torn out by a ghost dog but she had no desire to find out—she would have been perfectly happy to try and bring a flicker of light to the darkness in which this little spirit existed.

She sat down in the middle of the circle, because that seemed to be the thing for storytellers to do. Then she thought for a few moments as the ghosts waited, still as the graves which were their homes.

"Once there were three people," she said at last, "one of whom wanted the other dead, and one of whom brought about the death of the other."

"I like it already," said the young ghost.

And this was the story she told, more or less, although to be truthful, she told it as an eight year old would tell it, with stops and starts and going back and filling in bits that she had previously missed, and with as many important words as a child with a wide vocabulary could muster. Still, there were limitations due to her age. So we will present you Mary's tale as a grown-up storyteller would, and will hope that neither you nor Mary take offense or believe that we thought her not up to the job.

Chapter 5

How Mann Planned to Destroy Wise Man

Once there were three people, one of whom wanted the other dead, and one of whom brought about the death of the other. They all lived in a village somewhere in Eastern Europe, at a time when life was both easier and harder than it is now.

The first of these people was the teacher who, for the purpose of this story, we shall call Mann. Now there are many great and good teachers in the world, but Mann was not one of them. He taught the children of the village reading and writing and arithmetic, but he did so joylessly and not very well and sometimes incorrectly. But he was filled with so much bluster and arrogance that he was unable to realize when he was wrong, and the mere suggestion that he might be mistaken on any topic was enough to cause him to fly into a rage.

The second of these people was a wise man who, for the

purpose of this story, we will call Wise Man. Wise Man was very learned, having gone to schools all over the world. Because of that, even though he was not the official teacher of the village, many of the young people came to him in order to learn. But he did not teach them reading and writing and arithmetic, for he knew that that was the job of Mann, and did not desire to intrude on Mann's duties. Instead he would hold court in his humble home and speak to them of many things, of fools and kings. He would teach them how to think, which sadly, a lot of students never get taught. Most students just have facts dumped in their heads; far too few learn what to do with them other than just spit them back out onto tests. And Wise Man taught them the latest scientific theories, and how they fit together with the oldest beliefs. The youths loved him for expanding their minds and helping them to think of things that they never would have thought of in a million years.

Mann hated him. He hated Wise Man with a fiery passion. He hated his wisdom. He hated his philosophies. He hated that the village youth seemed to like Wise Man better than he. And when Wise Man said to him, "We should speak for a time, for I am sure there is much that we can learn from each other," Mann hated him more than ever before, because if there was one thing Mann knew, it was that he knew everything he needed to know.

The third and last of the people of this tale was a young boy who never spoke, or even moved. His name was Small, given him because he had been born early and thus much smaller than most babies. Other than his size, though, he seemed healthy enough and was coming along nicely. Then, at one year of age—on his birthday, in fact—he became dreadfully ill, with a fever so terrible that it seemed to his parents that he was to be carried off to heaven before the night was out. But the night passed, and another night and then another, and the fever faded. The boy, however, never recovered. Instead he simply lay there, unmoving, unspeaking, some even claimed unblinking although that was not true, he did blink from time to time. He had a beloved stuffed toy bear that he kept at his side, in the crook of his arm, but he never played with it. His parents were grief-stricken but hopeful, and every day they would pray that this was the day their child would come out of his waking coma, and every night they would pray that the following day would be the day he would come out of it. And they never lost faith, for they were sure that this was all happening for a reason, and they loved their son the best they could.

And this situation would have continued very much the same forever, except that Mann's jealousy of Wise Man grew with every passing week. Every time he saw Wise Man passing through the village, doing his normal errands, smiling and greeting the people, his jealousy grew. Every time he saw how the youths of the village grinned in Wise Man's presence, his jealousy grew. And worst of all, every time Wise Man would see Mann, he would nod and smile warmly, showing no anger or even the slightest awareness that Mann was his mortal enemy. This infuriated Mann so greatly that he could taste it in his mouth and feel it churning in his stomach.

So Mann began to do everything he could to turn the people of the village against Wise Man.

"Look at Wise Man," said Mann. "He does not live among us, but instead in a house separated from the rest of us. Does he think he is too good for us? Perhaps he is planning dark and terrible things."

The adults of the village grew worried, and they came together in a crowd and went to Wise Man and asked him. Wise Man shrugged and said, "This was my father's house, and his before him, and his before him. I live here because this is where my family has always lived. I honor their traditions. Do any of you have trouble with honoring traditions?"

They said no, they did not, because truly it was no business of theirs, and even though the seed of suspicion had been planted, still they walked away satisfied.

But Mann was patient. So he waited a time and then he said, "Wise Man does not pray in the way that we do. He does not come to our house of worship, and being right thinking, we must hate him for this, and make him go away, lest he destroy the minds of our children."

The adults of the village grew greatly disturbed, and they came together in a crowd and this time did not ask but demanded of Wise Man that he give answers to these things and accused him of destroying the minds of the village youth. And Wise Man listened to them and said, "My beliefs are mine, and yours are yours. The only one or ones who knew the truth of how the world came to be is the creator or creators. And if He or She or They are satisfied to let each of us believe what we will believe, and not pass judgment on us by hitting us with lightning bolts or causing the earth to swallow us up, then who are *we* to pass judgment on each other? As for your youth and matters of faith, I have taught them what everyone believes, so that they may have a greater understanding of the world in which they live. Would you have them know less of the world?"

And indeed there were some adults who would have preferred their children know less of the world, because they felt the world was a dark and scary place and the less that was known of it, the better, but the majority of adults said, "No, of course not, that makes no sense, knowledge is strength and we want our children to be strong." So the minority kept their tongues still, but in all of the adults, the seeds of suspicion that had been planted now began to grow. They walked away, but far less satisfied.

Mann sensed that growth, and now his patience was beginning to wear thin. He knew that if he waited, the people would grow to remember why they liked Wise Man in the first place, and the growing distrust would whither and die if it did not receive more fertilizer in the form of hatred and fear. He knew that he was going to have to do something extreme.

Then one day he saw the parents of Small in the central square of the village, and the mother's belly was swelling, for she was with child. And the father of Small was saying that he was going to have to build an additional room onto their house for the new child, because ordinarily the new child would simply have shared Small's room, but he was worried that the baby would grow up sad, watching the unmoving form of his or her big brother simply lying there day after day after day.

And Mann decided that he could solve two problems with one simple action.

So he waited another week, and one night, when all was still, Mann snuck into the house of Small. He stood over the child and, taking a pillow, whispered, "This is all for the best," and covered the child's face with it. Ordinarily when you try to smother the life from someone, they toss and thrash and fight, but Small simply lay there and Mann watched until the rising and falling of Small's tiny chest stopped. Then, satisfied that Small was dead, he stuffed the child's body in a sack, along with the toy bear as well, and then snuck out of the house. Hidden by the darkness, he made his way to Wise Man's house, where he had already stashed a shovel behind a tree. There, as clouds covered a moon that was little more than a sliver of light, Mann dug a shallow grave behind Wise Man's house and placed the unmoving body of Small into it. Then he filled in the dirt and placed the bear atop it as a marker.

He returned to his home, washed the dirt and sweat of his

efforts from his body, and waited for the rising of the sun. Shortly after dawn, the village was awakened to cries of alarm sounded by the parents of Small. They knew their child could not possibly have gotten up and walked out by himself, and there were howls of "Someone has stolen our child! Help us!"

Quickly the villagers gathered in the town square, and there was much fear and terror from the villagers, because not only were they frightened because of what had happened to their neighbor, but also naturally they were worried about the safety of their own children. Mann promptly seized the opportunity that he himself had created, and he said, "Obviously the person who did this is not someone who lives among us, but separate so that he can do his terrible deeds in privacy. And very likely, he is someone who does not worship as we do, but instead needs children to sacrifice to his terrible prayers. Who, I wonder, does that sound like?"

"Wise Man!" cried out one, and "Wise Man!" shouted another, and moving as one, all of the people gathered and headed for Wise Man's house. They showed up at his doorstep and pounded on his door, and Wise Man opened it and, even in the face of such group anger, merely looked concerned about the villagers being upset rather than worried about himself. "How now, my friends?" said he.

"Look how calm he is!" cried the mother of Small.

"That alone is proof that he is responsible for our son's disappearance!" cried the father of Small, and others started saying the same thing, which is always dangerous because no matter how ridiculous something is, if you say it enough times then sooner or later people believe it to be true.

"We must search the area!" shouted Mann above the crowd, and he led them around, and did not go immediately to the place where he knew the child's body lay, because that might have seemed a bit too obvious, even for a mob. But eventually the search led them to where Mann wanted them to go, and Small's parents let out a great cry upon seeing the child's bear there, lying atop a plot of newly turned dirt that was just large enough for a child's body.

And Wise Man was brought forward, and angry fingers pointed at the mound and demanded to know what explanation he had for this horror. He looked around at the angry faces, and saw that one, the face of Mann, was smiling, and he knew at that moment what had truly happened. Slowly he shook his head and said, "Were I to say that this was a sin of Mann, you would believe that I am somehow accusing the whole of mankind, and in a way, you would be right, for what we have here is a grave injustice in every sense." After which he offered no further words, for he felt that they would be of no use, and Wise Man valued his words and did not throw them about as if they were dried leaves.

"*Hang him!*" cried out Mann, who Just So Happened to have brought a rope along, and others took up the idea. And even as they strung a rope on a nearby tree and prepared to hang Wise Man, the mother of Small clawed at the ground with her bare hands, for she wished to look upon the face of her child once more. She tore at it and dirt was flying everywhere, and moments later she had uncovered that sweet face, eyes closed as if in slumber. She howled like a dying wolf then, her husband by her side, for she was seeing the end of hope, crushed like a castle of sand under the hammering of the waves.

And as the mob pushed Wise Man toward the waiting noose, she brushed her child's face with the small bear.

Immediately the child's eyes snapped open.

Small's mother shrieked, and so did his father, and the shrieks brought the hanging to a halt as the mob turned to see what Small's parents were babbling about.

And then everyone shrieked with one voice as Small's tiny hand erupted from the dirt, shoving upward and through, and clutching at his prized bear. Small gasped and coughed and his parents, paralyzed by what they were seeing, simply stood or sat there in shock and horror as Small clawed his way out of his shallow grave.

For Mann had been ignorant of a great many things, as has already been said, and one of them was how to be utterly sure that someone was really, truly dead. In those days that was not always an easy task, even for a man of medicine, which Mann definitely was not. He had thought he had killed Small, but he had in fact failed to do so.

And when the fresh air had struck Small's face, it had recalled him from the twilight land which doctors called "Coma" but which is really called the Noplace. But the Noplace is not easily escaped from; one has to fight his way out of it. This did Small now do. He battled his way out of the Noplace, clawing at the dirt, clawing at the air, and in doing so it caused something in his brain to truly awaken for the first time since he had fallen ill.

His actions shook his parents from their shock, and they reached down and pulled him back into the world. He coughed violently and hugged them.

Panic seized Mann, and he shouted, "Do you not see? That is not their child! It is an undead creature brought back through the evil schemes of Wise Man! Do not be fooled!"

The superstitious mob trembled at the notion, but Wise Man said calmly, even with the noose dangling in front of him, "Were he undead, his skin would be cold to the touch. Is it?"

His parents touched his skin and his mother kissed his dirt-stained cheek, and it was as warm and human as anyone's there, which they said. And even though the mob was sore afraid, one by one, they approached the child and touched his face and saw that what his parents had said was true.

But Mann held back, which Wise Man saw, and Wise Man said, "Why do you not see for yourself, Mann? Are you afraid to come near the child?"

"He is a ghoul, a monster!" said Mann, but his voice was shaking and filled with fear.

"He is nonesuch," said Small's mother. "Come see! Approach him!"

Slowly, with the gaze of the entire village heavy upon him, Mann neared the child, a finger extended to caress Small's check.

And Small, still in his mother's arms, drew back upon Mann's approach, crying out in alarm, and he pointed a single finger at Mann and spoke for the first time.

"Don't let him hurt me again," said Small with a frightened wail.

Mann backed up then, so quickly that he stumbled over his own feet and fell upon the ground.

Small's father slowly approached Mann, whose eyes were wide with terror, and in a low, flat voice said, "What did you do to my son?"

And what Mann wanted to say, what he perhaps should have said, was that he had done nothing, that the child was lying, that Wise Man was casting a spell on him, that they were being duped, deceived, fooled...all this and more might have been to Mann's advantage had he actually uttered it.

Instead what Mann blurted out, before even realizing it, was, "I was trying to make things better for everyone!"

He then tried to go on to explain exactly what he meant by that. He kept talking as quickly as he could. He talked as they pulled Wise Man away from the noose, and he talked as they lifted him off his feet and dragged him toward the waiting rope, and he talked as they shoved his own head in there, through the noose, drawing it tight, and he talked as they yanked on the far end of the rope, hauling the noose high and him still in it, and that was when he stopped talking.

Eventually he was cut down, since Wise Man had no desire to have a body left hanging there. And it was not felt that one such as Mann deserved even a proper burial, so his body was carried to a distant area of marsh and swamp—a bog, is what they called it—and he was tossed into the bog and sank from sight.

Wise Man was made the teacher of the village, which was no great trouble for him since he was as well schooled in reading and writing and arithmetic as Mann had ever been, and actually better. He remained in his house, and many years later, when his time came to depart the world forever, he left the house to Small, who had grown up well and strong and full of words and ideas and had been Wise Man's best pupil. And Small likewise became a teacher, and Wise Man was always spoken of fondly and well.

And Mann was scarcely mentioned by anyone at all, except every so often in order to scare very small children who were misbehaving. They would be warned, "The boggy Mann will get you if you aren't good and don't watch out," and over many years and many repetitions it got changed to bogeyman, or boogieman, depending on where you lived and how you pronounced such things.

And that's where that came from, in case you were ever wondering.

Chapter 6

How Mary Left the Cemetery

There was a long silence after Mary had finished telling the story. Finally she heard some soft murmurs, and what might have even been sounds of approval, but she didn't think she could be sure.

Finally Hekate spoke.

"That was good," she said, and then went on to say, "that was very good, actually. All the things that an audience like this looks for in a story: Death, premature burial, and something left behind to scare children at night. Yes...that was well said and well done. And you?" She was speaking not to Mary but to the childish ghost who had wanted a story told in the first place. "Were you satisfied?"

"Very much so," sighed the ghost. "Truthfully, I would have liked to hear more about Mann's last moments. How he strangled and whether his neck snapped out loud. Whether his legs pin-wheeled, or spun as if he were on a bicycle, or splayed out to either side. That would have given the story more body."

"Perhaps next time," said Mary. Inwardly, she thought it was kind of awful, to be so interested in all the details about how someone had met his end, even a deserving villain such as Mann. But she felt no need to say that aloud, lest she wind up hurting the ghost's feelings. Then she felt something slimy against her arm. She turned and saw that one of the green, glowing mastiffs was licking it.

"He's taken a liking to you," said Hekate. "He's being affectionate."

This was good as far as Mary was concerned, since she'd thought that the thing was getting ready to eat her and was tasting her first. "That's nice," she said. Then, feeling bolder thanks to Hekate's words of praise, she said, "So are you going to keep your word and aid me?"

"The best aid I could do for you," said Hekate, "would be to tell you to return home and forget this mad adventure. So your friend lives without imagination. So what? Imagination simply makes life difficult for you as you grow up, because all it does is get you to see the world the way it should be, rather than the way it is."

"What's so wrong with seeing the world the way it should be?"

"What's so wrong is that *They* don't like that," Hekate told her. "*They* like the world the way it is, and it is in *Their* best interests to keep it that way."

"I'm not sure I understand what you're talking about," said Mary, who could not see the capital "T" in *They* and *Their* since she was hearing it spoken rather than reading it written down, and wasn't thinking about what the old woman had said to her four years earlier. (In her defense, she had a lot on her mind, and there were only so many directions she could think at once.)

Hekate studied the child for a short time, and then said, "You assume that Anna's imagination simply ran away. Yes?"

"Yes."

"Things don't just run away," she said. "They need a reason for it. Things either run away *toward* something, or they run away *from* something. In this case, it was a case of running away."

"But why would Anna's imagination run away from her?"

"It didn't."

"But it did!" Mary insisted. "It..." Then her voice trailed off and she understood. "You're saying that it ran away from...something else. Something it was trying to escape."

"Yes. I was there, within Anna's mind, when her imagination fled. Something frightened it into running away. Except what it did not fully understand is that it wasn't simply running. It was being herded. Driven, as hounds drive a fox, toward a particular place."

"What was it running from? And where did it run to?"

The edges of Hekate's mouth twitched. "So much you wish to know, and only so much am I willing to tell you. A compromise must be reached." She appeared to be giving the matter a great deal of thought, although Mary had a feeling that Hekate already knew exactly what she was going to say and was simply dragging it out. Finally she said, "You have asked two questions: Who and where. You may choose which question you wish answered."

Mary thought about it and decided that the most important thing was to go after the runaway imagination. Granted, it meant that she would not know who or what she was going to be going up against, but she would just have to deal with that.

"Where?" she said.

Hekate drew herself up as if she were about to say the most important word ever spoken in the history of words ever spoken.

"*Afrasia*," she said, saying it with such foreboding that she was able to drag the word out from four syllables to eight.

Searching her memory, Mary tried to recall the name from her geography lessons, from her texts, and finally from the stories that her father had told her. Although some of them sounded kind of familiar, none of them were exactly the same. "Afrasia," she echoed. "Is it another place? Another planet? Another world?"

"All and none of that."

"And how would I get there?" This could have been a serious problem. Reaching the cemetery, or the bottom of the ocean, or the moon...these were places she could conjure up from her imagination and thus guide her refrigerator box there. But Afrasia was a mystery to her; she didn't know anything about it. "I've never been there and I can't picture what it looks like. I...I guess I could launch the *Argo* and just hope..."

"That would not be a good idea," Hecate warned her. "Your vessel could wind up stuck between the lines, drifting neither here nor there. You might be trapped between forever."

"Could that really happen?"

"It's possible. With an active imagination, anything is possible, as you well know."

"That's true," she said.

"Afrasia," Hekate said, "is a land betwixt and between. It is the continent to which Atlantis was attached before it sank. It is to the right of Lilliput and the left of Brobdingnag. The rainbow bridge that leads to Asgaard stretches over it, and Odysseus stopped at it for a time during his lengthy trip home after the Trojan War. It is a land with different areas of different weather conditions, so it is more or less impossible to dress for whatever you may run into. For the most part, it is a land where only beings of myth and legend or those who have passed into other realms can reach, and so you would have no way to—"

"I will be her guide."

It was the small ghost boy who had spoken. He was fluttering around Mary, and it was hard to make out what his expression was because his features were somewhat blobby. "I can take her to Afrasia. I have passed into another realm, what with being dead and all. I will bring her," and then he dipped in the air toward Hekate, "if it is acceptable to you."

"I would not suggest you do that," said Hekate. "Things can go very badly for a random spirit, particularly in Afrasia."

"I..." He hesitated and then said firmly, "I wish to go with her."

Once again the corners of Hekate's mouth twitched upward. Then, all business, she said, "You cannot leave this place as you are. You would need to possess something. And I believe," she went on, "that I know just the thing."

And she looked straight at Mary, and then pointed at her.

There was a rush of air, and the ghost hurtled straight toward Mary, clearly in Hekate's control. Mary stepped back, unafraid (naturally) but still unsure what was happening, and then she felt her chest become warm and cold all at the same time, and a strange pressure, as if she were being stabbed with an icicle that was wrapped in a hot towel.

And then, just as quickly as it had been there, it was gone.

Mary turned in place several times, trying to see where in the world the ghost had gone. And then she suddenly felt something thrashing about in her knapsack. She shrugged it off her back and opened it wide.

Hunter sprang out.

She stepped back, gasping in shock. Even fearless people can be surprised, and this Mary most certainly was. It took her a few moments to realize what had happened, although we're certain that you have already figured it out. Mary hadn't been sure of what to expect when the child ghost said he wished to go with her, but possessing her plush winged lion was definitely not it.

He was certainly acting the part. He lowered his head and stretched his non-existent spine, one imaginary bone after the next. He thrust his paws forward and then, to Mary's utter astonishment, claws popped out from the end. The first thing that occurred to her was that maybe his spine wasn't so imaginary after all, and the next thing that occurred to her she actually gave voice to: "Where did the claws come from?"

"From in you," said the lion. He stretched his wings then and began to beat them furiously. He made a slow, hovering lift off, scattering bits of dirt around as he did so, and then he was huffing and puffing with the effort. With an annoyed grunt, he thumped to the ground and shook the bits of dirt from his paws. "I went through you, and you have more than enough imagination to spare, so I took some of it."

"*Took?*" Mary was not thrilled by the sound of that.

"Borrowed," he immediately corrected himself. "I borrowed some of it." Looking immediately apologetic, he said, "That's okay, isn't it?"

"Well, next time, ask first," she warned him. She wasn't sure what else she could or should say at that point. She had to be careful because she had far more need for this strange creature than he did for her. Without thinking about it, she rubbed her chest where the ghost had gone through her, and tried to see if she could feel something missing from within her. Nothing seemed to be, and she supposed that if her imagination were truly unlimited, then she wouldn't miss it if some of it were gone from her. After all, if you hauled a bucket of water out of the ocean to make a sandcastle, did the ocean look any shallower from the absence? Of course not.

She was still a little concerned, but decided there was no

point in worrying about it.

The newly created lion cub now bounded around Hekate's feet and wagged his tail proudly. "Did I do a good job?" he said eagerly, snapping his tail around like a whip. "It's my first possession. Did I do well, Hekate?"

"Very well, especially considering it's your first time," she said, but then her voice took on a cautious note. "Have a care, little one. For you can still be hurt."

"How? I'm already dead."

"Except there are those who can force you from your vessel," she said. "They are called," and she paused for dramatic effect, "exorcists."

The mere mention of the word sent a chorus of "ooooos" through the cemetery, for the ghosts knew all about exorcists, and shuddered at the mere mention. So if you ever desired to know what frightened ghosts, now you do.

Even the ghost within the lion trembled slightly, and the body he was inside of shook as well. "What would happen? If that happened?"

"You would be unable to return to your vessel, unable to return here. Eventually you would dissolve, like tissue in water, and that would be the end of your afterlife." She paused and then added very softly, "That is a terrible risk to take for someone whom you just met, little one."

"I know," he said, although it was hard to tell if he really did know or was just saying that because it was the sort of thing one is supposed to say. "But she needs me. And I cannot recall ever having been needed before. I rather like the feeling, and I don't want to let it go just yet. There is far more to being dead than just not living, you know."

"I am not quite sure I do know," said Hekate patiently. "However it is not my unlife at stake, but yours. So if you feel that you *do* know, then that will have to be enough."

And then, very suddenly, Hekate was no longer where she had been standing, but was instead directly in front of Mary, and her hand clamped upon Mary's throat. Mary would have gasped, but she was unable to draw in air. She quickly realized that if Hekate did not release her grasp upon her very quickly, this entire adventure would end before it had truly had a chance to begin. There was an alarmed and very small roar from the lion cub, but he made no move because one simply didn't interfere with a goddess when she was going about her business.

"I put it upon you," she said tightly to Mary, "to have a care for the little one's welfare. For although he is centuries old, he is very inexperienced in the way of the world. His trust in you stems from that innocence, and if something terrible were to happen to him, then my vengeance would be terrible."

With that warning, she released her hold on Mary, who sagged to the ground, clutching at her throat.

Any other young girl would simply have been grateful that she was still among the land of the living. Not Mary. Instead she spoke, and even though her voice was raspy, it was also defiant. "And if something wonderful were to happen to him, would my reward likewise be wonderful?"

Hekate actually looked stunned, an expression that is very odd when seen on the face of an ancient and ageless, all-knowing being. "I am now unsure whether you are remarkably fearless or remarkably stupid."

"All of one and some of the other," said Mary.

Studying her for a moment as if she were looking down upon her from atop a very high mountain, Hekate finally said, "We shall see."

Mary took that as a good sign. Certainly a better sign than having a goddess's hand clamped upon her throat, threatening to choke the life out of her.

"Be off with you then, before I change my mind." Hekate said.

That seemed a good a time as any to get out of there as quickly as possible, and Mary did exactly that. The lion cub bounded around her feet, licking its chops with a delicate pink tongue that had not been there before since it didn't actually have a mouth; just a single line of black thread across his muzzle to represent a mouth. Out of curiosity, Mary reached down and petted him. His plush fur was now real, and fuzzy, and remarkably warm to the touch. It was a warmth that she felt deep within her chest, and she wondered if she was connecting with the animal that he was, or with the part of her that was within him.

"Thank you, thank you, thank you for this chance," he said as he bounced about with all the energy of an eight-week old kitten. "I won't let you down, I promise."

"I'm sure you won't, Hunter."

He stopped in her path and looked up at her, wide eyes unblinking. "Is that my name?"

"It's what I called the lion that you're inside of. But you said you don't have a name that you remember, so if you wish me to keep calling you Hunter, I'd be happy to do so."

"Hunter," and he rolled the name around in his mouth. "Hunter. Huuuunteerrrr." He did this over and over the entire walk back to the grave where the *Argo* had landed, saying the name every way he could think of, with every different accent, dragging out this letter and that letter, as if he were trying on a coat a hundred different ways in addition to the normal one of the left arm in the left sleeve, the right one in the right sleeve, and the opening in the front. Finally, by the time they had gotten to the edge of the grave, he nodded in satisfaction and said, "All right. I can live with Hunter."

Mary did not bother to point out that he wasn't really living with anything, but she kept that to herself since she didn't want to take a chance of hurting his feelings.

They arrived at the edge of the grave and Hunter looked down at the open coffin. "You came here in that?" he said. "I didn't know coffins could do that."

"They can't. That's my ship," she said. "It changes to what I need it to be."

"That's very convenient."

"It is, rather."

Six feet was a bit of a jump, but Mary was too pressed for time to try and climb back down. So without hesitation she leaped down into the coffin and landed with a loud thud, bending her knees and rolling in order to absorb the impact. Her knees were a bit banged up as a result, but nothing that she couldn't live with. The lion cub landed next to her a moment later, not the least bit put off by the distance of the drop.

He was staring at the stub of her right arm. "What happened to your hand?"

She was going to tell him the truth, but remembering the kinds of things he liked in a story, she said, "It was bitten off by an alligator."

"Really?" He grinned. "Wow."

"Yes, I thought you'd like that. So...take us to Afrasia."

"Where in Afrasia?"

"I don't know," said Mary. "If I knew anything about Afrasia, I'd be able to go myself, right?"

"I suppose."

"So we get to Afrasia and then you'll help me track Anna's runaway imagination to wherever it is. How are you going to do that, by the way?"

Hunter growled low in his throat. It wasn't an angry growl, but more of a thoughtful one. "I'm not really sure," he finally said. "Maybe it will have a scent I can pick up."

"Maybe?"

"Probably."

"Which is it?"

"Probably," he confirmed and then added, "I hope."

Mary rolled her eyes. This wasn't exactly filling her with confidence, but she didn't see that she had a great deal of choice. Hekate had told her as much as she was going to; Mary was just going to have to take the rest on faith.

She crouched down into the coffin and pulled the lid shut over herself, plunging them into darkness. She didn't turn on the flashlight yet again, continuing to be careful about not using up the batteries. The lion cub was pressed up against her and she liked the feeling of it. Mary had never had a pet; her parents had never offered and, naturally, she had never asked. And she was well aware that this was not actually a lion cub, but the ghost of a young boy inside the body of a toy. Still, it was somewhat like having a pet: A pet that she could talk to. If all pets were this smart, she might have been more interested in the idea of being a pet owner.

"Would you be insulted," she said, "if I petted you?"

"Not at all. I would rather like it, actually."

She couldn't really make out much of him; he was a sort of mass in the darkness that was a bit different from the rest of the darkness. Mary reached out and ran her hand repeatedly down the back of his head. A noise came from the cub's chest, a deep rumbling like the echo of a subway, and his head snapped up in surprise. "What was *that?*" he said.

"What was what?"

"That sound coming out of me!"

"I'm pretty sure that was purring."

"How am I *doing* that?"

"I don't know. I'm not sure anybody knows."

"All right, well," and he shifted his back legs, "it was a little disturbing, is all that I'm saying."

"You'll probably get used to it. So," and she continued since she saw no point in dragging things out, "can you get us to Afrasia? How are we going to do this?"

The lion cub thought about it and then said, "Well...this vessel responds to your imagination. And I took a portion of it to take over this toy. So if I put my mind to it, and you put your mind to my putting my mind to it, then it should just...take us there, I guess."

"All right," said Mary, who wasn't entirely sure about any of it, but what he was saying certainly seemed reasonable. "Then just imagine us to Afrasia."

"I'm doing it," said Hunter. She could see even in the darkness that he had closed his eyes, because they had been glittering in the dark and were now invisible. "I'm pretty sure I'm doing it."

Again he was talking about being pretty sure. Pretty Sure wasn't going to get the job done. "You have to commit to it," she said.

"What happens if I don't?"

"Nothing good."

"Then I commit to it," said Hunter with as much conviction as he could muster. "I'm ready. I'm definitely ready. I can see it. I can see it so clearly. We're going to Afrasia."

"Okay then," said Mary, and she threw her body to one side, sending the *Argo* once again tumbling off the edge of reason.

The box fell through unknown space for a much longer period than she had ever known. So long, in fact, that she was starting to wonder if they would ever land, and then the *Argo* halted suddenly and violently. Mary struck her head against the side and realized that it was now solid metal. She rapped on it and it echoed back to her. It felt extremely thick, like it couldn't be hurt by anything. *It can't be hurt by anything*, she thought fiercely. *That is what I need. Nothing can hurt the Argo. Nothing can get through it. As long as I'm in here, I'm totally safe.*

How marvelous it would have been—to say nothing of very convenient—if Mary could have affected the world around her in that way. To simply say, "This is how it will be," and that was enough to shape the world to her liking. Were that the case, she could have wished for Anna's runaway imagination to be brought to her immediately, and that would have been the end of that. But it was not that easy, because a grand adventure is never that easy. She could, however, affect the *Argo* because she had brought it with her—even more so since she had left the real world behind—and now she put her mighty imagination to work, making sure that, no matter what, the *Argo* would be a safe place for her. Of course, she couldn't accomplish what she needed to do by hiding inside of a refrigerator box.

She placed her one hand against what had been a lid, except it no longer was. Instead it was a hatch, like a submarine, fastened by a large wheel. She reached up and, gripping the rim with her left hand and placing her stump right arm inside one of the wheel spokes, she grunted and worked on turning it.

"Do you need help?" said Hunter hopefully.

"No...I've got it," Mary grunted between gritted teeth. Just when she thought that it might be hopeless, the wheel suddenly turned. Once she had gotten it started, it turned very quickly until it was practically spinning. She turned it as far as it would go, and then pushed up against the hatch. It opened easily, but with a squeak that nearly deafened her inside the cramped box. She made a mental note to imagine the inside of the *Argo* as larger, and with lights if possible so she didn't have to keep deciding whether or not to use the flashlight.

"I smell something," said Hunter, his nostrils flaring. "Something burning. A lot of something burning. And something stinks... what *is* that...?"

Mary had never smelled that particular aroma before and yet somehow, instinctively, she knew what it was. "Sulfur," she said. "It's a chemical used in things that burn, like matches."

Every instinct told her that she should remain within the *Argo*, but hiding and waiting for something to happen simply wasn't how the game was played. Instead, taking a deep breath, she stuck her head out of the vessel to see what was around her.

The first thing that hit her was a blast of air so hot that she could barely breathe. Mary covered the lower part of her face with her hand. She had to squint against the waves of heat that pounded her face so hard that tears started to roll from her eyes. There was also smoke drifting up around her that further stung at her eyes, and she waved it away with her handless arm so that she could have a clearer view of her surroundings.

High above her was a round opening that revealed a night sky. She couldn't see any stars.

Far below her, although not quite as far as she would have liked, was a huge mass of lava. As wide across as a football field, it was bubbling and churning and there seemed to be a distant rumbling coming from beneath that scalding pool of death.

The *Argo* was sitting on an outcropping of rock, a shelf extending from the wall, which seemed solid enough for the moment but there was no way of telling just how long it was going to stay that way.

Mary, Hunter and the *Argo* were trapped inside of an active volcano.

"This isn't good," said Mary.

Chapter 7

How Mary Met Purl

Mary thought about her surroundings for a time, as well as her options. She wasn't thrilled with any of them. Meanwhile the smoke continued to rise, the lava continued to bubble, her face continued to become streaked with dirt, and her hair was getting frizzy.

Hunter rubbed around her ankles. Apparently the longer he was a lion cub, the more feline and less boy-like he was becoming. She wondered if there might reach a point where he would forget that he had ever been a boy at all. "Stop that," she said, trying not to sound impatient. "You're making it hard for me to think."

He stepped away from her ankles and blinked up at her from the floor of the vessel. "Can you change the *Argo* into a flying machine?"

"If we'd first arrived in the skies over Afrasia, *then* it would be a flying machine. Since we arrived in a volcano, it became something that won't be destroyed in a volcano. Unfortunately," and she looked up toward the distant opening, "it's not something that will get us *out* of a volcano. It couldn't become an airplane now; there's no runway. And a helicopter, the motor could choke out from the smoke."

"Even an imaginary motor?"

"There have to be *some* rules, Hunter."

"It sounds like you're making them up as you go."

"Well, sure," said Mary. "Obviously it has to be as I go, since I don't know ahead of time what I'm going to run into."

"Okay," said Hunter, who didn't even pretend to understand he knew what she was talking about. "Can we climb out?"

"I'm not sure. It's an awful long way. And if we slipped off, we'd fall into the lava."

"That would hurt."

"Not for long," said Mary, practical as always. "We would be reduced to ashes almost instantly."

"Well, that's very comforting," said Hunter, who didn't actually sound all that comforted.

It is hard to say just exactly how long Mary might have remained there trying to figure out the best way to proceed. As it turned out, she didn't have to wait very long at all.

To be specific, she waited about a minute and a half, and that was when she heard chants and shouts and howling and shrieks, all coming from high above. And when you think about the noises that were surrounding her from within the volcano, you can imagine just how loud those things had to be in order to attract her attention.

She looked up and saw that there were people surrounding the rim of the volcano. It was impossible to make out any details of their bodies, because they were completely hidden behind hoods and robes that were a bright blue with gold trim. They were waving around long, thin metal rods that seemed to be, from this distance, some sort of spears.

It was hard to make out exactly what they were chanting with all of the howling and shrieking, but as near as Mary could determine, it was all some gibberish about pleasing "them" and asking that "they" be generous and compassionate and forgiving.

Mary had no idea what they were talking about.

And then something tripped in her mind, something clicked together, and she remembered what the old woman had said those four years ago and also what Hekate had been saying in the cemetery, about *They* and *Them* and it suddenly occurred to her that there might well be a connection. She thumped herself on the side of the head with her stump in annoyance for not realizing it earlier. Sure, she'd been distracted by ghosts and a goddess, but she still didn't excuse herself for not figuring it out sooner.

It was fortunate, as it turned out, that she had those few moments of relatively free thought to think about things, because something else happened almost immediately that would have distracted her even more.

There was a young girl being shoved toward the edge of the crater.

She was older than Mary, apparently just on the edge of being a teenager. She was wearing a loose brown tunic, belted with an orange sash, and long, flowing sleeves that had slid down to around her shoulders. Her skin was very dark, and her hair was long and thick with curls. That was all that Mary could make out from such a distance, and even that wasn't easy with all the smoke that was billowing around.

She could, however, hear, because the volcano was a vast echo chamber. The girl's voice was rising above those who were pushing her toward the crater. One might have expected—and indeed it would have been understandable—if the girl had been pleading for mercy, begging for them to release her, because it was clear what they were planning to do. They were going to push her into the volcano so that she would plummet to her death in the boiling molten rock.

But there was neither pleading nor begging. Instead the girl was shouting commands that they stop what they were doing and she was fighting back every step of the way. At one point she actually managed to shake loose of the people who were holding her and slammed her elbow into the hooded face of the nearest of her captors. He (or she) went down and the girl spun and lashed out with her right foot, catching another attacker in the knee and sending him tumbling. He nearly fell into the crater but caught himself at the last moment.

The girl tried to leap away from them, but one of them tackled her across the waist and then more of them grabbed her by the arms and legs and hoisted her high. If she was indeed afraid, there was no telling it from her expression.

Mary saw the way the brutes above were holding her, she guessed the direction in which the body was going to fall, and made her best guess about exactly where the girl was going to be when she fell past Mary toward the swirling cauldron of death below.

Even as she did so, she reached into her knapsack and yanked out the crowbar, which still had the rope attached to it. Looking across the way, she saw a likely anchor point. Unlike her earlier experience with the tree, she wasn't going to have time to try it over and over; she was going to have to get it right the first time.

Standing atop the *Argo*, she held the crowbar loosely and then started to whirl it, slowly at first but then faster and faster, building up confidence and letting out more of the rope as fast as she could.

The villains high above were now moving all together, doing a sort of "one, two, three" countdown in getting ready to toss the girl in. Apparently if you plan to throw someone to her death, it's only Good Form to do so all together. Mary was able to hear them shout, "One," and, knowing that she couldn't wait any longer, she let fly the crowbar. Like the crow for which it was named the crowbar hurtled across the inside of the volcano, and landed with a clank on the far side. The wedged hook end of the crowbar lodged solidly in the crack. Mary yanked on it and the rope drew tight, and then quickly wrapped the other end around a rocky projection right above her head.

Meanwhile the shouts of "Two!" and "Three!" sounded from above, and then the dark-skinned girl was hurled headlong into the volcano.

She fell straight down, like a diver, rather than flailing her arms and legs around and screaming at what seemed to be her oncoming death. Apparently if she was going to die, she was going to do it stylishly.

She must have seen the rope directly in her path at the last possible second. Instead of catching it, as Mary hoped she would, the girl struck it hard and bounced off. Smoke belched up, blocking the view, and Mary let out an alarmed cry of frustration; she had so wanted to save the girl, and now it seemed she had failed.

And then, as the smoke drifted upward, Mary couldn't quite believe what she was seeing.

The girl was hanging by her feet. Specifically, she had her ankles wrapped around the rope and was trying to bring her body up so that she could reach the rope. Unfortunately, the way she was dangling there, it was impossible for her to bring her body up and around to get to it.

"Hunter! I need you!" Mary called out, and Hunter leaped out of the ship immediately. She pointed to the girl who was hanging over the lava far below. "Can you help her?"

"Of course," said Hunter. He leaped onto the rope and started making his way toward her, one paw placed carefully in front of the next. Moving quickly and with perfect balance, he made his way toward the middle where the girl was dangling. Then his wings began to flap, and he hopped off the rope, descending toward her. He took the back of her tunic in his teeth and started to pull.

But instead of dragging her upward, Hunter began to sink. It seemed that she was too heavy for his wings to lift the both of them up.

"You can do it!" Mary shouted encouragingly. "You can save her!"

Mary's confidence in Hunter was uplifting for him in every way. Hunter's wings began to beat with greater strength than ever and slowly but surely he drew the girl upward until she was able to wrap her fingers around the rope. It took her only seconds to pull herself up and then, displaying as much skill tightrope walking as Hunter had, she sprinted along the rope right behind him toward Mary and safety.

Unfortunately the volcano was continuing to act as an echo chamber and when she shouted, her voice bounced upward and caught the attention of the villains who had just been in the process of leaving. They turned back and clustered around the crater, shielding their eyes and trying to make out just what was going on below in the heart of the volcano. The smoke briefly blocked out their view of the girl, but they were able to see Mary and then, in short order, saw the girl approaching her.

The girl covered the remaining distance with a single leap and landed on the rocky shelf next to Mary. She looked at her in wonderment. "Are you a goddess?" she asked Mary.

"No. I'm a girl."

"Oh." Her face fell. "That's much less interesting."

Mary was slightly annoyed by this remark. A goddess, after all, could do whatever she wanted and there was no real challenge to it. She was a normal, human girl who had no vast power, but instead had to depend upon her wits and her imagination. The more she thought about the girl's attitude, the more it annoyed her. And then she thought of something.

"Are you a princess?" she asked.

"Yes. I am. You recognize me, I assume?"

"No. It was just a feeling, is all."

"I," and she paused for dramatic effect, "am Princess Purl." She then added with an important voice, "*The* Princess Purl."

"All right," said Mary, who wasn't quite sure what to say to that. "I'm Mary. But not *the* Mary because there's quite a few of us. And this is Hunter. We saved your life."

Purl glanced from one to the other and then said, "You're waiting for me to say something. I can tell. What would be the right thing to say?"

Mary blinked in confusion. "Well...'thank you' comes to mind. You know: show some gratitude."

"Ah." From the pocket of her clothes she produced what seemed to be a small sheaf of papers, folded up. She also had a small pencil and she scribbled on the paper while murmuring, "When being saved from falling, be grateful, and say 'thank you.'" She nodded, satisfied, then folded the papers, tucked them and the pencil away, and then said, "Thank you" without sounding the least bit thankful.

Mary had never seen such a strange way of behavior and decided to focus instead on getting back her crowbar. She snapped the rope a few times until she managed to dislodge it. As she hauled it toward her, she asked, "Who were those people? Why did they throw you in here?"

"They're the Galoots," said Purl. "They believe that this volcano is about to erupt, and that the only way to stop it from doing so is by making a sacrifice to the monsters they believe live in there. I was to be that sacrifice."

"You're their princess?"

Purl gave her a blank stare. "Do I look like a Galoot to you?"

Unsure of what Galoots looked like, Mary just shrugged.

The Galoots, meantime, remained at the top of the crater, shouting and waving their arms angrily. Then they started pointing the thin shafts down at the girls.

"That seems rather useless," said Mary. "Do they really think those spears are going to do them any good?"

"Spears...?" said Purl and her eyes widened as if she suddenly remembered something. "Take cover! Quickly!" And she shoved Mary back behind an extension of rock.

This annoyed Mary greatly, for she felt such treatment was highly rude. That was what she thought until something crackled directly over her head, and a large piece of rock was blown off the wall just above her. Hunter gave out a startled cry and ducked behind the *Argo* while Mary brought her arm up to shield her eyes from the fragments. There was a telltale stench of ozone from electricity in the air.

"Was that...*lightning?*"

"Yes," said Purl tersely. "Those aren't spears. The Galoots wield lightning rods. They store up and throw electricity."

"Where in the world did they get those?"

"From *Them.*"

This time Mary quite clearly heard the capital "T" in the word.

Then the cries from the Galoots came down to them. They

were begging, pleading. "Please!" they shouted. "Please throw yourselves in! The Mighty Ones are getting angrier and angrier! *They* are getting ready to erupt! Save us by sacrificing yourself!"

And it seemed that there was something to what the Galoots were saying, for Hunter was looking down from between his paws that were covering his eyes and saying, "I think the lava is getting higher."

Mary looked down. He was right; she was sure of it. The lava was starting to rise, the smoke becoming more intense, and there was a distinct rumbling that was beginning to build, as if a gigantic ball were rolling toward them from somewhere far below.

With the realization came immediate action. Mary, scrambling to her feet, yanked at Purl's arm. Purl pulled her arm away with annoyance and said, "What do you think you're—?"

"Get in," said Mary brusquely, having no time and less patience.

"That is not how a sidekick talks to a princess."

Mary stared at her, her jaw dropping. *"Sidekick?"*

"Yes. You have been dropped into my adventure; clearly you are a sidekick."

"No, *you* were dropped into *my* adventure, and you're just a distraction," said Mary, starting to take a serious dislike to the princess. "I don't need anyone coming with me."

"Hey!" said the lion cub in protest.

"Sorry, Hunter."

"Apology accepted, but maybe," and Hunter cast a worried glance downward, "we need to focus on other problems..."

Two things happened at the same time which brought truth to Hunter's words: Another round of lightning bolts thrown from above that barely missed Purl's head; and another fearful rumble from beneath that seemed even louder than before. The lava surged and a huge blast of the molten slag leaped upward, like a geyser, stopping short of them by only a couple of feet. The air became so hot that Mary was sure she felt her eyebrows starting to scorch.

"Time to go," said Mary firmly, "with or without you." Not bothering to see if Purl was following her, Mary climbed through the hatch of the *Argo*. Hunter, glad that it looked like they were getting ready to leave, leaped in after her.

Mary paused to see if the princess was following them. When she didn't appear to be, Mary reached upward to pull the hatch tightly closed. Just before she could do so, however, a dark-skinned leg extended from above into the hatch, followed by the other. She saw that Purl was wearing sandals with straps that ran all the way up to just under her knees. They were quite attractive. Within seconds Purl had clambered in next to her, looking around the cramped quarters in annoyance. "Not a good deal of room in here," she said.

"It's enough for Hunter and me. If you have another means of escaping, you're free to use it," Mary said sharply.

Purl looked like she was about to fire back with a snippy response, but she seemed to think better of it. Instead she said, "How is *this* going to be our means of escape?"

Mary hated to admit it, but it was actually a fair question. She wasn't going to take the time to answer it, though, since she felt it was going to be made clear in short order. Instead she moved past Purl, reached up and grabbed for the hatch. Just as she did so there was another violent quake, and the sound of distant explosions that weren't *quite* as distant as she would have liked. She yanked down on the hatch and it slammed with a clang that nearly deafened her. Hunter, whose hearing was sharper than hers, let out a yelp. Mary then spun the wheel so that the seal would be solid.

"You haven't answered me," said Purl.

"I was figuring events would do that for me."

Mary was correct.

If the Mighty Ones, whom the Galoots seemed to fear, were indeed living deep inside the volcano, then it was becoming obvious that they had reached the end of their patience. There was a roar from outside, and for the life of her Mary could not determine whether it was the natural fury of an explosion or the unnatural howl of anger from some creature deep within the pits. All she knew for sure was that there was a hellacious noise all around them. It was as if she had been dropped into the middle of a gigantic blender with a virtual wall of sound all around her.

She didn't have to see it to know exactly what was happening: The volcano was erupting. A massive blast of lava was spraying up from below and lifting them, propelling them, toward the top. Hunter let out a frightened mew and hid his head under his paws. Mary reached out, trying to brace herself against either side of the vessel, but quickly she withdrew her hand because the walls were becoming superheated. Fortunately the floor was lined with blankets, else they would have had nowhere safe to sit.

You would think that seeing Mary yank her hand away from the wall would be enough to stop Purl from doing the same thing. Instead, to Mary's surprise, Purl stared at the walls and then reached out, placing her hands flat against them on either side.

"Be careful!" said Mary.

Purl did not appear to listen. She kept her hands pressed against it. Mary couldn't fathom it. "Are you *trying* to hurt yourself?" she called out over the roaring of the volcano around them. The *Argo* was jolting with even greater violence than before.

"I want to see what it feels like."

"What *what* feels like?"

"Warmth."

"If that's what you wanted, you could just have let yourself fall into the lava!"

Giving her a very distant look, Purl said, "I thought about it, actually."

Before Mary could question her in greater detail, suddenly, just like that, the roaring was gone. The *Argo* began to slow.

"I think," said Mary, "that we just got blasted out the top of the erupting volcano. Perhaps the Galoots were right. Perhaps something down there is angry."

"Now what happens?"

"Well," said Mary thoughtfully, "either the ship develops wings and we glide...or else we simply fall. I think it could really go either way."

In short order the *Argo* came to halt. It hovered in midair for a few seconds, and then the front end tipped forward and gravity seized hold of it.

"Looks like we're falling," said Mary.

They fell.

It was the exact sort of situation where normal people would scream.

Mary, of course, did not.

Hunter, who seemed to have forgotten that he could not die, was mute with horror.

Purl laughed.

This struck even the fearless Mary as an odd reaction. She twisted around to face the young woman and said, "Why are you laughing? I mean, I'm not afraid of death, but even I don't laugh in the face of it. It seems rude."

Upon hearing her words, Purl stopped laughing. "That was the wrong thing to do?"

"It's unusual."

With a shrug, Purl said, "I was sure that the moment called for *some* manner of reaction. I couldn't recall which one was the correct one and took a guess."

"You are a very strange person."

"I'm not a person. I'm a statue brought to life through magic."

Mary and Hunter exchanged looks.

"That would explain it," said Mary, except it really didn't explain all that much and she hoped that she would live long enough to find out what Purl was talking about.

That was when the *Argo* landed.

It was not the smoothest of landings.

Instead they were jolted around violently, bouncing around off the sides of the vessel, slamming into the walls and each other. Hunter managed to leap this way and that, avoiding the repeated collisions through his feline reflexes.

The impacts were repeated and quick: Hit, fly, hit, fly, hit, fly. Mary quickly realized it was like a rock being skipped across the surface of a lake.

"I think we're on water!" she said.

"Does this thing float?"

"When it needs to."

Purl stared at her, her eyes seeming to glow in the darkness. "This is a rather strange vessel you have here."

"Yes, I know."

The *Argo* began to slow and soon came to a halt. Except it was not quite a halt; instead it felt as if it were drifting, which seemed to support the idea that they were on some body of water.

Mary reached up to start opening the hatch. Purl stared at the stub of her right arm. "You're missing a hand."

"Yes."

"And how should I react to that? Fright? Disgust? Curiosity?"

"Curiosity, and what's wrong with you?"

"Nothing, but then again, I have two hands. I'm curious: Is everyone missing a hand where you come from?"

"No, and are you curious because I told you to be?"

Purl was busy scribbling on the notepaper once more and didn't bother to answer.

Deciding to ignore her, Mary poked her head out to see what was what, and Purl was directly behind her, likewise looking around.

They were on a river. Impenetrable jungle lined it on either side, and there appeared to be unblinking, animal eyes watching them from deep within the darkness. Far, far behind them was the volcano, with lava pouring down the sides.

"I wonder if the Galoots managed to get clear."

"Who cares?" said Purl indifferently.

Now the Galoots were not Mary's favorite people, what with their trying to throw an innocent person into the heart of a bubbling volcano to what would surely have been her death. And certainly if anyone was going to hold a grudge, it would be the person who they'd been trying to kill. Still, Purl could have shown a little compassion. Or maybe she might have gone in the other direction and been outright overjoyed, feeling that the Galoots had it coming. It wouldn't have been very nice, but at least it would have been understandable.

"I would have thought you cared," said Mary.

Purl stared at her. "You would have been wrong."

"But why? I don't understand. You're a princess. You're supposed to care. You're acting like..."

"Like a statue brought to life?"

"You keep saying that. What are you talking about?"

Purl looked around them and saw that the wide, winding river was carrying them at a slow, steady pace further into the darkness.

"This is what I'm talking about," she said, and she told her exactly what she meant.

And this isn't quite how she told it, but it's close.

Chapter 8

How a Princess Lost Her Kingdom

Most stories tell of a country that is very distant, but this one will not. Instead let us speak of a close country, the name of which isn't that important since it is not there anymore, or at least not in a way that makes any difference. So for the purpose of this story, it shall simply be referred to as Close Country. As it so happened, Close Country was filled with Close people, and they were ruled over by a Close king and a Close queen.

And the country was peaceful, and Close.

And the country was rich, and Close.

The people went about their business. The builders built. The farmers farmed. The merchants merched. There was peace and there was a sense of unity and oneness of purpose.

Every so often, other countries would make noises of war, and send emissaries or even soldiers to try and take from the Close Country. When they did, though, they encountered a king and queen and people who said, "We are a land of plenty. What is ours is yours; we will be as neighbors to you and not take up arms against you." And the intruders would laugh or sneer at the cooperation of the people, because at first they thought as all other bullies did: That to display nothing but love and compassion and a refusal to fight was weakness. But the land was so filled with closeness, from the highest tower down to the deepest roots of the crops they grew, that newcomers could not help but become filled with it as well. Some of them would wind up staying in the Close Country and becoming productive citizens. The rest would return home with their bellies full and their minds happy, and if they ran into any who even spoke of going to war against the Close Country, they would do their best to talk them out of it. And if they failed to talk them out of it, then they settled for wishing them well and then killing them when their back was turned.

In that way did the Close Country remain peaceful.

And it was very important to the king and queen that it continue to remain so. They were not foolish people, this king and queen, for they knew that they were fortunate to rule over a country that was so Close. And they knew it was important that the Closeness be kept up. This is not always as easy as you might think, because times change and rulers change, and a country that knows peace and wealth one day can know terrible times not soon after. Much of a country's ability to maintain that peace and wealth depends on the quality of its rulers. So they knew how vital it was that those who followed them as rulers would feel the same closeness to their people as they did.

Now king or queen is an inherited title, passed on from father to son or mother to daughter. In this case the king had inherited his title from his father, and he was perfectly happy with the idea of either passing the title of king onto his son or queen onto his daughter.

So the king and queen set about trying to have a child in the normal way, or at least whatever the normal way is that your parents have told you such things are done.

One would have thought that it would not have been all that difficult because however you may have learned that such things happen, we can all agree that children come from love and closeness, and as we have already made clear, there were none closer than the king and queen of the Close Country.

But no child showed up.

They came close on occasion, but producing a child is one of those times where close was simply not good enough.

They were very frustrated. They tried everything they could think of. They used prayer. They used begging. They used songs. They used special diets. They used fasting. They used sleeping in different positions. They used not sleeping at all. They used Raoul Mitgong but he wasn't much help.

And still no child showed up.

The people of the kingdom were supportive, for they knew how much this meant to their king and queen, and they gave their best wishes and hopes that matters would turn out as their rulers desired. But slowly the fact that no heir was being provided really began to start bothering the people in the Close Country. They started worrying on behalf of their rulers, and wondered whether this was some manner of cosmic punishment. Which of course led them to start wondering just what the king and queen might have done to deserve it. No one knew of anything, but rulers can be very skilled at keeping things secret. Which in turn led the people to wonder what sorts of secrets were being kept from them.

And the king and queen knew that these thoughts were intruding upon the peaceful day-to-day life of their people, and they were truly grief-stricken that they were responsible for causing any sort of problems

"We must do something," said the king.

"Yes, we must," said the queen, "but what?"

The queen and king thought and pondered and discussed, and they kept coming back around to the same conclusion, and when they did they would hurriedly run away from it and try to come up with something else, but finally no matter how far their running took them, back to the same conclusion did they come. This happened more times than can really be counted, (we lie; it was seven) and finally they realized they would have to do what they didn't want to do.

They would have to talk to Them. Or, to put it another way, they would have to talk to *Them* (spoken with emphasis and, if you wish, a slight dramatic pause before "to" and "*Them.*" Also *They.* There are rumors that *They* and *Them* are two different groups, but that is just what *They* want you to think in order to confuse you. Why? Because that's the way *They* are.)

So the king and queen set out on their own, without their retinue or followers or anyone that normally supported them and protected them and assured them that everything they were saying or doing was entirely right and proper. They journeyed across the length and breadth of Afrasia, seeking *Them* out, and they met up with a variety of challenges and hazards about which we need not go into detail, except to say that they were challenging and hazardous. And the king and queen had to deal with all of it themselves, which served—we suppose—to prove that they were worthy of obtaining the goal that they had set.

And finally, they reached the land of *Them.*

It was unusual for the king and queen to be in the position of asking for something from someone else, for usually they were the ones to whom people came, hat in hand, asking for help. The closer they drew to *Them*, the more they disliked the notion of being in that position, but there was nothing to be done about it by this point. They had decided that this is what they had to do, and it was too late to get cold feet about it. (Again, we lie. They did, in fact, get cold feet, but that was because the country of *Them* was extraordinarily cold, being in the midst of a cold snap, leaving the king and queen with cold feet, icy stares, and chilly dispositions.)

The great home of *Them* was a vast building called City Hall, which was widely known for being something that no one could possibly fight, because *They* were simply too powerful. There were guards outside, each looking extremely dangerous, but they stepped aside when the king and queen approached, indicating that they should pass through unhindered.

They did so.

They were expecting that it would be very difficult to reach *Them*, but it turned out that *They* were expecting them. Without wasting time, the king and queen told their concerns, their fears, and their desires. *They* listened without comment, and after giving the matter much thought, this is what *They* said.

"Wait here."

They waited.

They lost track of how long they waited. Their bellies growled for food and their throats desired liquid to slake their thirsts, but they said nothing, asked for nothing, since they already felt that they were asking for so much that it would be Bad Form to ask for even more. Instead they remained silent, stoic, and as regal as they possibly could.

Eventually *They* returned, and *They* had brought with *Them* a block of marble. It was three feet tall and two feet wide. Marble is typically white, but not this. With this particular block the surface was gleaming ebony and seemed to absorb the light that shone upon it. It was rolled in upon a small cart, and *They* said the following:

"Have the greatest sculptor in your Close Country carve a child for you from this. Then put it out under the light of the full moon, and you will have that which you most desire."

"And what is the price for this?" said the king.

"The price will be that you will have that which you most desire. The rest will be made clear later on."

The king and queen exchanged puzzled looks, clearly hoping that the other understood, but neither of them did. But they didn't want to ask what *They* were talking about. Which is a shame, because if they had done so, they might have found out and been spared some heartbreak.

Instead they took the marble block and left with nothing more than a brisk, "Thank you." The king and queen hurried back to their kingdom as quickly as they could, considering that they were hauling a block of marble on a rolling cart. But the weight of it didn't matter, for their hearts were light and so everything else seemed lighter as well.

Along the way, the king and queen discussed what gender the child should be—that is to say, whether it should be a boy or a girl—and realized that they could not decide. So they decided to leave it entirely up to the sculptor, which made sense to them since there is a sort of grand sculptor who makes us all that typically decides upon the gender of all children.

They arrived back in Close Country in the dead of night. Hurrying to their castle, they then called in the greatest sculptor in the land, and gave him his instructions and promise of great reward if he did it successfully.

The sculptor took on the job eagerly and decided immediately that what the Close Country needed was a young and healthy prince. So he pictured what the young prince would look like and chipped away everything in the block that didn't look like the prince was supposed to look. He chipped and chipped and, at the worst possible time while he was chipping, he sneezed, and he looked down in horror at the vital piece that had hit the floor as a result of his errant strike. Then he shrugged and decided that a princess would be just as good.

And time passed, and the king and queen watched the sky and saw the full moon come and go and there was no child to put beneath its rays, which was disappointing, but these things take time. And so it went for another month, and then when the third full moon since their return was rapidly approaching, they were told that the sculptor had returned. Eagerly they summoned him to the throne room. He came quickly, wheeling on the very same cart the statue, covered with a cloth so that he could provide a dramatic revelation. The king and queen sat forward upon their thrones, consumed with eagerness, and the sculptor waved his hands over the covered statue like a magician and then pulled the cloth away.

The royal couple gasped in delight, particularly the queen who clapped her hands upon seeing that their child was to be a girl.

There upon the cart stood a perfectly formed female, looking about two years old, with delicate, carefully carved features, slender arms and legs, and a slightly rounded belly that would doubtless flatten out as time passed.

Thanking the sculptor profusely and giving him the promised sum, they hastened to the upper reaches of the castle with the statue and set it down carefully, spreading a blanket beneath it in order to provide it something soft to lie upon. Then they sat near it and waited, the queen resting her head upon the king's shoulder, watching as the sun set and the moon slowly crawled into the sky.

The king and queen were determined that they would not take their eyes off the miracle that was about to occur, but even as the statue was bathed in moonlight, the exhausted rulers drifted off to sleep.

When they awoke, they gasped at what they saw.

In the cold morning air, a two-year-old girl of flesh and blood was standing in front of them, naked as the day she was born, which of course made sense since this was the day she was born. There was such a chill, the air so thick with dew, that the royal teeth of the king and queen were chattering.

The girl's teeth were not. Instead she simply studied them with large, dark, thoughtful eyes. She was so unbothered by the cold air that she hadn't even bothered to drape the blanket around herself in order to provide warmth.

Her parents immediately ran to her, swaddling her in the blanket even though she did not seem especially interested in it. They welcomed her to their family, and they told her how loved she was, and how she was going to be a princess and be the eventual ruler of Close Country.

And were we ending the story here, we would be able to say, "And they lived happily ever after." But whereas stories end, people's lives do not (a third time, we lie: They do end, which is usually sad, which is why "happily ever after" is the biggest lie of all. Who, though, wants to read stories that end, "and they lived happily until they were unhappy because one of them died and then the other died," no matter how truthful that might be?)

The princess grew, as children typically did. She was slender and beautiful and everyone who saw her immediately fell in love with her.

She, however, fell in love with no one.

She didn't even fall in like with anyone.

It's not that she was nasty. She wasn't.

It's not that she was mean-spirited, or abusive. She wasn't those either.

What she was...

...was cold.

Marble has no heart, no soul. It doesn't breathe, it doesn't weep. Nothing can affect it...

...save for water. That is because, when it comes down to a war between water and anything else, water always wins.

Pounding waves will overwhelm the most determined of swimmers, just as they can pound down the most determined of barriers. Even the hardiest of rocks will eventually be worn down by the steady drip, drip, drip of water. Running rivers create vast gorges. Melting glaciers rearrange landscapes.

Water always wins.

If you remember nothing else of what we're saying in this chapter, remember that. It's important.

And now back to the princess.

There are some who look upon statues carved of marble and believe that they have a certain warmth, and perhaps there is something to that. But still, when you come down to it, it is stone, cold stone. It is not human.

The princess was human, but she carried her origins within her. It wasn't that she was invulnerable to harm. She could be hurt. She could be wounded. She could die. But there is more to life than worrying about losing it.

The problem was this:

She did not feel heat.

She did not feel cold.

She did not feel pain (although one assumed that she could be knocked unconscious).

She did not feel anything.

Instead she acted as if the world had very little to do with her, and her with it. If she saw people in pain, she felt no sympathy for them. If she saw people celebrating, she did not share in their joy.

She wasn't cruel about it or harsh or scolding. She didn't mutter "humbug" and snarl about how useless people were. She didn't attack them because she was annoyed to see them rejoicing or mourning things that she couldn't possibly share. She attended all functions that she was expected to attend and fulfilled the duties that a princess was expected to fulfill.

She just didn't care about any of it.

And when we say that she didn't care, we don't mean that she was deeply depressed or sad. We mean that she simply didn't see how any of it, including anything having to do with the human condition, mattered to her.

Life had little meaning to her. She understood that other people had deep emotions, and she knew that she did not. She didn't feel that made her any better than anyone else; just different. It was a difference that did not bother her at all.

It bothered her parents a lot.

It bothered the people of Close Country even more.

Because all of them—the king, the queen, and the people—were all used to the closeness for which their country was known. So to see a complete absence of that closeness in the princess was very, very disturbing.

The king and queen worried about this a great deal, until they couldn't think of anything else day and night, night and day. They were getting no younger, and sooner or later, their princess would be the ruler of the Close Country. It was a reign that frightened them to think about, because it seemed as if their daughter was totally lacking the compassion that any good ruler needed to rule well.

How would she be able to handle appeals for her help when she did not care about people's problems?

How would she be able to tend to their needs when their needs didn't matter to her?

How would she be able to care about what happened to her people when she couldn't shed a single tear?

There were rulers who were cold of heart, yes, but things usually went badly for them and for the people over whom they ruled, and the king and queen were horrified to think that such a fate might be awaiting their people once it came time for the princess to become ruler of the land.

Now there are many tales regarding princesses who have some manner of personal problem. These problems are solved through different means.

Sometimes the princess is locked up in a high tower, left alone to think about her situation, in the hopes that the aloneness might lead her to realize what was wrong with her life and make her decide to better herself.

But the king and queen could not bring themselves to send the princess away.

Another popular thing to do was bring in a whole bunch of possible grooms in the form of princes, with the occasional prince disguised as a beggar tossed in for good measure, and somehow those princes always managed to find a way to get the princess to smile, or laugh, or dance, or something.

So they tried that. Admittedly the princess was a bit young to be thinking about getting married, but the king and queen were hoping that the princes might stir some interest or romantic feeling in the heart of the princess.

Nothing. Princes came and princes went, and she was polite but indifferent to all of them, and whether they went on quests in her name or sang romantic songs or were willing to crawl across floors covered with jagged glass to prove how much they adored her in the hope that, at some future point when she was older, they might be joined in marriage, none of it made the slightest difference.

She was as cold as stone.

The queen cried and cried, and the king was grief-stricken, because they felt that they had made a great mistake in bringing her into their lives, and now they had no idea what to do with her.

Finally they were faced with a terrible decision.

They made it.

One night at dinner, the princess drank deeply of a beverage that tasted a bit odd to her. She had no idea why it did, but since she didn't care, she drank it down, as her parents knew that she would.

Then she felt a deep slumber embracing her and she barely had time to register that her parents had drugged her before she succumbed to the blackness of unconsciousness.

She awoke three days later.

The first thing that she realized when she came around was that she was incredibly hungry, which made sense since she had been sleeping for so long. (Even someone who had no feeling for hot or cold knew that it was time to eat.) Before determining why her parents had caused her to slumber, she wanted to eat something. She called loudly for servants to bring her food.

No voice answered save her own in the form of an echo.

She found this curious. She wasn't particularly upset about it, but even someone as unfeeling as the princess was used to things happening in a specific way.

So the princess looked around and found some food and water down in the kitchens. Much of it had been cleaned out, but there was quite a bit remaining. In the process of searching for food, she found no servants or ladies in waiting or any of the usual castle staff. This would obviously explain why no one had responded to her, but it did nothing to explain where they had all gone in the first place.

Once she'd eaten just enough so that she wasn't hungry anymore, she went out into the city to see where her parents and everyone else had gotten to. The princess emerged from the castle and blinked against what seemed an unusually bright sun that morning.

She saw no movement.

There was no movement in the public square.

There was no movement in the market place.

There was no movement on the great lawn where so many celebrations that she had attended without really caring about them were held.

A disturbing silence had settled upon the whole of Close Country, for no one was near.

She thought about this odd turn of events and then returned to the castle. As she passed through the great dining hall where she had last seen her parents, she spotted something that had fallen to the floor, perhaps blown off the table by a passing wind. It was a curled up document, and she went to it and picked it up, reading the contents carefully.

Here is what it said:

Our beloved daughter,

Every time we look upon you, we are filled with sadness, for we know that you can never be the queen that our country will need you to be. We have studied the situation very closely, and have consulted with Them, *hoping that* They *could tell us what to do since we cannot find it in our hearts to banish you from the only home that you have ever known. And* They *have given us advice, and although it is hard for us to accept, we believe it is the only way.*

And so, while you slept, we moved away.

We have gathered all of the people of Close Country and we have departed. We will go to Them *and* They *will in turn help us to create a new home in a Distant Country, and we will remember you fondly, but purely from a distance.*

Please know that we will always love you, even though we know that you never can, and never will, love us.

Your parents—the king and queen.

The princess read the note over and over. Then she turned it around and stared through the blank side, reading the words backwards to see if they made any more sense to her. Then she flipped it back and read it a few more times.

Then she lowered it, stared into the air at nothing in particular, and wondered one thing and one thing only. And she wondered it aloud, and what she wondered was this:

"Should I care about this?"

She wasn't sure. For so many years her parents had been telling her that she should care about this or that or some other thing. She had depended upon their guidance, and even though she hadn't actually cared about any of those things, she had kept a detailed list so that perhaps, at some point in the future, she would find the ability *to* care about these things. After all, her parents felt it was important, and so it probably was, even though she couldn't understand why. Over time, the list had become the only thing she really *did* care about. Not emotionally. She just liked the idea of having something she could refer to.

But they weren't around to tell her whether being abandoned in your sleep by an entire kingdom was worthy of concern, and if so, how one should react.

"I need to find this out in order to maintain my list," she said.

And so she returned to her room, got her list, folded it carefully, tucked it into the pocket of her traveling clothes, and set out. Seeing the marks of wagon wheels and such leading out of the city, she had no trouble figuring out which direction they had gone.

Within an hour, the princess who felt nothing had left the tallest spires of the Close Country far behind.

She didn't care.

Chapter 9

How Mary Reacted to Purl's Story

"Oh," said Mary. "And...did you find your missing people and family?"

"Not so far. I do not know where *They* reside and those that I have run into have not been forthcoming. I reached a vast granite desert and lost track of them. So I wandered in a different direction and after a series of events, wound up with the Galoots. The rest you know."

They bobbed along on the river for a while, the three of them—Mary, Purl, and Hunter. Hunter had stuck his head out and he was looking around. The thick jungle lined the river on either side, darkness hanging heavily upon it. Hunter growled low in his throat, his tail alternately swishing and stiffening. "We're being watched," he said finally.

"Are you sure?"

"Yes," he said with certainty. "I can smell them. I can smell everything," he added with a faint sense of wonderment. "This body that your imagination cooked up for me...it's amazing. I feel more alive than I ever did when I was alive."

"I'm glad you're happy, Hunter," Mary said a bit more short-tempered than was needed. "But I'd be more interested in what else you know about the people watching us."

"Right." His nostrils widened a bit more and he inhaled deeply, as if he were standing over a newly baked pie and enjoying the scent wafting from it. "There's a lot of them, whoever they are." His ears were twitching as well. "I can hear them, rustling around in there. I wonder if they have any idea how noisy they are."

"Do they have any weapons?" said Purl.

Mary stared at her. "How could he possibly know that?"

"If they have bows and arrows, the sound of bows creaking back to let fly. Guns would have triggers being cocked. Spears would be noiseless, but the river is wide, we're out of range of any but the strongest of arms, and they're not terribly accurate anyway."

"That all makes sense," said Hunter, and Mary hated to admit it, but he was right. It did. Hunter continued to listen carefully and then shook his head. "Nothing like that. They're just watching. If they do have weapons, they're not using them against us."

"Let them watch, then," said Purl with a shrug. "Of what possible interest to us could it be?" With that pronouncement, she sank back down into the ship.

Mary stared at her for a time. Then she turned to Hunter and said, "Keep watch, will you?" Hunter nodded and she dropped down onto the floor of the ship, facing Purl who had drawn her legs up cross-legged and stared at her, her narrow eyes glittering in the dim light.

"I don't believe you," Mary said flatly.

Purl raised a single eyebrow so high that it seemed to brush against the edge of her scalp. "Excuse me?"

"I don't believe that you don't care about anything."

"I don't see how that's my concern."

"You're in my ship. That makes it my concern."

Purl considered her words and then said, ""It's simply that I don't know what I am supposed to care about, or how I should feel about those things I am supposed to care about. It was what my parents and my people wanted me to do, and..." She paused and then pulled out her notes and checked them over. "...and it would have been nice if I had been able to do so. Nice?" She looked questioningly at Mary, who nodded. "Yes. Nice. That's what I thought," and she pocketed the notes once more. "But I can't and I don't. I care enough to want to go on living, if only because there are questions about me that will go unanswered if I should die. If, on the other hand, something were to transpire and I were to die, well...," and she shrugged again, "these things happen."

"It sounds so cold, the way you say it."

"Yes, well..." and she pointed at herself. "Stone."

Mary reached out and took Purl's hand and squeezed it. "It feels like normal skin to me. Cold. Colder than most. But there's lots of people who are cold. In fact, I once overheard one of my father's friends say his wife was frigid. So it's not all that unusual."

"The coldness isn't on the outside. It's on the inside," said Purl so matter-of-factly that she might have been talking about someone else. "The thing is, I'm rather used to it. It's all I know, and so for the longest time I didn't think it was all that unusual."

"Like someone who was born blind?"

"I suppose." Purl looked a bit mystified. "But somewhere along the way, I began to understand that other people didn't think the same way I did. They seemed to have all kinds of feelings that I didn't."

"Oh!" Hunter said to Mary. "She's like you!"

"She's nothing like me," Mary said quickly.

"Sure she is. You're fearless and she's—"

"I care about things, Hunter. She doesn't. If I didn't care about things, I'd never have gone looking for Anna's imagination in the first place, so stop saying I'm like her, okay?"

"Okay," said Hunter.

Purl acted as if they hadn't spoken at all. "I would watch other children with their parents, and their boundless range of reactions, and I knew that there was something missing from me."

"And that bothered you?"

"No. And shouldn't the fact that it didn't bother me...bother me?"

"Oh, bother," said Hunter, who was still a bit grumpy over the way Mary had spoken to him so sharply. "Girls only ever want to talk about their feelings. It can get a little tiresome, if you ask me."

"Nobody did," said Purl pointedly.

Mary started again. "But have you considered—?"

Sounding ever so much like a princess, Purl announced, "We are done talking about this. It will accomplish nothing and so is not worth my time. Instead you will tell me why you are here."

"Do you care?"

"Not really, but since you did save me, I will do my best to pretend that I do." She put her hand to her chin in what she believed to be a thoughtful manner and widened her narrow eyes as far as they would go so as to look interested. "You said something about the imagination of someone named Anna?"

"Well, yes." She proceeded to tell her everything that had brought them to this particular place. She was pleased to see, as she spoke, that Purl genuinely appeared to be listening. She knew that Purl said she was only pretending to do so, but she doubted that was the case. Nobody, thought Mary, was that good an actress.

Mary was so thorough in the telling that she finished by saying, "And then you said, 'Not really, but since you did save me, I will do my best to pretend that I do.' And then I told you, and here we are." She took a breath and let it out slowly, because it indeed had been a very long tale. Reaching for her canteen, she took a careful swig of water. She knew it was important to ration what she had, but then out of politeness she extended it to Purl. If anyone was likely to be thirsty, it was the princess, because certainly escaping from the inside of a raging volcano was thirsty work. Yet Purl said no, waving it off. This struck Mary as odd. "You're not thirsty?"

"I am, but I figure you will need it more."

Mary smiled warmly. "Thank you. That's very considerate."

"I know." She held up her list. "It's right here. *Giving food to others because they need it more = considerate.* The hero is supposed to make the sidekick feel as if she is worthwhile, and showing consideration is the simplest way to do that. My list is quite useful, isn't it?"

"You're unbelievable." Mary was annoyed all over again. "And I'm not your sidekick."

Purl didn't seem to have heard her. "So you are here, now, trying to find your friend's runaway imagination. Do you have the slightest idea which way you're going? Whether you're heading toward it or away from it?"

"Not really," Mary was forced to admit. "Hunter got me here, but it's too much to hope that Hunter could lead us to Anna's imagination..."

"Sure, I can," Hunter said chipperly. "We're on our way there right now."

"What?" Mary was astounded. "How is that possible?"

"I picked up her scent once I was here."

"*Her* scent?"

Hunter, who had been perched at the top of the hatch, dropped down lightly once more and smiled. Mary never realized quite how odd smiles looked on lions. It made it seem as if he were looking forward to eating them. "Yes. I couldn't smell it from the cemetery, but now that we're here..."

Mary said, "How could you have the scent of the imagination of a girl that you've never met?"

"The girl's been here, in this vessel," Hunter said promptly. "She's spent a good deal of time here, hasn't she?"

"Yes." Mary smiled at the recollection. "Yes. Many, many hours. We traveled oh-so-many places together."

"Well, I figure that whatever isn't your scent, or yours," and he nodded toward Purl, "has to be hers. And her imagination shares her scent. It's very, very far away, but I smell it on the faint breeze of the night, for imaginations are both powerful and personal. I don't know where this river is taking us, but it's in the direction of what you're looking for."

"And in the direction of what Purl is looking for as well?"

"I wouldn't know." Hunter sounded apologetic. "Sorry, princess."

"That's all right," said Purl with her typical coldness. "I will go where the river takes me and deal with whatever I find at that point."

"All right then," said Mary as if she was settling the matter rather than being carried along by the flow of events. "That answers that, then. You are welcome to join us on our journey..."

"I'm not joining you," Purl said. "You're joining me. You're my sidekick."

Mary stared at her as if the words were hanging in the air. "Why do you keep calling me your..."

"Sidekick. The person who comes with me on my adventure.

My mother," said Purl, "read me many stories and they were very specific about that sort of thing."

There was really no reason for Mary to feel annoyed about this and yet she was. Fearless she might have been, but she had as much pride as any typical child. "I'm not your sidekick. If anything, you're my sidekick."

"Hey!" Hunter protested, his fur literally ruffled.

"My human sidekick," she corrected herself. "I started this adventure without you, and I can complete it just fine without you. Now if you want to come along, that's perfectly okay with me, but I don't see what gives you the right to act like you're the boss or something."

For response, Purl pointed to the top of her head.

Mary stared at her in confusion. "What are you doing?"

"Pointing to my crown."

"You're not wearing a crown."

"I left it at home because it's heavy. But when I'm wearing it, it's up here."

"And your point is what?"

"That a princess is no one's sidekick. It doesn't work that way. Side kickage flows down, not up."

"First of all," said Mary heatedly, "I'm pretty sure there's no such word as 'kickage,' and second, how much of a princess are you if your entire kingdom ran away from you?"

Purl's lips thinned and she said regally, "It's fortunate that you can't upset me, because if you could, I would be very upset right now."

Mary chuckled at that. "It sounds to me as if you're not quite as uncaring as you say you are, my friend."

"We are not friends."

Now understand that when Mary had said "my friend," she

hadn't really been thinking about whether she and Purl *were* friends. "My friend" was just something that one says. If you say, "Hey, buddy, get out of my way" to a total stranger, obviously he's not actually your buddy.

But still...

To hear Purl just dismiss the notion of their being friends out of hand like that, as if the idea were ridiculous...as if *she* were ridiculous...

It hurt her.

It hurt her more than she wanted to admit.

And she thought, *How could Hunter say I'm like her? Because her feelings don't get hurt and mine do.*

But she had absolutely no intention of showing the slightest sign of weakness in front of Purl. She wasn't going to give Purl the satisfaction of knowing she had that sort of power over her.

"Thank you for clearing that up," Mary said as archly as she could. "I won't make that mistake again."

"Good."

"And if you find my company so annoying," Mary continued, "you're perfectly welcome to jump out anytime you want."

"I can't do that, obviously. I wasn't looking for a sidekick, but now that I have one, it would be extremely Bad Form to simply leave you behind. No," she sighed, "it appears that I am stuck with you."

"You poor thing," said Hunter, with a sarcastic purr. (Sarcasm is sounding like you mean something, but you really don't; you mean the exact opposite.) Mary had never known there was such a thing as a sarcastic purr before, and was impressed that Hunter had mastered it, especially considering that he had been a lion for such a brief period.

"Don't feel sorry for me," said Purl, who seemed to have no

understanding of sarcasm. "I know I certainly don't."

Feeling annoyed that she had gone to all the trouble of saving Purl, Mary slumped against the interior of the *Argo*, drew her legs up and wrapped her arms around her knees.

"Are you tired?" said Hunter, looking at her with concern.

"No," said Mary, because that's what you're always supposed to say when you're a child and someone asks you if you're tired. But it was a lie, and she knew it was a lie, because she could feel sleep pulling at her eyelids. She was literally fighting to keep her eyes open, and she knew it was a fight she was going to lose. The bottom line was that she was up way past her bedtime and it was catching up with her. With the realization that she wasn't going to last much longer, she hastily added, "But I might become tired soon. We need someone to keep watch—"

"*I'll do it!*" Hunter said immediately, his tail straight out with excitement over the idea of being trusted to watch over Mary. "I'm the best one for it! I can see best in the dark, and hear the best, and I smell the best—"

Purl sniffed. "Actually, I think you could use a bath."

"I didn't mean 'smell' in *that* way," Hunter said. But then he started licking at his coat just in case.

Not wishing to keep talking about it, Mary quickly said, "That would be fine, Hunter. Go to it."

Hunter stopped cleaning himself and bounced over to the hatch. Flapping his wings, he fluttered upward and draped his upper half over the rim of the hatch, and maintained his perch with his hind legs.

"Can he be trusted?" said Purl warily.

"Yes," said Mary. "And you know why? Because *he* cares about what happens."

She waited for some sort of snippy or imperious response from

Purl. Instead, to her surprise, Purl considered that briefly and then said, "From my understanding: He is fortunate."

With that rather curious declaration, Purl slid down to a sitting position. She crossed her legs into a yoga position, draped her hands on her upper legs, and looked straight ahead. "What are you doing?" said Mary.

"Thinking," said Purl.

"About what?"

"Whatever occurs to me."

Mary was about to ask more about it, but sleep was pounding toward her and she could push it away no longer, particularly since the slow bobbing of the vessel was lulling her. Her head thumped back against the hull of the ship, her eyes slammed shut, her breathing slowed and in less than a minute she was sound asleep.

She was awakened by a very loud sound. Confused, briefly forgetting where she was, she couldn't figure out what the noise was or why it seemed to be coming from everywhere. Then Mary realized: the river had gotten noisier.

A lot noisier.

And the *Argo* was moving faster.

A lot faster.

But, she told herself, *we're not in any danger, because if we were, Hunter would have warned us.*

Then she heard a soft snoring and looked down. Hunter was curled up on the floor next to her, his eyes closed. The sides of his body were rising and falling in time with the snores.

Mary's head snapped around and looked toward Purl. The princess was in the exact same position she'd been in before; Mary could easily believe that Purl had begun life as a statue. But her eyes were also shut.

Sunlight was flooding through the hatchway. This greatly

concerned Mary, because it meant that the only hope she now had for returning home before night was over was if time passed differently in Afrasia than it did back home. That twelve hours in Afrasia was the same as twelve minutes back home. Kind of like how dreams seem to take a very long time but actually pass through the sleeping mind in seconds. She would have no way of knowing if that was the case until she got back.

It couldn't be helped now, though.

"*Wake up!*" shouted Mary as she got to her feet. Her legs felt numb; they were still asleep and her knees almost gave way. As Purl and Hunter looked around in confusion, she shook off the feeling like a million insects running up and down her legs and hauled herself to standing. Then, stumbling, she got over to the hatch and stuck her head out, even as Hunter was babbling apologies over having fallen asleep for just a few moments, and Purl was demanding what in the world was going on in just this way: "What's going on up there!"

"I don't know!" Mary shouted back and she looked accusingly at an embarrassed Hunter. "*Someone* was supposed to be watching!" Hunter whimpered and slunk back from the irritation in her voice.

"Well, *find out!*" Purl ordered. Cold to emotions and feelings she might have been, but she was still a princess and used to ordering others about and having those orders obeyed.

And that was when Mary made her first serious mistake (assuming that you didn't count her setting out on the entire mad adventure as a mistake). What she really should have done was batten down the hatch and ride out the situation. Instead she did as Purl instructed, partly out of reflex because Purl sounded so princessy that it just seemed the thing to do, and partly because she was genuinely curious to know.

Without even thinking about it, she grabbed her knapsack and slung it over her shoulders. Then she climbed up the hatch and looked out.

Now: Some quick information about waterfalls and how they're normally shown in movies.

Usually when the heroes are on a collision course with disaster with a waterfall, there's time for them to realize their danger. This is done for dramatic purposes, to get the audience all worked up about it. Will they go over the falls? Will they find some way to avoid it? Will this waterfall mean certain death and, thus, will they all die, even though that would make no sense at all since—if they do die—there's really nothing left save for the villain to say, "*Mwwa-hahah!*" and roll the final credits. What fun would that be for the audience?

Anyway: This is not a movie, and so things can, and do, happen a bit differently.

So it was that between the time that Mary stuck her upper body out the hatch and the time that the *Argo* hurtled over the edge of a Very High Waterfall was no time at all. There was no big build-up, there was no realization that the slow, lazy river had changed into speeding white water rapids, there was no sudden understanding of the peril before her. There wasn't even time for her to shout, *"Waterfall!"*

Basically the instant she came out of the ship to see what was happening and the instant the ship headed over the edge was the selfsame instant.

As a result, Mary had no time to grab hold of anything. She was sideways before she even realized what was happening, and the next thing she knew she was airborne, pitched headlong out of the *Argo*. There was no doubt in her mind that Hunter would have cried out in alarm while Purl would have said something like that she had not given permission for her "sidekick" to be thrown out of the boat, but Mary couldn't possibly have heard it over the crashing of the waterfall all around her.

Then the *Argo* disappeared into the raging waters of the falls, and Mary was alone, falling, with the bottom of the falls looming below her and getting closer very, very quickly.

Chapter 10

How Mary was Captured

There is one other thing you should really know about Mary before we go any further. We have not brought it up earlier than this since it was not really all that important before now. But pretty soon you're going to see Mary doing some pretty impressive things, and you may find yourself wondering, "How is that possible for such a young girl to do all this? When could she possibly have learned it? It seems very unlikely."

Except it isn't. If you actually know how Mary's brain works, then you will understand that it all makes perfect sense.

Let us start by putting it as simply as we can:

Mary had an exceptional memory.

There are different names for the type of memory that Mary had. The ordinary name is *photographic memory*. The scientific name—because scientists cannot, simply *cannot* stand being ordinary—is *eidetic memory*. What that means is that when Mary saw something then, if she chose to, she remembered it completely.

Mary's memory was very orderly and precise and more mature than most adults, which is likely why she spoke the way she did.

If Mary saw something that she had no particular desire to remember, she would remove it from her brain as one would erase a drawing. She didn't waste one single cell of the gray matter in her brain on those things she decided weren't important.

On the other hand, she was able to remember perfectly anything she felt *was* important. And the way she did it was by taking a sort of mental snapshot of it. If she read a book that she felt was worthwhile, she could recall every word on every page after staring at it for about thirty seconds, so that she never again had to pick it up and read it. It was the big reason, aside from her fearlessness, that her imagination was so powerful. She could visualize perfectly whatever she wanted. It made her imagination not simply a child's ability at play, but more like a force of nature.

More than that, however: If she saw someone extremely skilled performing some impressive feat, and she watched it for long enough, then she remembered every detail of how it was done. And if she chose to picture herself doing it, then her muscles would be able to imitate it to perfection.

Which, when you think about it, is actually a fairly good way to handle challenging situations as you go through life. You do not need an eidetic memory to picture yourself, say, hitting the ball squarely and driving in the winning run, or receiving an A-Plus on a test or quiz. Envision it hard enough, believe in it enough, and you can accomplish anything.

Except leaping off a building and flying. No matter how much you picture yourself doing that, it's not going to work.

Same thing with stopping a speeding car with your body and not being hurt.

Or wrestling a snarling monster of a dog to the ground.

You know what? Now that we think about it, maybe it would be best if you forgot everything we just said. Which, as it so happens, you can probably only do if you have the sort of very ordered and tidy mind that Mary had. If you don't, then none of what we've said really matters all that much. Then again, nothing we say in general means all that much, so at least we're being consistent.

Where were we?

Ah yes. Mary was falling to her apparent death, with the bottom of a thunderous waterfall yawning beneath her.

The year before Mary wound up in Afrasia, the summer Olympic games were being held. Her parents watched them constantly, and so Mary watched a bunch of the greatest athletes in the world doing amazing things. She watched them and memorized everything they did.

Are we saying that Mary could have gone and competed in the Olympics? Of course not. She had school and so had no time for games.

But she could call up from her memory everything that they had done and order her muscles to imitate those marvelous athletes in every way.

Had she been afraid of impending death, of course, she could not have managed it. Her mind would have locked up; her body would have done the same, and when she struck the water below it would have been with such force that she might as well have landed on a mattress made of rock. By the same token, if she'd flipped around in midair, she could have snapped her spine or broken her neck and been dead before she made it to the water.

Instead, her mind seized upon what she'd seen the Olympic divers do. The smooth way they positioned their bodies, the way that they split the water when they struck.

Do that, her mind ordered her body, and her muscles obeyed her command, kind of like the way a printer does when a computer sends information into it and moments later a perfect picture comes out.

Her arms snapped out in front of her and she twisted her body around in midair so that she was head down. Her legs obeyed her brain's command and stuck out behind her, and her back stiffened. As precise and perfect as a missile, she headed straight down toward the churning water far below her.

This didn't mean that she was not in any danger. Oh no, most definitely not.

To begin with, she had no idea whether she was going to hit a deep enough section of water to cushion her fall, or if she was diving head first into a bed of rocks. It didn't matter how fearless she was or how perfect her dive; smashing directly into jagged stones would put an end to her just as much as if she'd been a terrified young girl landing like a flopping fish.

Second, if she was lucky enough to hit a deep section of water, it was all churning around so fiercely that it might drag her under and keep her there. She was a strong swimmer even though she only had one hand, but she was only as strong as a child could be. Bravery wasn't a substitute for muscle.

She knew these were risks. She knew she might well be falling to her death, and that she could end up a bloody pulp on rocks below, or perhaps wind up with water filling her lungs and sinking like a stone. *One thing at a time*, she thought, which is how fearless people tend to deal with things. Fearful people, when faced with something dangerous, can become paralyzed by thinking about one thing after another going wrong, and in becoming paralyzed, can't even handle the first thing. A fearless person, such as Mary, just figures that she will come through each challenge and face the next one head on. Although, we have to admit, that Mary's way of dealing with it wasn't always the cheeriest. For instance: *At least if I hit rocks and die instantly, then I won't have to worry about drowning.* See what we mean?

As it turned out, she hit water, not rocks.

Down under the water she went, the roar of the waterfall becoming less and less as she submerged, water filling her ears. She took a moment to glance around and see if the *Argo* was anywhere around underwater. There was no sign of it. That didn't bother her. As long as Purl and Hunter remained inside, they would be fine.

Unless, of course, water came flooding in through the open hatch.

Don't think of such things, she ordered herself. It bothered her that she had to remind herself not to think about things going wrong.

Then, in the murk, she had a vague view of the bottom of the riverbed racing up toward her. She had barely enough time to twist around, her head and upper shoulders taking the impact. A cloud of silt rolled up around her when she hit and she felt dizzy and confused. For a moment she lost the sense of which way was up and which down, but then her thrashing feet touched bottom. She pushed up with all the strength in her legs, aiming for the surface.

The knapsack was heavy on her back, trying to drag her back down again. For a moment she thought about shrugging it off her shoulders and leaving it behind, a sacrifice to the gods of the river. Then she considered everything that she had to face in that calm, logical way she had, that caused her thoughts to be so orderly even in the face of incredible amounts of trouble. *I am most certainly going to need some, if not all, of the things in my knapsack to survive. If I die now at the bottom of the river, or I die later because*

I didn't have what I needed to face a challenge, I'll wind up just as dead either way. So I might as well try to keep the knapsack around and just deal with it.

The decision made, she kicked furiously toward the surface, knapsack secure on her back. The knapsack jostled around against her spine, but she ignored it, determined to just power through.

Then she felt the current grabbing hold of her. Fortunately it wasn't trying to pull her down; instead it was pulling her sideways. It was far too strong for her to fight, and so she allowed it to yank her along, tugging her further from the falls, which was good, but not allowing her to get closer to the surface, which wasn't so good. It was hard for her to see how close to the surface she was; everything around her was murky, even though it was daytime.

Wait for your first chance and then kick toward the surface, she told herself, keeping her cool. At the same time, however, her lungs were starting to burn more and more, demanding that the stale air inside them be released and new air be drawn in. But unlike the *Argo*, which she could transform with the power of her imagination to become what was needed, she couldn't command herself to grow gills and be able to breathe underwater. She had to get to the surface.

She rode with the current for as long as she could afford to do so, and then decided that it was now or, quite possibly, never.

Mary kicked her legs even harder than before, pumping her arms like a frog's, trying to angle herself toward the surface. For a moment that seemed to stretch out into forever, it seemed like the current was going to keep holding on to her. Someone else might have given up or gotten so desperate that they would have panicked and drowned; yet Mary, for some reason that even she didn't quite understand, suddenly had a mental image of a great sailing vessel, like the kind that pirates steered back in the old days, and it was sailing straight and true, keeping to its course even though it was in the middle of a storm. She followed that picture in her mind, and it helped her keep her sense of mental balance and determination.

She was kicking with all the strength she had left in her body. Her lungs were on fire, her chest feeling heavier by the second, as if there was an anvil inside it trying to weigh her down. She wondered if having two hands would have helped her get the job done, and then tossed aside such thoughts as being not at all helpful. She had to do the best she could with what she had at hand or, more exactly, didn't have at hand.

And suddenly the surface was right there, just inches away, and she snapped her legs together in one final display of her determination and lunged for safety.

Her head broke water and she thrashed, gulping in deep lungsful of air. There was water in her eyes and she was gasping, and as a result didn't see the large branch hanging low over the water and right in her path.

Mary slammed into the branch at the full speed of the river current, banging her head into it, the second such impact within the past minute or two. At least the riverbed had been soft; the branch most definitely was not.

It wasn't as if she even had any kind of chance to avoid it; at the point where she made it to the surface, her back was to the oncoming branch. She struck it with such force that for an instant she could feel her brain sloshing around inside her skull.

She felt blackness falling upon her and blindly she grabbed out. Her hand snagged one of the upper portions of the branch, which she barely had time to realize was a fallen tree limb. She reached up with her other arm, and this time actually cursed the fact that she was missing a right hand; it would have made her life a lot easier. Instead she shoved her right up and kept shoving with the remains of her rapidly fleeing strength until she was able to wrap her arm fully around it. Then she managed to pull her right leg up. Her left leg was still dangling in the water and mentally she commanded it to move, but it ignored her. It was like her brain was shutting down and a wall had sprung up between it and the rest of her body. *I hope a crocodile doesn't show up*, and that was the last thought that flittered through her head before she blacked out.

Waking up from being knocked out isn't at all the same as waking up from falling asleep. Falling asleep is a gentle process and, unless you're in the grip of a nightmare and are fighting to escape it, waking up is likewise a gentle, even relaxed thing.

Not so when coming around from being knocked cold due to a whack in the skull. First of all, there's the pain that starts at the point in your head where you got hit and just sort of creeps out like painful fingers squeezing on your skull. Sometimes your neck is stiff as well, which was the case with Mary in this instance. Then there's the whole thing of feeling confused. You have no idea where you are or how you got there. This usually comes from the fact that someone has found you unconscious and declared, "We must bring this person someplace where they can be helped!" And so when you do wake up, you have to figure out where you are and how you came to be there, and that can take you a while because it's hard to think because your head hurts.

So there was Mary, in pain, uncertain of where she was, trying to stand up and being rewarded with even more pain for her efforts. She realized that she was still alive, which was certainly a plus since there had been every reason to think that she would wake up dead.

She began to stand up and discovered that that was impossible. There were thick ropes pulled tightly across her chest, binding her arms to her sides, and it turned out she had been tied to a solid upright pole. Mary frowned and then pulled at it just to see what would happen. There was no slack. She had no means of yanking clear of it. Whoever had attached her to the pole had done a very complete job.

It was at that point that she looked around, trying to get an idea of where exactly she had wound up. She saw that there was a series of tents all around her, encircling her, about a dozen in all. Each tent looked large enough to fit comfortably three, maybe four people. She was impressed by how exact the layout of the tents was. They weren't scattered around; instead they were, as near as she could see, in a perfect circle with her at the exact center, like the hub in the middle of a wheel, and there was exactly the same distance between each tent. The outsides of the tents were white and crisp, with not a scrap of dirt or mud on them, so either they were newly pitched or else—and she suspected this to be the case—the occupants were really into keeping them clean.

"Hello," she called out. "Is anyone here?"

There was a slow rustling from within the tents and then, one by one, she saw people coming out.

They were dressed in crisp white pants with white boots, and red jackets with broad shoulders and gold epaulets that gleamed in the sunlight. They were adjusting their hats on their heads; the hats were high and white and conical and had gleaming red stones set in the middle of them. Each person had a curved sword dangling from a scabbard on his belt.

And every single one of them was an old man.

They had a variety of facial hair, ranging from bristling mustaches to thick sideburns or even mutton chops. Some of them looked so much like goats that she half expected them to start saying "baaa."

They were clearly soldiers of some kind. The tallest of them strode forward and came to within a few feet of her. Of the lot of them, he was certainly the sturdiest looking. It was very likely that, when he was in his prime, he was quite a tough opponent. But his prime was...she wasn't sure how long ago. Maybe centuries. He studied her this way and that and "harrumphed" a few times.

"Who are you?" she said.

"Now see here, young lady," said the tall one, "we'll be the ones asking the questions here."

"All right," said Mary, who didn't see much point in arguing about it.

He glared at her from underneath his thick eyebrows as if he thought that she was trying to trick him. "Very well," and he drew himself up to make himself looking even taller. "Who are you?"

"Mary Dear."

"Now see here!" he thundered, clearly annoyed. "You shouldn't be using such overly familiar terms of affection, considering that you are not only our prisoner, but we have just met!"

She stared at him, not knowing what in the world he was talking about, and then she understood. It was all she could do not to laugh, but she managed not to since she felt it would be impolite. "'Dear' is my last name. Mary is my first name. My full name is Mary Dear."

"Yes, yes, I understand. I'm neither a fool nor deaf, you know."

Mary in fact knew neither. He seemed rather foolish to her, and his advanced age might indeed have promised some measure of deafness, but she saw little reason to point out either fact since she was tied up.

"All right," she said, which seemed the only smart thing to do since there was no point in getting him more upset.

"Now what," he said stiffly, "are you doing here, Mary Dear?"

"Nothing. I'm tied to a post."

"I mean, why are you here?"

"Someone tied me to it."

"You are not giving me any useful answers."

"Then perhaps," said Mary, whose patience was beginning to wear thin, "you might want to come up with better questions."

There were a few snickers from the other soldiers, but an angry look from her questioner silenced them. He leaned in toward her and said, "Do you have any idea who you are being rude to, young lady?"

"No."

"I," and he grew a foot taller because he was standing on ceremony, "am Captain Mykeptin, commanding officer of the Old Guard. Certainly you've heard of us."

"Certainly I have not."

All of the soldiers gasped, stunned that they had run someone who knew nothing of their legend. "We," said the captain proudly, "are the main personal protectors of," and he paused for the usual moment of drama, "*Them*."

"*Them?*"

"Yes. Without us, *They* would be lost."

"So...we're near *Them?*"

"No, not at all. *They* are quite a distance away."

Mary blinked several times, giving her time to consider this bit of information. "I would have thought," she said finally, "that personal protectors would have to be closer to the people they're protecting. But you're here and *They*...aren't."

His mustache bristled a bit more. "You are a child and do not understand anything of the way things are."

"I understand that you are trying to stop me from reaching *Them*."

"*Aha!* So you *are* trying to get to *Them*." There was nodding from all around.

'Yes," said Mary. "I wasn't trying to keep it a secret. I have business with *Them*. I have reason to believe *They* stole my friend's imagination, and I'm here to get it back."

They started to laugh.

"Stop laughing this instant," she said sharply and with absolutely no patience.

They stopped laughing immediately. Then the Old Guard looked at each other in surprise, wondering just what it had been about the tone in her voice that had commanded immediate respect.

Even the captain had stopped in surprise when she had spoken so. He was well aware, though, that all eyes were upon him and he was about to say something clever and commanding in return.

That was right before a full-throated, very loud roar froze every other man in the camp.

"*The Furies!*" one of them shouted, and the others took up the call, which meant nothing to Mary.

"Stand fast, men!" Captain Mykeptin cried out, but even he was clearly upset by the animal sound that had pierced the air.

So it was that they were all backing up when Hunter came down from overhead, his wings fluttering fiercely to slow him down. He dropped directly toward Mary and, as he fell past her, he popped his claws and raked them across the ropes that were keeping her tied to the pole. Instantly Mary stood, shaking off the last of them. Her knapsack was a short distance away and she grabbed it up. Hunter scrambled around, momentarily losing his footing in the dirt but quickly regaining it and then crouching defensively in front of Mary. He bared his teeth, looking around warningly.

"That's not a Fury!" one of the soldiers said.

"What the blazes is it?"

"Whatever it is, it's an odd combination of terrifying and cuddly."

The soldiers were clearly confused by what they were seeing, to say nothing of the conflict of fear and cuteness that Hunter represented, and were so even more surprised when a sharp, commanding voice said, "Come no closer."

There was a rustle from tree branches overhead and then Purl dropped down into the clearing as well. She was holding a long branch sideways; it had been stripped of leaves and bark and was fairly straight. It could serve as a walking staff but also—even more dangerously considering the way she was holding it—as a weapon. "You heard the terrifyingly cuddly creature. Stay away from my sidekick."

"I'm not your sidekick," Mary said, unsure whether to be grateful or annoyed.

"Here now, she says she's not your sidekick," said Captain Mykeptin. "Is it possible you have her confused with someone else?"

"No, that's definitely her," Purl said with the sort of certainty that came from her being a princess. "And you will release her to me now or," and she waved the makeshift weapon meaningfully, "there will be problems."

The captain did not appreciate threats from a slip of a girl armed with a stick. "Sergeant," he snapped at one of his underlings. "Arrest that youngster and that...thing," he waved vaguely toward Hunter, "with her."

The sergeant came toward her. Hunter growled threateningly and looked ready to spring, although he seemed a lot less dangerous when he had shown himself to be a small winged lion than when he'd been roaring from hiding and been mistaken for a Fury, whatever that was.

Purl took two quick steps forward, keeping the staff leveled. In response the sergeant yanked out his sword, waving it threateningly. Purl ignored it as if it were not there, reversed the direction of the staff, and jabbed it forward like a pool cue. It struck the sergeant squarely in the middle of the chest. He gasped, the wind knocked out of him. Just trying to defend himself, he swept his sword around in a broad arc that Purl easily ducked under and then she struck again, whacking the rod soundly against the sergeant's knees. His legs buckled and he went down, with Purl using the staff to slap his sword out of his hand as he fell. It bounced across the dirt, Hunter hopping over it easily to avoid it.

In spite of herself and her mixed feelings about Purl, Mary had to admit she was impressed. "Nicely done," she said.

Purl had immediately snapped back into a defensive pose. "I was well trained," she said and then, as an afterthought, she pulled out her notes with one hand and glanced at them. "But I think this is one of those moments when I should say 'thank you.' Is that right?"

"It's generally considered the right thing to say, yes."

"Then thank you." She promptly tucked the notes away.

The captain had pulled out his own sword, and the rest of the Old Guard had their weapons out as well. Purl watched them warily and Mary was not pleased about the odds. Purl was a skilled fighter and powerful, certainly, and these guardsmen were elderly. In a full-out battle, though, anything could happen, and even one stray and lucky slash of a sword could open a vein in Purl's neck before she could strike it away. And who knew whether Hunter would be of any real use when it came to combat, although what with his being dead already, he certainly had very little to lose.

Still, she had gotten herself into this situation, and she felt it was her job to get herself out of it.

The picture of icy calm, she stepped between Purl and the captain, whose mustache seemed to be taking on a life of its own, and said, "They're only here because I am. And I am only here," she continued, "because of you. One of you pulled me out of the river, I take it?"

"That is correct," said the captain, not lowering his weapon, apparently thinking she was planning some sort of trick.

"Then I am grateful to you for that. And I have no argument with you. But if you wish to harm me or my friends, then you're leaving me no choice but to—"

"To what?" He chortled, amused by so much defiance from such a little girl. "To challenge me to a duel?"

"Yes," said Mary without hesitation. "Here. Now. And when I win, you will let us leave without giving us any more problems."

"*When* you win?" The captain let out a huge guffaw, which was promptly picked up by the rest of his men. Within moments the air was filled with laughter by the amused soldiers.

Mary wasn't laughing. Instead, the picture of calm, she undid her knapsack. As the soldiers continued in their merriment at her expense, she removed the leather strip, lay it down on the ground and then placed one of the lug nuts carefully in it. Then, in her one hand, she picked up either end of the leather strip and let it dangle there, the lug nut sitting securely within. "Do we have an agreement?" she said. The question did nothing to slow down the laughter, even though her strong voice carried above it. And so she added, "Or are you too much a coward?"

That brought the laughter to a quick halt.

The captain's mustache now looked ready to leap off his lip and attack her all on its own. His cheeks flushed furiously red, his eyebrows knit so closely together that they looked like one single line of brow across his face. He tried to say, "How dare you!" but he was so filled with anger that he wasn't able to get any of the words out.

And then, with a roar of pure fury, uncaring of the fact that he was facing a little girl who was holding nothing but a piece of leather and a lug nut, he charged straight at her, waving his sword above his head and clearly ready to bring it swinging down in a killing stroke.

Mary never flinched. Instead she braced her feet firmly, drew back the leather strap, whipped it around several times in order to get enough speed, and then snapped it forward as hard as she could, allowing one of the ends to drop from her hand and send the lug nut hurtling through the air.

It sailed straight into the captain's open mouth.

He stopped dead in his tracks, his war cry instantly replaced by silence, followed by gagging. Then he staggered, clutching at his throat, trying to cough up the lug nut that had lodged firmly in his windpipe. The sword dropped from his hand and he tried to shout orders to his men to do something, anything, to save his life. But he couldn't draw any breath since the lug nut was blocking his air. His men were used to being told what to do, and since he wasn't telling them to do anything, they stayed right where they were.

Captain Mykeptin fell to his knees, and his face began to turn a horrible shade of blue that made his mustache and sideburns look even whiter.

Then he slumped onto his back, staring at the sky, his chest slowing. His hand stopped its clawing at his throat and fell to one side.

"Good." It was Purl. Her voice was flat, detached, even practical. "One less enemy is one less enemy."

That was the moment that Mary abruptly ran forward, as fast

as her legs would carry her. And then she jumped and brought both feet down squarely on the captain's chest.

There was a sudden rush of air from inside the captain, as if she had stomped on a balloon, followed by a popping noise. And with the sound came the lug nut, exploding from out of the captain's mouth into the air.

Mary deftly caught it. Then she calmly wiped it against the front of her clothing in order to dry it. Once that was done, she stepped down from his chest and replaced the lug nut in the box from which she had taken it.

Meanwhile the captain had managed to sit up. He had his hand to his chest and the blue tint was slowly vanishing from his face, allowing it to return to its normal color. He was wide-eyed, having heard the furious hoof beats of death riding toward him, only to be turned away at the last moment. He coughed a few times to make certain that his lungs were clear, and then he looked to his men. "You did nothing while I was in trouble—?"

"You always tell us to do nothing without your orders. You weren't giving us orders," said the sergeant.

"I couldn't *breathe! I was dying!*"

"Well," said the sergeant reasonably, "if you had died, *then* the chain of command would have fallen to me, and *I* could have given orders. But as long as you were alive and weren't talking, we were simply awaiting instructions."

Once again the captain was speechless, but not for lack of air. Then he pulled himself together and slowly got to his feet. He looked down at Mary, but there was new respect in his face. "You could have let me die."

She said nothing. She didn't think anything needed to be said.

"Sergeant!" he promptly called, his voice still a bit scratchy.

"Yes, sir!" said the sergeant with a great deal of enthusiasm.

"Clear out of your tent. We have honored guests, and you will provide them your quarters."

"Yes, sir!" said the sergeant with a good deal less enthusiasm.

The captain nodded once approvingly and then he turned back to Mary. He saluted crisply and she returned it. "It is getting late in the day," he said which Mary had to take his word for. She didn't know how long she had been unconscious, nor did she know how long days in Afrasia lasted. "Tomorrow morning, if you still want to go there, we will escort you to *Them*. It's not something we should really be doing," he added with a *harrumph*, "but your behavior was in extremely Good Form, and deserves to be recognized."

"Thank you," she said.

His chin stiffened. "Do not be so quick to thank me, child. Reaching *Them* may well be a case of getting your wish not being everything you wanted it to be."

Mary, Purl and Hunter went into the tent that they'd been assigned. A meal of tea, scones and some manner of beef—Mary wasn't entirely sure what kind it was—was given them. But it tasted decent enough, and she hadn't realized how hungry she was until that moment. Hunter showed some mild interest, commenting that he had forgotten how things tasted. Purl ate just precisely enough to keep her body going, and nothing beyond that. "I see no necessity for things that aren't necessary," Purl said, and it was difficult for Mary to argue about that.

"Speaking of things that are necessary: Where's the *Argo?*" said Mary.

"Hidden," Hunter said. "It helped us survive going over the falls, but we got banged up somewhat and knocked out. When we came to, we had drifted a ways down river. We brought it to shore and hid it in the underbrush, and then came looking for you.

I managed to track your scent here." He smiled as much as his mouth allowed. "Am I not clever?"

"Ever so. But how did you know even to look? How did you know I hadn't drowned?"

"I would have known," Hunter said flatly. "If you were dead, I would have known."

"Because you yourself are dead?" said Mary.

Hunter nodded and then licked his paws. "Yes. Although it's odd. I'm dead, but I feel alive as well. And I don't know if I'm remembering how it felt, or only imagining that I remember it."

Mary considered it. "What's the difference?"

"Not much, I suppose."

Purl took a minimal sip of the tea and then said pointedly, "You ignored me."

"Pardon?"

"When I told you to let the soldier die. You ignored me."

"Oh. Yes," she said, recalling the incident. "I did do that."

She had pulled out her notes and had a pencil poised. "Why?"

"Because," said Mary matter-of-factly, "I didn't want to do what you said."

"But I'm a princess, and you're my companion on an adventure. You're supposed to do what I say, because I know better." She didn't sound particularly arrogant or high-handed about it. She just clearly didn't understand why things weren't happening the way she believed they were supposed to. For someone who was older than Mary and presumably more experienced in the world, she was remarkably naïve. "So should I feel angry that you disobeyed me?"

"I don't have to obey you."

"Yes, you do."

"No," said Mary firmly, "I don't."

"I think you're wrong."

"Well, I didn't obey you, so obviously I'm right."

"I'm just going to hide over here," said Hunter and he placed himself as far from the girls as he could.

Purl stared at her. "You're not going to tell me how I should feel about your disobeying me?"

Mary thought about it and then said, "You should be patient and interested in what I have to say."

"Not angry? Because I would have thought angry."

"No, not at all."

"Okay," said Purl and she quickly scribbled what Mary had told her in her notes. Mary tried to hide her smile. That had been way easier than she'd thought. Purl folded up the notes, put it back, and then said, "So...I am patiently interested. Why didn't you do what I said?"

"Because then I would have killed him. And I didn't want to be someone who killed someone else. Not if I could find a way to avoid it."

"*He* didn't care about avoiding it."

"Well, I did. And that's all that was important to me."

"Dying isn't so bad," said Hunter. "You could have let him—"

"No," said Mary, more sharply than she had meant to. "I couldn't. Even though..." She paused.

"Even though what?" Hunter prompted her.

"Even though I missed."

They both stared at Mary, not understanding. "What did you miss?" Purl said.

"I wasn't aiming at his mouth. I didn't know he'd be yelling. I was trying to hit him in the head, like David did with Goliath."

"Like who did with who?" said Purl. Apparently the stories that her mother had read her hadn't included the bible.

But Hunter knew well what she was talking about. "Didn't

David kill Goliath when he did that?"

"Yes."

"Oh. So...you were trying to—"

"Yes," said Mary, and she felt a bit ashamed. "I was just thinking about...not letting my mission fail, and I was ready to stop him, no matter what. And my shot missed and went in his mouth and down his throat, and I saw a chance to save him so that I wouldn't have to...so I saved him. All right?" She was starting to sound a bit annoyed about it. "And it all worked out."

"But it might not have," Purl pointed out. "He might have picked up his sword and come at you again, and then what would you have done?"

"I don't know. I would have figured out something."

"Well," said Purl, "I suggest you work on figuring it out ahead of time, because if you wait to figure it out while it's happening, it could well be too late."

"And why," said Mary, "would that matter to you? Oh wait, I forgot. It wouldn't matter to you, because nothing matters to you because we're not friends. Except if that's the case, then why did you come looking for me at all? Obviously you were concerned about what had happened to me."

"I was curious. It's not the same thing at all."

"And you were fighting for me. What does that mean, if you say you don't care?"

"Why were you," Purl shot back, "afraid to kill the man who was trying to kill you? You, who say you're fearless."

"I am."

"But afraid to kill."

"Not wanting to isn't the same as being afraid to."

"It sounds all the same to me," said Purl, sounding rather indifferent about it.

"The two of you!" Hunter said. "You keep acting like you're nothing alike, and you don't even want to realize how much you have in common. What's a Fury?"

The question came so completely out of nowhere that it stopped both Mary and Purl in mid-discussion as they were preparing to throw more accusations back and forth. They looked at him and he said, speaking very carefully, "They said they thought I was a Fury. They sounded very worried about it, and very relieved to find out I wasn't. So what is one?"

Mary, who was very well-read, or at least very well read to, said, "They were something out of Greek mythology. Angry women who avenged the dead, or something like that. They weren't very pleasant."

"And they thought that's what I was? That doesn't make a lot of sense."

"None of this makes any sense," said Mary, feeling a bit annoyed with everything and every one around her. Moreover, her concern over her parents was growing. She wasn't any closer to Anna's runaway imagination, and now so much time had passed that her parents couldn't help but be worried about her. This entire business wasn't going at all the way it was supposed to. "Time is slipping away," she said, giving voice to the end of a string of thoughts that she hadn't bothered to share with the others.

"It has a way of doing that," Purl agreed. It was perhaps the very first thing they'd agreed upon since they first met. "It's there, and then it's gone. You're young, and then you're old, sometimes in the blink of an eye, and you're left wondering where your life has gone."

"Do you think," said Mary, partly lying down, propping up her head on her hand, "that that would be something you would finally care about? I mean, even rocks are worn down by time. So maybe its passage would affect even you."

Purl scratched her chin thoughtfully. "I don't know. I suppose I will find out if and when I should run into it."

Mary shook her head, sighing heavily in a way that sounded much like the way her mother would sometimes sigh with her. She was surprised to discover she had her mother's sigh, but then she put it aside. "I really don't understand you, Purl."

"It's not my job to explain myself to you. I do not need you to understand me, nor am I asking you to, nor do I care if you do. Don't try to make your problems into mine."

Something in her voice set Mary's teeth on edge, and the girl said sharply, "It must be nice not to care about what people think of you, or about other people's feelings, or anything at all."

Purl was silent for a time, and then she looked at Mary levelly and said softly, "No. It's very hard."

Mary had no idea what to make of that reply, and she was about to ask, when suddenly a series of high pitched shrieks tore through the air, and then before they could react, and before they knew anything at all, the Furies were upon them.

Chapter 11

How the Old Guard Became Old

There are some who say that Afrasia was a far more generous, even pleasant place before *They* showed up and took it over. And *They* being *They*, no one even knew about *Them* until it was too late and everything that happened in Afrasia simply happened because that was the way *They* wanted it. And if pressed, no one would even have been able to say precisely when *They* came onto the scene. Previously *They* had been somewhere else, but at some point *They* had decided that Afrasia would be their new place to live. And so it was. And you certainly couldn't fight *Them* because *They* always won. It was a war that had been fought without any being declared, and won without a shot having been fired. That's just how good *They* were.

There was another theory that said that *They* had always been there. That *They* had somehow come into being in *Their* stronghold of the unfightable City Hall just like that, out of nowhere, with origins as mysterious as that of the universe itself.

Here, though, is what the Old Guard would have said, had they been given the chance to discuss the matter:

Before City Hall was called City Hall, it was called something else. And it was overseen by someone or someones who were far more generous and considerate than *They* were. And this person or persons were protected by Captain Mykeptin and his soldiers who were, at the time, simply called the Vanguard. And then something changed, something that no one in the Vanguard could readily recall, either because they were getting on in years and such things were harder for them to remember, or else because reality had changed in such a way that what they thought was true, was no longer the case.

All the Vanguard knew for sure were these things:

First: *They* were now in charge, and it seemed as if *They* had always been in charge.

Second: The services of the Vanguard were no longer required. Instead they were told to depart City Hall immediately.

Third: *They* had new defenders, and they were known as the Furry Furies.

The Furry Furies, or Furies for short, were simply just there, as out of the blue as *They Themselves* had been. In truth, not all of them were furry, but they were all animals, and they were all furious, or at the very least fought as if they were filled with fury. They were utterly at the command of *Them,* and it seemed no enemy could stand against them.

Told that they were now old and out of date, the Vanguard didn't want to leave. But *They* unleashed the Furry Furies on them, and the Vanguard—finding themselves beaten back by the attack of an army unlike any they'd ever seen—sounded the retreat.

They had never retreated before.

The act of doing so broke something within them. No longer were they the Vanguard, the first and best line of defense for Those In Charge. Instead they were simply the Old Guard, cast aside in favor of something newer and better.

They retreated deep into the jungle and set up a camp there, and they embraced the old saying that they also serve who stand and wait. The newly christened "Old Guard" told anyone who would listen, which was mostly themselves, that they were serving as a sort of outer guards for *Them*, since the truth of the matter—that they had been cast aside like worn out shoes—was simply too painful for them to think about.

And while they remained in the jungle, pretending to be something they were not, they aged rather quickly. Nothing will age you quite as much as retirement will, especially if it's something forced upon you. As a result the Old Guard was, in very short order, living up to its name. They looked old. They felt old. They acted old.

They *were* old.

It happens in real life more often than you would think. The period of time between when something is young and something is old is constantly shrinking. How quickly does a song that you once loved become one that you can hardly stand to listen to? Or a television program you used to enjoy suddenly seems old and uninteresting. For that matter, you do it to yourself, all the time: Something that you used to love—some toy, or a fictional character, or a cartoon—is tossed aside because now you are "too old" for such things. Deciding that you are "too old" for something that you once enjoyed is the first step toward becoming too old to enjoy anything.

You would never think that inside every old person, there is a young person betrayed by a body becoming too old and fragile to do all the things it once did, but that is often the case.

Make no mistake: The Old Guard was as brave a group of old soldiers as you could possibly expect to find. But the Furry Furies were their great weakness. They had no idea how to deal with the creatures because they didn't fully understand what they were or where they had come from, and their sheer overwhelming animal nature was too much for the Old Guard to deal with. Plus just thinking about the Furies would remind the old soldiers of how they were tossed aside, their services no longer needed. So all the Furies had to do was show up and the Old Guard's confidence was so shattered that they were less than useless.

Now you know exactly where matters stood when the Furry Furies came tearing into camp that night.

Here is what happened next.

The roars from outside immediately alerted Mary, Purl and Hunter to the idea that something was wrong. They were coming from everywhere, and they were thunderous and terrifying to anyone who was of a mind to be terrified.

Hunter's immediate impulse was to curl up in a ball. He backed up, hunching his spine, lowering his head, his wings angling down in as submissive a manner as possible. "Something out there wants to kill us!" he said.

"You're already dead," Mary said.

"But I'm getting used to not feeling that way, and I'd appreciate it if you would stop reminding me of that."

"All right." Mary didn't want to seem unreasonable about it.

"Stay here," Purl said, brandishing the staff that she had fashioned from a branch. "I'm going to see what's happening out there."

Mary was about to ask her why she cared, but then remembered that Purl had said there was a difference between caring and simply being curious. She wasn't entirely sure she understood it, but obviously it was good enough for Purl, and so she didn't see much point in arguing about it.

Even as Purl headed out of the tent, Mary undid her knapsack and withdrew the crowbar. She took an odd comfort in the weight of it. "We may have to fight for our lives," she told Hunter, "or at least I'll have to fight for mine, and you for whatever it is that's existing under your pelt."

When she said that, there was a complete change in Hunter's posture. Instead of looking frightened and submissive, he padded forward and took up station at the entrance to the tent. His wings extended, and when he stretched out his paws, his claws stuck out from them. "I will fight for you," he said firmly. "They will not hurt you, whoever or whatever they are. I will not let them."

Mary had never felt quite so touched. She reached down and scratched Hunter on the back of his head and he flattened his ears in response. "Thank you," she said.

"You're welcome. Get ready. And don't be afraid."

"Not really a problem."

She whipped the crowbar back and forth several times, liking the sound it made in the air. For some reason, when she looked at it, she could almost see herself holding a sword in her hand. It felt oddly comforting.

She and Hunter stayed where they were, facing the opening, waiting for an attack that they were both sure would come. The roaring and howling of animal voices continued. "Is your nose telling you anything?" she asked Hunter.

He inhaled deeply. "Animals. Lots of animals. Different types. And..." He scented once more. "Human scents."

"Coming from the soldiers."

"No," he said. "Coming from the animals."

"You mean they're part human, part creature? Like werewolves?

Or centaurs?" Her knowledge of all sorts of mythic creatures was coming in handy.

"I'm not sure what I mean," said Hunter. "It's just...strange. If I had more practice at being a lion, it might be easier..."

"Whatever it is," she said, squeezing the crowbar tighter, "sooner or later, it's going to come in here. And then we'll deal with it." There was not the slightest doubt in her mind that she would be able to handle it, whatever it was.

The longer they waited, though, the more concerned Mary became. She had been hearing shouts torn from human throats that she had been certain were the soldiers, but she had heard what sounded like a challenging battle cry from Purl. For someone who claimed not to care about anything, she seemed to take a grim pleasure in combat.

But then she heard fewer and fewer voices that sounded like human, nor was she hearing Purl's war cries at all. Suddenly, rather than waiting calmly for an attack so that she might have the upper hand, she started getting the feeling that she had waited too long.

Purl ordered me to stay in here. Why did I even listen to her?

With that thought, she bolted for the opening of the tent. Hunter let out a startled cry, telling her to stay back, but Mary was through taking orders from companions, whether they were princess or possessed toy.

She emerged from the tent, waving her crowbar around, ready for a target to strike as hard as she could. Realizing that she wasn't going to remain in hiding, Hunter ran out after her, his teeth bared, ready to take on anything that was going to attack her.

Nothing did, because nothing remained. Or at least, nothing that was going to be a threat.

There was no sign of the Old Guard anywhere. She looked around quickly, wondering if she would see great pools of blood or chewed upon bones. But there was nothing like that at all. Instead all the tent flaps were shut. The campfire was blazing and because of that, it gave her enough light that she could see the silhouettes of the soldiers within the tents. They were visibly shaking with fear, probably worried that they might be seen by whatever it had been that had come tearing through the encampment.

"What in the *world!*" Mary cried out, astounded by what she was seeing. "You're supposed to be soldiers! What sort of cowards are you!?"

The captain came out of his tent, clearly trying to grab hold of his fleeing dignity with both hands. He squared his shoulders and straightened his jacket. "You do not understand..."

"Of course she understands. You're perfectly happy to fight a young girl," Hunter said. "But anything other than that—"

And the captain shouted at them, "I had two hundred men under my command! *Two hundred!* The best, proudest soldiers in the history of Afrasia! And when *They* first tried to send us on our way, we fought back! We wanted to continue to serve the land. And those...those things, those Furry Furies, servants of *Them,* fell upon us and tore into us! My men stood against them, and then we broke, and then we ran!" His voice was trembling with shame. "Scarcely two dozen of us survived that massacre! What you saw here was all that was left of a once proud fighting force. So when those creatures came at us again, here in this...this pathetic place we call home, we hid and we prayed they would leave us alone! And I didn't see you, Missy," and he pointed his sword at Mary, "stepping out to fight them!"

"Purl told us to stay inside," Hunter said defensively.

"And you obey her, do you? Or do you only do so when it's convenient for you?"

Mary had no ready response for that. Why *had* she remained

inside when Purl told her to? That wasn't something a fearless adventurer would do. A fearful sidekick, yes, but not her.

"Or maybe," continued the captain ruthlessly, "you were hoping something would happen to her so that you could get her out of the way and not have to worry about her anymore."

"That sounds right," Hunter said, his tail twitching happily.

Mary turned to him and said impatiently, "No, Hunter, that's *not* right!" Hunter drew back, surprised by the scolding, and his ears flattened. She felt regret over having possibly upset Hunter, and in order to show there were no hard feelings, she scratched the back of his head. He purred softly and rubbed against her legs. Then she turned back to the captain and said, "Purl wanted to handle it. I decided to honor her request."

"Lucky for you, then, that the Furry Furies took her away. It was obvious that you didn't like her, and now you don't have to worry about her anymore."

"Of course I'm worried about her," said Mary.

"Why? She was arrogant and high-handed to you. Why would you worry about her?"

"Because..." She hesitated, and then said softly, "because she came looking for me when she didn't have to. Which makes me wonder if she *really* doesn't care about anything, like she says, or if she just keeps *saying* it because it's easier *not* to care about things. I don't know. What I do know," she continued sounding more sure of herself, "is that, if these Furry Fury things captured her, then I have to go after them and free her. Are you coming?"

"Me?" said the captain. "Why would I come along?"

"Because you said you were going to bring me to *Them*. And since the Furies work for *Them*, then obviously they're connected in some way..."

"It was one thing to bring you to them as guides. Quite another to have to fight the Furies. We'll pass on that, thank you, very much."

Mary glared at him. "You," she said, "are just cowards."

"You should be more like Mary," Hunter said proudly, still rubbing against her legs. "She's fearless."

The captain snorted. "And you think that somehow makes her better than us?"

"Well, yes, obviously," said Hunter.

"Well, that's how much you know," the captain told him. "If you're not afraid of anything, then you don't have to be brave to do great things. Being brave means overcoming your fears. If you have no fears to overcome, then nothing you do means anything."

Mary was very annoyed to hear this comment. "So here we've got you, who's so scared you can't do anything. And then we have me, who has no fears and so I can do anything, or at the very least, try. And when the things I'm trying to do are all to help other people, what does meaning matter?"

"It matters," said the captain gravely. Then, as if that was the final word on the subject, he turned away from her with his head held as high as he could possibly manage it and vanished into his tent.

Even Mary's very organized mind was starting to feel a little overwhelmed. It was like she was having quest piled on top of quest. This had begun with her trying to track down Anna's runaway imagination. Then she had picked up a fellow traveler in the form of Hunter. Then she had stumbled into the middle of Purl's own adventure, and the princess in turn had tried to draft Mary's quest as part of her own. And somehow all of this was tied to *Them*, who might well have been the one or ones responsible for Anna's imagination running away, and now these Furry Furies had—what? Kidnapped Purl? So now she had to go save Purl again? Or was that even possible, since for all Mary knew, Purl had been killed or eaten or worse.

"I need the *Argo*," Mary finally said. It seemed a reasonable decision to her. Her ship was her center of calm. Her journey began there and, with any luck, would end there. Once she returned to it, climbed inside and used it to focus her own powerful imagination, she knew that everything else would become clear. "Where did you say it was?"

"Up the river," Hunter said confidently. He was bounding around, obviously pleased that whatever annoyance Mary might have felt for him earlier, it had passed. "We hid it well, under some brush, but I know I can find it again."

"Good. That's what we'll do." Thinking out loud, she repacked her knapsack to rearrange everything since much of it had gotten thrown around as she pulled things out and tossed them back in. "Once we're back to the *Argo*, I'll turn it into some sort of land vehicle. We'll use it to drive after Purl and find out where they've taken her."

"You can drive?"

"If the vehicle is imaginary, sure. What would be the point in imagining something that I couldn't work?"

"That does sound silly," he said.

The soldiers did nothing to stop them in any way from leaving the camp. Mary thought she could hear a collective sigh of relief being breathed as Hunter and she left. She didn't believe that she was in any way responsible for bringing the Furry Furies down upon the Old Guard, but perhaps the soldiers thought otherwise.

Hunter led the way. It was easy not to get lost, because they were walking along the shoreline, and all they had to do in order to keep going in the right direction was follow the way that the river was running. The sun was just starting to rise, which Mary far preferred. If the Furies, whatever they were, attempted to attack them, it would be harder for them to get the element of surprise if they didn't have the darkness to hide their movements.

They continued along the shore until Hunter said, "Here. Right here, near that large rock. We hauled the box into the forest. Look there. You can even see the marks in the ground where we dragged it."

He was right. There were track marks on the ground, broken branches littering the way. Even if Hunter had not been with her, finding the *Argo* would have been no great trick.

They made their way through, and minutes later, Mary saw the *Argo* lying sideways in a clearing. It no longer looked like a submarine or a boat or any kind of transportation. Without Mary's imagination to keep powering it from within, it had become a refrigerator box after Purl and Hunter left it, although—let's face it—it was a truly amazing refrigerator box. "I thought you said you hid it."

"We did," said Hunter. "We dragged it behind—"

Then he stopped so suddenly that Mary nearly tripped over him. "Hunter! Why did—!"

He shushed her. "Something's wrong," he said. "There's a scent coming from the box. Something that wasn't there before. Something," and he paused, his tail twitching furiously. "Something alive."

"Is it one of the Furies?" Naturally she wasn't afraid, but she was very interested to see what one of them looked like, after having heard so much about them.

"I don't think so. For one thing, it doesn't smell at all furry, or even warm blooded," he said. He flicked his tail to indicate that she should follow him and she did, both of them moving as carefully as possible. *Fearless, not reckless.* The advice of the long-gone woman was as fresh to her now as if it had happened just the previous day.

Then Mary saw a few strands of something rippling from within the box. "What is that?" she said, pointing.

"Some kind of white thread."

"It wasn't there before. Where did it—?"

He was wandering toward it, staring at it with great interest, and suddenly Mary called out, "Hunter, wait! Back up! Don't get near it and don't touch it!"

Hunter immediately obeyed even though he didn't understand why. But then the smell came to him even stronger than before. The white threads had distracted him, the way such things can do when it comes to cats—even winged ones.

There was a skittering from within the carton, and it moved this way and that for a few moments. Instantly Mary was reaching into her knapsack, yanking out the crowbar and holding it defensively.

Something large and ugly and hairy slowly unfolded itself from within the refrigerator carton. Tufts of white silken thread were clinging to it, waving in the breeze like tiny flags. A thick black liquid was dripping steadily from its maw, and its mandibles were clicking together like castanets.

"What *are* you?" Mary said, her eyes wide in surprise. She had never seen any creature like this. It had multiple, slender legs covered with black hair, each of them hinged in several places. It looked a lot like a spider, but it was as big as an automobile and, worse, there was what appeared to be some manner of curved stinger on its back, flicking in one direction and then the other. It pointed at Mary, then at Hunter, who cowered fearfully, then back to Mary, who neither cowered nor was fearful.

The creature seemed to find this interesting and turned its full attention to Mary.

It spoke, its voice thick and whispery.

"What have we here?" it said.

"*We* have my ship," Mary said making no attempt to hide her annoyance. "And *we* had best get out of if immediately."

"Finders keepers," it reminded her. "That is simply the law of the universe."

"Not this time," she said defiantly. "That is my ship."

"Really? Did you buy it? Have you a receipt for it?"

"No," said Mary, a little less defiantly.

"Then how did you wind up with it?"

"I..." She hated to admit it, but there was nothing else she could say. "I found it."

"Ah." That seemed to settle it. "And now I have found it. So it is mine."

"She makes a convincing case," said Hunter, and then saw the annoyed look Mary was giving him. "I'll wait over here."

"Please do." Then she returned her attention to the gigantic creature. "What are you, anyway? A spider?"

The creature's mandibles clicked more forcefully, apparently irritated at the suggestion. "A common spider? Me? The very idea! I am a Cob! You've seen the webs of my kind, certainly."

"Yes. I thought they were just spider webs."

"Spider webs are spun by spiders. Obviously cobwebs are made by something else. My kind is that something else. Are we not magnificent?"

"Yes, you are," Mary had to admit.

"And we are also hungry. We have become tired of eating the occasional birds that fall into our webs. We were hoping," said the Cob eagerly, "that you would enter our new home and join us for dinner."

"Sorry to disappoint you," said Mary, who in fact wasn't sorry in the least. "And it's not your new home; it's my ship."

"Only if you ignore the finders keepers rule, which seemed

just fine with you when you did it, but now you would deny us that same rule." Its large head twisted around and its solid, black, soulless eyes fixed on the stump of her right arm. "Did something else get a taste of you?"

"No. I was born this way."

"And you will die this way as well."

"Not willingly and not easily," said Mary. She whipped the crowbar back and forth.

There was a beating of wings nearby her; it was Hunter. The wind from his wings blew her hair about and he said softly in her ear, "Her head is quite small and attached to her body by a very thin neck. I'm sure I can cut through the neck and then crush the head between my paws."

"If I don't crush it first with my crowbar." Mary had no taste for killing, but the Cob disgusted her. Even though it was capable of speech, she wasn't going to hesitate to do whatever she had to so that she wouldn't wind up in the belly of this beast. Plus she was well and truly angry that it had staked a claim on her ship.

"You are going to make this difficult, aren't you?" The Cob tapped one of its limbs thoughtfully on the ground, and then said, "It is far too nice a day to get involved in fights and such. What if I were to offer you a challenge?"

"What sort of challenge?" Mary was hesitant. "Not a quest. I'm already juggling several quests and don't need one more."

"You juggle? With one hand?"

"Not actually juggle. I meant..." She blew air through her lips in annoyance. "As long as the challenge isn't a quest—"

"It's not. I will ask you a riddle. If you are able to answer it, then you may have your home back and I will walk away. If not, then you will not fight me as I eat you alive."

"Fine," she said.

"*Not fine!*" Hunter said. He landed on her head and looked down into her face. "Are you out of your mind? Riddles? Being eaten alive? Do you *want* this to end badly?"

"No. But I'm not going to run from a challenge."

"It's a challenge where that creature holds all the advantage!"

"If I had all the advantage, it wouldn't be a challenge."

Hunter couldn't argue with that logic, but still, he was not pleased. "And if you lose, then I'm supposed to simply stand by and watch that thing devour you?"

"I expect you to honor the challenge. Anything else would be Bad Form."

She then brushed him off her head, and he fluttered to the ground a short distance away. "All right. Go ahead."

"You have made a mistake, little one. A very bad mistake." The Cob chuckled deep in its thorax, which is what it had instead of a chest. "For there are none in Afrasia more skilled in riddles than I. You will be able to measure the rest of your life in minutes."

"So you say. Do your worst."

"Very well," said the Cob. It fastened its heartless gaze upon Mary and then said, "*What...is at the center...of every problem?*" Its stinger twitched in excitement. "You may take as much time as you wish to think about it. In fact, the longer you take as you realize how doomed you are, the more I will—"

"The letter 'b'."

The Cob looked as if air had been released from it. "What?"

"The letter 'b' is in the middle of the word 'problem.' That was easy."

"It was not easy, and it was not even the riddle. I was simply testing you," said the Cob defensively. "To see what level of difficulty I should provide you when giving you the *real* riddle."

"That's ridiculous."

"Do you want the box back?"

Mary rolled her eyes. "Oh, very well."

The Cob rolled back and forth a few times on its legs and then said, "*What is broken every time it is spoken?* And this time I will give you only five minutes to—"

"Silence. Silence is broken every time it's spoken."

"Will you *stop that!*" The Cob looked as if it were ready to fly apart on its own out of pure frustration.

"I answered your riddle. I answered two. Now get out of my ship."

"Best three out of five."

"Oh, come *on!*" Hunter spoke up in exasperation. "This is ridiculous!'

"I swear," the Cob intoned, "by all the honor of the Cob, that if she can answer this, I will leave immediately."

Mary, her arms folded, was tapping her foot impatiently. "That's what you promised two riddles ago."

"Yes, but I didn't swear."

Feeling very annoyed but deciding to play matters through to the end, Mary said, "Fine. Go ahead."

Hunter, sharing her annoyance, flopped onto the ground and covered his eyes with his paws.

The Cob drew itself up and said in a low, deep voice, "*What walks on four legs in the morning, two in the afternoon, and three in the evening?* And you only have ten seconds to—"

"Oh, for crying out loud, the answer is 'Man,'" said Mary. "In the morning of his life, when he's a baby, he crawls on all fours. In the afternoon of his life, when he's grown, he walks upright. And in the evening of his life, when he's old, he walks with a cane—"

The Cob glared at her. "That's wrong."

"It's *not* wrong! It's not even *original!* That's the riddle of the

Sphinx! It's thousands of years old, you stupid bug. Now," she said triumphantly, "you promised by the honor of the Cob that you would leave. So leave."

The Cob spoke with a low and deadly calm. "You think you know so much, don't you, little one. Well...there is one thing I know that you do not."

"And that would be?"

"Cobs have no honor."

And with that announcement, the creature came at Mary.

With an alarmed roar, Hunter flew straight at it, going for the head, figuring that he would be able to crush it and put a swift end to it. He hurtled toward it and was almost upon it, and then one of the Cob's legs swatted him aside, sending him tumbling end over end and crashing into a tree.

The rest of its legs came after Mary, trying to pick her up, grab her, tear her apart.

Mary blocked the attacks with her crowbar, trying to bat each thrusting leg aside. But there were eight of them and only one of her. Even as she was quick enough to deflect seven attacks, an eighth would manage to slip through, and in less than a minute she already had a number of small cuts on her arms. They were painful and slowed her down, but she was determined to ignore them and tried to push through by sheer will power.

There was a fearsome roar and Hunter charged in yet again. He darted between the thrashing legs and leaped forward, clamping his teeth onto the slender neck that attached the Cob's head to its body. He expected to bite through it and end the fight right there and then.

It did not work out that way, for as thin as the creature's neck was, it was strong as steel, and Hunter's efforts had no effect. The Cob reached up with one of its legs, knocked Hunter off its neck, and kept him pinned even as he tried to free himself. "You," it warned him, "will be dessert." Then it turned its attention back to Mary.

Mary and the Cob faced each other once more, Mary breathing heavily, the Cob barely winded. Mary's hair was, hanging in her face, and she brushed it away from her eyes as best she could. The crowbar was feeling heavy in her hand. The Cob studied her, and if it had been capable of smiling, it would have.

"You fought well, little one," it said, "but you never had a chance."

Then it changed tactics, catching Mary flat footed. Rather than trying to reach her again with its legs, the Cob whipped its stinger around, like a scorpion. The stinger seemed to lengthen as it drove hard and fast right for Mary's chest. It was moving too quickly; there was no chance for Mary to get out of its way.

And suddenly something moving very fast was between her and the Cob, shouting defiance, and waving a sword most threateningly.

It was Captain Mykeptin of the Old Guard. It seemed he was rather good at tracking as well.

"Keep back, monster!" shouted Captain Mykeptin, and then he gasped and choked and looked down in surprise as the stinger buried itself in his chest.

Instantly his body was paralyzed and the sword dropped from his nerveless hands. Yet before it hit the ground, Mary tossed aside the crowbar and caught it deftly. If she'd had two hands, she wouldn't have had to make a choice, but since she didn't, she opted for the weapon with the cutting edge.

She charged straight at the Cob.

Seeing that she was doing so, the brave soldier found new strength where none should have been. His arms came to life entirely through force of will, and he reached up and grabbed the creature's tail, holding it firmly even though it was in his own body. The Cob tried to pull it free so that it could use the tail against Mary, but was unable to do so. "*This shouldn't be possible!*" the creature snarled. The captain made no reply, all of his energy focused on remaining upright and keeping the Cob's most vicious weapon useless.

At that moment Hunter, still pinned, twisted around and managed to bring his jaws together on the leg that was holding him. The Cob let out a howl and between the struggling soldier and the infuriated lion, it didn't know where to look first. As a result, it momentarily lost track of Mary.

That proved to be the monster's undoing as Mary lunged forward, the sword sweeping through the air. The Cob's neck might have been sturdy enough to resist Hunter's attack, but the blade's edge was razor sharp and it seemed to whistle as Mary brought it down. Without slowing in the slightest, it sliced down and through, separating the Cob's head from its body. The head rolled away and yet the body still continued to move, as if the head was giving it instructions from a distance. This was quickly settled by Hunter who, now freed from the leg, bounded across the ground and landed upon the head with all four paws, squashing it like an overripe tomato. Instantly the body went stiff and then collapsed. The legs stretched out in all directions, shuddered a few times, and then stiffened.

The Cob was dead.

Mary had no time to feel triumph. Instead, dropping the sword, she ran straight to the captain, who had fallen to the ground, stiff as a board. She fell to her knees next to him and touched his bristling mustache. "Just hang on," she said urgently. "We'll get you help..."

"No help, young miss," he said, his chin quivering. "The poison is quite fast acting. Nothing to be done."

"Oh Captain Mykeptin..." she said sadly. "Oh, the bleeding drops of red...but...why? Why did you do it?" She couldn't understand it. "After the things I said..."

"It was because of that. And it was because..." He was struggling to find both the energy and the words. "...because it has been quite some time...since I cared about something enough...to do something about...anything. You made me want to feel...proud. And to have someone feel proud...of me..."

"I am. I do," she said, her voice firm.

"I hope..." He coughed roughly. "I hope that someday you do know fear...true fear...because once you do...then you can know the feeling...of overcoming it....it is...the single greatest triumph...anyone can feel...without that...anything you accomplish...is just a hollow victory..."

"I..." Mary's voice broke and, in a rare instance of acting her age, she said, "I don't know what to do...should I...should I bury you...when you die...?"

"Silly child," he said gently. "Don't you know? Old soldiers never die....we just...fade away..."

And it was true. His face, his body, were becoming more and more transparent with each passing moment. "Captain—?" Mary said, her arm under his head. But the captain did not answer; his lips were pale and still. He did not feel her arm. He had no pulse or will. The proud colors of his uniform became more muted, and within seconds he was a pale reflection of himself. Mary could see the ground beneath him. From somewhere came the strength for his chest to rise one more time and then slowly he exhaled and, as he did, his body vanished entirely as if drifting off into the morning air.

The old soldier had indeed faded away.

Mary drew her handless arm across her face, wiping away the tears and only partly succeeding. Trying to help, Hunter licked the tears away with his little tongue and then Mary embraced him, sobbing into his fur and letting all the exhaustion and difficulties of the last few days come out of her in one gush of emotion.

When she was finally done, she apologized for getting his fur wet, pulled herself together, and then went to her knapsack. She took out a length of the rope, cut it free, tied it around her waist and, having thus made a crude belt, stuck the sword of the fallen soldier into it so she could carry it with her. Then she and Hunter climbed into the box and set out after Purl, even as birds landed on the carcass of the fallen Cob and began to eat it, one final act of the prey becoming predators at last.

Chapter 12

How the Furry Furies Tried to Stop Mary

M ary did not immediately leave the scene of the old soldier's passing and Cob's attack.

First she had to clean out all the signs of Cob's having been in the box. She pulled out large clumps of web from the box and then found some flat, broad leaves that she was able to use for wiping out the inside. Hunter pitched in by using his tail as a brush, reaching into the corners of it to remove the last remains of the Cob's having been there.

The entire time that she worked on getting the box fixed up, Mary burned with quiet anger that continued to build. Nothing was going the way it was supposed to go. She still hadn't found Anna's imagination. She had crossed paths with Purl, toward whom she now felt some manner of responsibility because, well, that's what happens when you saved someone's life. Your own life becomes all tangled with theirs.

And now the old soldier, whom she had barely gotten to know, was gone, having lay down his life in order to save hers. That put even more responsibility upon her. If she failed in her quest, then not only would she have let down Anna, but also the Old Soldier's noble sacrifice would have been a waste as well. That was just way too much failure for anyone to have to deal with.

And all of this, *all* of this, apparently had to do with whoever *They* were. It was frustrating. She didn't know what *They* wanted. She didn't know why *They* were doing any of this. Instead she felt as if she were running about in darkness and somewhere *They* were sitting and somehow watching everything she was going through and laughing at her.

The angrier it made her, the more it made her focus on the refrigerator box. She had been thinking of it purely as a means of getting around until that point, but now her fury caused her thoughts to turn in darker directions.

Inside the refrigerator box, she rested her hand on one side and her stub on the other and allowed her anger to burn within her like a white-hot furnace that, at the same time managed to be icy cold, and then fill her entire insides before slowly moving from her insides to the outsides. She fancied she could actually feel it traveling through her veins, through her skin and going into the *Argo*. Her vessel responded, reflecting the anger pulsing in her.

Hunter stood outside the *Argo* and his eyes widened as he saw it transform all around Mary. The quiet of the jungle was filled with the steady clanking of metal as plate upon plate snapped into existence. The vehicle grew and grew, larger and larger, powered by Mary's unleashed imagination—because, as we've said, an imagination that isn't restricted by fear in any way is a very powerful weapon—and Hunter had to scramble to get out of the way before he found himself wedged under the treads.

He let out a low whistle when he saw the result.

"What *is* that?" he said in wonderment.

Mary's head was poking out of the hatch. "It's a tank," she said, looking it over with a sort of grim pride. "It's an armored vehicle. My brother, Paul, when he was younger, had toy soldiers and they always rode around in one of these. Do you like it?"

"I'm not sure. It's scary."

"So am I," said Mary.

"What's that long thing sticking out of the front?"

"It's a big gun. It shoots some kind of missiles."

"What kind? How do you load it?"

She shrugged. "Don't know. Don't care. It's an imaginary tank; I don't have to know how it works as long as it does."

"But can you shoot it if you don't know how to—?"

An explosion tore the air as the gun belched out a missile. The shell struck an extremely large tree twenty yards away, hitting at its base and blowing it into splinters. Hunter covered his head with his paws as bits of wood and debris fell all around him. When he looked up he saw that the path in front of them, which had been blocked by the tree, was clear. The sound of the gun continued to echo in the still air of the jungle for several moments before fading like a distant rumble of thunder.

Mary looked at him calmly. "There's a trigger. I made sure there was a trigger. I squeeze it, and it shoots. I didn't really think I needed much more than that."

"I guess not," said Hunter, slightly shaken by what he had just seen. He made a mental note never to get on Mary Dear's bad side, for he had no desire to find himself a target of the *Argo's* big gun.

He ran up the treads into the main hatch and dove in. He looked around the insides and purred in satisfaction. "Much roomier," he said.

"Glad you like it," she said, but her voice sounded flat. She didn't seem glad about anything.

Her tone concerned Hunter. "Mary? Are you all right?"

"I'll be all right when we do what we came here to do. Can you still track Anna's imagination?"

He climbed back up so that he was next to her. "Yes," he said, pointing with one paw. "It's that way."

"What about Purl?"

"She's that way, too."

"Finally," she muttered, "something going right."

She gunned the tank's engine and it roared to life, the huge sound of it shattering the calm of the jungle. Hunter was so startled by it that he leaped straight up, his wings fluttering, and he hovered in midair until he managed to pull himself back together. Then he darted down and landed squarely on the big gun that stuck out the front of the tank. He padded up and down it, making sure that he had a steady grip on it. Mary nodded; she liked the image of a winged lion sitting on top of a front-mounted cannon. It sent a definite message that she wasn't about to take any prisoners.

The treads rode right over the space where the tree had been moments before. There were still some smoking cinders remaining. It made a nice crunching sound beneath the treads.

Ordinarily, if someone were going to be making their way through a jungle on foot, it would be smart of them to have a machete or some other blade to cut through the brush in order to create a path. That wasn't necessary in this case; the tank made its own path, plowing through the brush and even trees. Obviously Mary wasn't giving any thought to trying to sneak up on anyone. Endeavoring to surprise the creatures she was chasing clearly wasn't part of her plan. At which point Hunter realized that he wasn't entirely certain she even *had* a plan.

"Do you have a plan?" Hunter asked.

"No," said Mary.

"Okay, then." Hunter couldn't say he was thrilled with that answer, but at least now he knew.

The tank continued to crash its way through the undergrowth, and as time passed, it began to thin out. Mary felt hunger growling in her stomach. She had supplies that the Old Guard had given her, not to mention some of the peanut butter and jelly sandwiches, but she was still angry over everything that had happened. And she wanted to stay angry. Because of that, she decided not to eat for a time, since being hungry just angered her all the more. She invited Hunter to help himself, though, if he felt hungry.

"I'm not really alive," he reminded her. "I've got claws and fur and all these other things because I have a piece of your imagination inside of me. But I don't really have a need for food or water, or even sleep when you get down to it, although I did find sleeping rather pleasant. It's like going on a vacation without having to pack."

She nodded, accepting all of that.

"I was wondering," Hunter said suddenly. "If you can turn this vehicle into anything as needed, why not transform it into an airplane? Wouldn't that be faster?"

"We might miss Purl along the way if we did that," she said, and then added grimly, "and besides, I feel like running over things right now."

"I don't blame you."

Time passed, and the jungle began to thin around them. Soon it was gone and a vast, arid desert stretched out in front of them, the ground brown and cracked. The sun, which had simply given light up until then, seemed to have become much hotter. It beat down upon them as if it had developed fists.

Mary drank water carefully from her canteen, knowing that she was going to have to ration it, because the desert stretched for miles upon miles.

Much time passed in silence between the two of them, and then Hunter said something that got Mary to thinking. And what he said was, "Why not your imagination?"

She thought about that and thought about that and, after much thinking, came back with what would very likely have been your reply as well, which was this:

"Huh?"

Hunter was confused for a moment, and he decided to explain himself. "Your friend's imagination: It ran away."

"It was stolen away," Mary said with firmly. "By *Them*. I'm absolutely sure of it."

"Okay, well...it doesn't seem terribly likely that she was the only one this happened to, right? There are probably many more victims of this kind of thing. People with no imagination."

"Probably," said Mary.

"All right then," Hunter said. "Now...if people steal something...then usually that thing has value."

"Right." Mary still wasn't certain where he was going with this.

"This Anna person...she is your best friend?" When Mary nodded, he continued, "Now...just for a moment, forget that she is that, because it might be hard for you to give an honest answer. I want you to ask yourself: Is there anything particularly extraordinary about her imagination?"

She realized the wisdom of Hunter's words. It was true: It was hard for her to set aside her personal love for Anna and give an honest judgment about her. But she had to try because it seemed important to Hunter that she do so, and after much frowning and forehead scrunching, she said, "It is...a perfectly good imagination,

I suppose. I don't mean to speak poorly of it—"

"And you haven't. And your loyalty to your friend is great," Hunter assured her. "But her imagination compared to yours...?"

"It's...normal. Average."

"But yours is above average?"

Slowly she nodded. "Anna is fine when it involves coming along. She shares things well enough. But she could never have set out on something such as this. She couldn't throw herself headlong into a full-blown adventure where the fantasy takes over, pulls you in, doesn't let you go until the quest is done. She would be too..."

"Afraid?"

Again she nodded. Then, quick to defend her friend, she said, "But who wouldn't be?"

"Indeed. That, though, brings me to my question..."

He did not have to ask it, because Mary had finally figured out where he was going with this. "Why not my imagination instead of hers?"

"Exactly," said Hunter. "If *They* are out grabbing imaginations, why not take one as strong as yours? Wouldn't that be more valuable to them?"

"Maybe it would. Or maybe..." Her voice trailed off.

"Maybe what?"

She looked down at him as the tank continued to barrel across the desert. In the distance, but coming up fast, was a series of mountains, stretching high. They weren't going to be much of an obstacle, though, because there was a path between two of the peaks that the tank could cross easily enough.

"Maybe," she said thoughtfully, "such an imagination isn't of value to them."

"Why wouldn't it be?"

"You said it yourself. My imagination is limitless. Something without limits can't be controlled. So maybe *They* have no use for it because *They* need to be able to rein an imagination in."

"It would be too powerful for them," Hunter said, his voice rising with excitement. "Which means that what you have within you is more than just a means of getting things done. It's a powerful weapon. Perhaps one *They* even fear."

"Which could give us an advantage that we—"

Hunter suddenly rested a paw on her hand, and his nose was twitching wildly. "What is it?" said Mary, immediately alert.

"I smell Purl. She is close. Very close. She's—" Then he stopped and pointed. "There. I see her."

And then Mary did as well.

In the mountain pass ahead, partly hidden in the shadow from an overhanging cliff, there was Purl. She was bound hand and foot with chains, and a gag had been tied over her mouth. She had just been lying there, but then she heard the grinding of the tank as it approached, and when she saw who was looking out from the top of the tank, her eyes seemed to widen in...surprise? Shock? Perhaps even alarm? All of these seemed odd reactions for someone who kept saying how much she didn't care about the world around her.

Purl began shaking her head furiously.

"She doesn't seem happy to see us," said Hunter.

Mary ground the tank to a halt; its large treads rattled to a stop.

"It's fairly obvious why," Mary said slowly. "It's a trap. Someone put her there to draw us in."

"*You* were tied up earlier. It wasn't a trap. Perhaps someone just left her here."

She was certain that he was wrong, or at the very least kidding himself. There was no doubt in her mind that Purl was being put there to lure her out of the tank. Hunter couldn't free her from her bonds the way that he had Mary; his claws would do him no good against chains. The links didn't look that thick, though; she was reasonably sure that by levering her crowbar into them and giving them a quick twist, she could break them. But that wasn't something Hunter could do. She had only one hand, but at least it had an opposable thumb.

So she would have to get out of her tank and when she did, it would be that much easier to attack her.

Brave, not reckless. Brave, not reckless.

For a long moment, Mary seriously considered going on her way and leaving Purl behind.

It made sense.

What was Purl to her, really? She had saved Purl from the Galoots. Purl in turn had saved her, or at least helped save her, when the Old Guard had her a prisoner. So they were even. All was square between them. Neither of them owed the other anything.

And it wasn't as if Purl was a remarkably pleasant person. The way she was constantly talking about how she didn't care about things, and how she and Mary weren't friends. If they weren't friends, and Purl didn't care about what happened to her, then why should Mary?

She looked straight into Purl's eyes, and Purl looked back at her, their gazes locking.

It was as if Purl was able to read the thoughts going through her mind. Mary could almost see them reflected in Purl's dark eyes.

Purl nodded. In fact, she nodded quickly.

The message was clear. She knew that Mary was thinking about leaving her there, and she was absolutely agreeing that it was the right thing to do. Her expression said it all, even though she couldn't speak: *Keep going. Save yourself. Whatever you do, do not try to help me.*

"What are you going to do?" said Hunter.

She looked down at him, and she was about to tell him that she was going to do the wise thing, the thing that was not going to stand in the way of her getting her main job done. And besides, again, Purl had said it herself: They weren't friends. Mary had to focus on the needs of the person who *was* her friend.

But something in the way Hunter looked at her threw her off for a moment, and she surprised herself when she said, "What do *you* think I should do?"

"I think you should do the right thing," said Hunter without hesitation.

"And how do I know what that is? How does anyone know?"

"Excuses."

"Pardon?"

"People always know what the right thing is," Hunter said matter-of-factly. "They just do. And sometimes they do the wrong thing anyway, and they try to tell themselves that it's right. And that's where the excuses come from. You don't need excuses to do the right thing. Doing the right thing speaks for itself."

Mary gave that about half a second's thought and then nodded firmly.

"Let's go," she said.

And she climbed out of the top of the tank, her crowbar firmly in her hand. She wasn't worried someone would steal the tank; it wouldn't work unless she wanted it to. With that safely in mind, she ran toward Purl, Hunter bouncing behind her.

When she saw her coming, Purl quickly started shaking her head. That told Mary—if there had ever been any doubt—that Purl had wanted her to keep going and leave her behind. The first thing that Mary did, when she got near enough, was to put down the crowbar and remove the gag from Purl's mouth.

"Are you *stupid?*" was the first thing Purl said.

Mary shoved the gag back in before Purl could get another word out. Purl's eyes narrowed in obvious annoyance. However much she said she didn't care about things, her training as a princess made it clear that she expected to be treated in a certain way and having a gag shoved back in her mouth was definitely not how you treat a princess.

Mary, however, hadn't gotten any training in how a princess should be treated, and so felt perfectly comfortable doing whatever was easiest when it came to dealing with Purl.

"I don't think I'm stupid, no."

Purl glared at her. Mary, feeling she'd made her point, pulled out the gag once more. The instant she did, Purl said, "This is a trap. They're going to come for you any second."

"I wasn't going to leave you here."

"Why?" said Purl.

"Because," Mary said, "it wouldn't be right."

That was when she heard the scratching sounds, the clicking, and the low growls, all of them coming from above her.

She looked upward even as she shoved the crowbar into the chain and tried to break it. But she was hindered by the lack of a right hand. She couldn't twist the crowbar around with any force; one hand wasn't enough to get it done. She moaned in frustration even as she watched danger coming nearer.

Fur-covered bodies were making their way down the rocky walls on either side of them. And they were coming from both ends of the valley itself, from behind and in front of them. Mary, Purl and Hunter were completely cut off in all directions.

At first glance the creatures coming toward them seemed to be extremely hairy human beings. But within seconds Mary saw that wasn't the case. They were, instead, animals that had somehow been transformed into human-like shapes, while keeping all of the pure fierceness of their animal nature.

They seemed to be, on average, seven feet tall. They were clothed in what appeared to be some kinds of uniforms: black breechcloths around their middles, and brown strips of leather that crisscrossed on their chests and backs. They came in all different types and breeds. Wolves, coyotes, tigers, all kinds of creatures were approaching, and all of them part human and part the beasts that they had been before they became what they now were:

The Furry Furies.

And the largest of them, good heavens, the largest of them...it was almost impossible for Mary to figure it out at first. It had thin but muscular legs that ended in hooves that then tapered upward to a narrow waist. But from that point up it started to widen and widen, and its fur was thick and curly black ringlets that covered its entire upper body. Its head was wide and flat, and it had huge, curved horns on either side, just above its small, narrow ears. The points looked extremely sharp.

Then Mary realized what it was: A buffalo. A human-like buffalo. Its small, red-rimmed eyes were locked in on her. It looked ready to charge her.

The rest of the creatures were getting closer, giving off a variety of snarls and roars and grunts, all of them looking eager to tear into Mary and her friends.

There was no doubt in Mary's mind: They were preparing to charge. They were going to rip her apart, trample her, maybe even devour her.

A person with fear might have panicked.

Instead Mary simply wondered aloud to Purl, "Why didn't they kill you?"

"I don't know," said Purl. "They haven't exactly told me a lot of their plans."

"Can they even talk?"

"Yes, but it's mostly along the lines of 'Want to kill you, but can't yet.'"

Now they were so close that Mary could smell stink coming off their fur. Her nose wrinkled in disgust. "They need to bathe."

"I noticed that. Then again, they're about to kill you, so it won't be a problem for you much longer."

There was a rubbing against Mary's leg. She looked down. It was Hunter, looking up at her, determined. "I cannot imagine letting them hurt you," he said. "I will stop them."

She realized she actually could imagine it. Then again, she had a lot of imagination.

"You're awfully small to be stopping them," said Purl. "If you were big enough, strong and powerful enough...if you were an alpha male...then perhaps you could. They would understand that, respect that, fear that. But that isn't you."

"No, it isn't," Mary agreed. Then she looked down at Hunter with dawning comprehension. "But it could be."

Mary was linked to Hunter, body and soul. He had passed through her and took a part of her imagination in order to live inside the lion body. It was because of that that he had been able to have claws and teeth and genuine fur rather than plush, all of them things that had not been part of the toy that he had taken over.

If that...then why not more?

She knelt down next to him, placed her hand upon him. His

fur felt warm beneath her hand.

"What are you doing?" said Hunter.

Mary closed her eyes. "You," she said firmly, "are more powerful than they are. Bigger...stronger...you are the most ferocious creature walking on four legs in the whole of Afrasia. Take them on," and her voice dropped to so low a growl that she could have been one of the Furry Furies herself, "and destroy them if you have to. Show them who is the true king of beasts."

Nothing happened at first.

And then it did.

Purl's eyes widened in astonishment as Hunter began to grow, and grow. The skin beneath his fur rippled, his wings extended to the size of an eagle's, and then an albatross, and then wider than that of the legendary griffin.

His body rushed to keep up. A mane began to grow in where none had been before, and his face matured from cub into full-grown male lion and beyond. His tail got longer, and when it snapped through the air it sounded like a whip.

When he opened his mouth, the challenging roar that was ripped from it was so loud that the mountains rumbled in response, and a thunder cloud that had been rolling in headed in the other direction, shamed into the realization that any thundering would sound lame in response.

The noises from the Furry Furies changed from snarls and roars to whimpers of confusion. They started to back up, to retreat.

All save the buffalo.

It pawed the ground, issued a bellow of challenge, and charged.

His full and gorgeous mane riffling in the wind, the rest of Hunter's body quickly caught up with his wings and head. Ten feet from tip to tail he grew, then twenty, then thirty, the size of a great white shark, and he bolted right at the buffalo to meet the charge.

Say what you will of the buffalo: That it was foolish. That it was too proud to realize it was overmatched, or too stupid. But it didn't back down. Instead it came straight at Hunter, determined to stab him with its horns or stomp him into the ground.

Neither happened.

Instead Hunter leaped through the air, propelled by the force of his wings and the powerful muscles in his body. He slammed into the buffalo, knocking it flat onto its back.

The buffalo never had a chance as Hunter, calling upon all the pure animal rage that was part of being a lion, tore the unfortunate creature apart. Within seconds all movement in its body ceased and a pool of dark red was spreading beneath it.

Hunter then leaped off the buffalo, turned toward the rest of the Furry Furies, and roared once more. He ran toward Mary and without hesitation she leaped upon his back. His mighty wings beat the air and sent him upward, toward the rest of the Furry Furies who were clinging to the mountainsides, watching in shock at how easily the vast winged lion had killed what was clearly their leader.

He roared again, and that was enough for the Furry Furies who were still furry but far less furious. Their response to the challenge was to run in the face of it. They had no problem with the idea of facing a weaker foe, but none of them wanted to risk those powerful jaws and terrifying talons.

And as Mary, grinning, watched them flee, she suddenly began to feel very dizzy. There was a pounding in the back of her eyes, and it started moving through her head. She felt some sort of wetness on her upper lip and reached up to touch it.

It was blood. Her nose was bleeding.

"That's very odd," she said, and then she passed out.

Chapter 13

How the Travelers Arrived at Their Destination

Mary awoke because something, a rough tongue, was licking her face. *Please let it be Hunter,* she thought, *and not some random creature tasting me just before it eats off my face.*

Slowly she opened her eyes and yes, sure enough, it was Hunter. He was no longer the monstrous form that she had come up with for him. Instead he had returned to his normal, lion cub size. But the Furry Furies had apparently not returned, as was obvious from the fact that they were all still alive.

"She's awake!" Hunter called.

Purl was now immediately leaning over her, looking down at her with...

...concern? Was that actual...*concern?*

Then, just as quickly as the expression was there, her dark face smoothed out and her typical uncaring look returned. "Good," she said briskly. "You did not die. I would hate to have to count on Hunter to tell me how I should feel."

Mary sat up and paused, putting her hand to her head, which was still hurting her a lot. She closed her eyes and felt tired for a moment, but she pushed it aside and fought her way back to full wakefulness. Then she realized something: "You're out of the chains," she said to Purl.

"I bit them through while I was still a giant," Hunter said proudly, bouncing back and forth. "My teeth were great, monstrous things, and when I bit down on them, they just crackled like popcorn in my jaws. Was I not truly wonderful, Purl?"

"Yes." And Purl laughed softly. She *laughed.* "You were."

"Are you feeling quite all right?" said Mary cautiously.

"I am fine, thank you." Now, however, she was frowning. "That is most odd."

"What is?"

For answer, Purl reached toward the side of her head. Mary didn't flinch; Mary never flinched. She just watched in curiosity as Purl drew a lock of Mary's hair forward for her to inspect. Mary took it in her hand and stared at it.

It had gone dead white.

Mary was startled. "Is *all* my hair like that? This isn't good at all. There is simply no way that my mother won't notice that."

"No. Just this one strand," said Purl. "Here." And with surprising gentleness, although her face remained impassive, she tucked it back behind Mary's ear. "It happened right around the same time that your nose started bleeding. Don't worry, I cleaned your face off."

Mary was glad to hear that, if for no other reason than she wasn't thrilled with the idea of Hunter having licked the blood off her. "I wonder why that happened? The nose bleed, the strand of hair turning white..."

"Maybe you strained your imagination," said Hunter.

"I didn't think that was possible."

"Obviously it is," said Hunter.

"It makes a certain amount of sense," said Purl. "Everything has to have boundaries, especially when one is on an adventure. Otherwise you could just imagine that everything was solved in one shot, and there would be no point in quests or voyages of discovery."

"I thought my imagination was limitless," said Mary, a bit disappointed to discover that something was not as she had believed it to be.

"Of course not. It is, after all, a 'nation,' just as the word implies. The Imagi Nation. And all nations have boundaries, so..." Purl shrugged, obviously feeling there was nothing more to say.

Mary hated to admit it, but what Purl was saying made a lot of sense. "But how do I know if I'm pushing my imagination too far? This time it was a nose bleed and a little white hair; what could happen next time?"

"I don't know," said Purl. "Depends what you did. Could be nothing; could be much worse. I suggest you try not to do too much."

"I will do whatever I have to," Mary said firmly. Then, more softly, she said, "Thank you for cleaning me up."

"It was..." Purl seemed to be fishing for the words, which was odd since she always seemed to know exactly what she wanted to say. "It was...different. For me to be taking care of someone else. Princesses don't typically have to do that. People take care of us, provide us everything we need. Helping someone else with their needs...that made me feel..."

"It made you *feel?* But...that's great news!" said Mary happily. "How did it make you feel?"

"I'm not sure. Perhaps you can tell me," and she started to reach for her notes again.

'Will you stop pulling that out? You're never going to be able to feel for yourself if you keep needing me to do it for you. Feelings aren't something you study. They're what you...I don't know...*feel*! Here!" And she tapped her chest above her heart. "If you don't feel it here, then knowing what you're *supposed* to feel is useless if you just go on feeling nothing."

"And is feeling nothing such a bad thing?"

"Of course it's a bad thing. How can you not realize—?" She shook her head. "I don't understand you."

"That is really not my problem. My back is not your bridge to understanding me."

Mary got to her feet. Even on her feet she was still considerably shorter than Purl, but she looked up at her and said, "You keep saying I'm your sidekick, but I'm not. You keep acting like you want to be alone, and you even drive people away, but you keep sticking with them or looking for them. Do you even know what you want?"

Purl did not answer immediately. Instead she thought about it for far longer than Mary was expecting. She and Hunter looked at each other in confusion over the lengthy delay.

Finally the princess said, "I do not. But I suspect that once I see it, I will know it for what it is, and perhaps even be..." She resorted to her list, pulling it out and looking it over before settling on, "...content."

Mary considered that and was surprised. "That actually sounds rather reasonable," she said. "All right, then. On to what's important: continuing tracking down Anna's imagination... "

"We have a problem," Hunter said. He said it with a depressed air, as if he had been dreading having to bring it up. "I've lost track of it."

"Lost track?" Mary wasn't exactly thrilled to hear that. "How—?"

"Because time has passed, and these things fade," said Hunter. "Not only that, but with all the Furry Furies, there were all sorts of additional scents mixed in that wound up covering it. I'm not sure where we're going. I'm sorry."

Mary was annoyed for a moment, but then she saw how saddened Hunter was over having—he felt—let her down. There was nothing to be gained by making him feel worse than he already did, assuming such a thing was possible. "There's nothing for it, Hunter. It's not your fault. You've gotten us this far. Since you are, in fact, a human spirit in an animal body and still learning your way around what you can and cannot do, it's great that you've gotten us this far. The question is, what do we do now?"

"It seems obvious to me," Purl said matter-of-factly. "You have soundly defeated the Furies. They work for *Them*. Were I the Furies, I would be running straight back to *Them* to let *Them* know that we are coming, and perhaps seek further instructions. So all we have to do is follow the Furies and they should lead us right to where we want to go."

"Excellent idea, Purl," Mary said.

"I'm a princess. All my ideas are excellent. Or at least so I have been told by people whose job it is to tell me all my ideas are excellent."

Mary could have argued that but decided there was no point.

"The Furies have left plenty of scents for me to follow!" said Hunter.

"It shouldn't be necessary to put your nose to work." Mary walked toward her refrigerator carton, gesturing for the others to follow her. They did so and, in short order, they were piled into the oversized carton.

Now you might think that, having just found out that bad things could happen if she used her imagination more than she should, Mary might have been slow to use it again so soon. If that's what you think, then you really haven't been paying attention. Unafraid of anything going wrong, Mary set to work turning her refrigerator box into just what she was going to need next. "This is the perfect time for it," she said as the box changed around them. "We have plenty of open land to build up speed and nothing to get in our way. This will be no problem at all."

And where there had been a simple refrigerator box, now a small airplane had formed around them. It had two sets of wings stacked one above the other, and a single propeller on the front. The plane was now tilted upward thanks to the landing gear that had sprung up beneath it.

Purl was shaking her head as she looked around from her perch in the cockpit. "You know, I see you do this, and I see you do this, and I still don't quite get *how* you do it. How do you turn this carton into an air vehicle simply by believing in it?"

"A dog does it all the time in comic strips with his dog house. Why should it be too difficult for me?"

"A dog? Comic strips?" Purl stared at her blankly. "What *are* you talking about?"

"Nothing. It doesn't matter." Mary got ready. "Contact," she said.

"Contact? What does that mean?"

"I don't know. In old movies, that's just what they say before the propeller starts up."

The propeller started up. The airplane (or actually the biplane if you want to know exactly what it was) lurched forward. It skidded from side to side at first since Mary was still getting the hang of the control stick in front of her. It didn't take her long, though, and soon the plane was speeding confidently forward, faster and faster, the propeller sounding like a swarm of a hundred thousand angry hornets. Hunter was shoved in next to Purl and he clamped his paws over his ears since his hearing was more sensitive than an ordinary plush winged lion. Purl looked down at him and then, feeling that she should do *something*, patted him on the head and said uncertainly, "It's going to be all right."

One, twice, three times the airplane bumped along the flat ground of the desert that was serving as a runway, each time trying to gather enough speed to lift off, each time failing.

"Uh oh," said Mary.

"Uh oh? What's 'uh oh?'" said Purl. Then she spotted what Mary had seen.

There was a vast crevice directly in their path, a huge canyon spreading out. Far off to the right, there was a narrow natural bridge that had formed out of rock, which must have been the way that the Furies had gotten across. But it was too far away and off to the side; Mary couldn't possibly change course to get over there in time. Unfortunately the small craft was also going too quickly to stop in time. The moment they reached the cliff, if they didn't have enough speed and power to take off, they would fall straight down into its depths and wind up smeared all over the bottom of the canyon.

"Now or never," said Mary. Rather than even try to bring the airplane screeching to a halt, she gunned the engine and sent it moving forward even faster.

Purl thought about checking her notes to see if there was anything about how she should feel over the idea of falling to her death but she was too crunched into the cockpit to reach them. Hunter, who hadn't heard or seen what was going on, looked up at her in confusion. "Is there something I should know about?" he shouted above the roaring of the propeller.

"I'll tell you later," said Purl.

The plane lunged over the edge of the drop and for a split second it seemed as if it might go in either direction, its fate as random as a coin toss.

(Now: It is entirely possible that Mary might indeed meet her end at some point during this adventure. Bad things happen even to good people, and at no time have we promised you that Mary makes it through the story alive. But we don't think we'd be giving anything way in telling you that if Mary were to die, it wouldn't be because of something as boring as falling into a canyon.)

Gravity tried its best to pull the plane down, but instead the determined little aircraft said, "Nice try, gravity, but not good enough!" With a surge of energy, the plane leaped skyward. The plane angled up, sharper and sharper, leaving the canyon far behind it.

The desert sprawled below them, and Mary looked at it with awe and wonderment. There was a beauty to it when one was able to look down at it from on high. Deserts look their best when you're watching them from a distance.

Once she was confident that she had the plane airborne, Mary leveled it off and then looked around. Her eyes narrowed as she tried to pick up some sign of the Furies.

"There!" said Purl, suddenly pointing. "Off in that direction! They made good time, I'll give them that."

Mary saw that Purl was correct. They were quite far away, moving in a steady line, running and galloping and galumphing and doing whatever means of movement came naturally to them.

Since airplanes were not all that common in Afrasia—assuming they existed at all—Mary wanted to keep as much distance between herself and the Furies as she possibly could while still being able to follow them. So she hung back and hoped that none of them bothered to look up or perhaps hear the propeller's noise. She got her wish. The Furry Furies were far more interested in where they were going than anything that might, by some wild chance, be spying on them from overhead.

The plane continued to follow them, and eventually the desert started showing signs of life. The flat, brown lifeless land gave way to patches of green. Small bodies of water were no longer small, few and far between, but instead larger and more frequent. Not only that, but the airborne travelers began to see roads and people walking on them, some of them hauling their wares on wagons being pulled by tired-looking horses. And those people would see the Furies bearing down upon them and scramble to get out of their way, looking very frightened as if worried the Furies were going to attack them. But the Furies ran right past, a column of animal energy, without so much as slowing down.

Soon the Furies were running down what looked like a main road, leaving even more pedestrians—there were no cars or trucks or anything with motors that Mary could see—frantically making the way clear. Mary wasn't sure if the Furies would have slowed down had anyone been unlucky enough to get in their way but she had a feeling that they would not. Anyone who was too slow would simply have been trampled. It angered her that they cared so little about life. She was beginning to wish that Hunter had destroyed the lot of them while he had been able to do so.

By this point there was a jungle in the way, stretching high and blocking Mary's view of what was past it. She angled the ship a bit higher so she could see what was beyond it.

She gasped in surprise when she saw it. So did Hunter, who was by that point crouched in Purl's lap, his fur blowing briskly. Purl simply grunted, as she tended to do.

There was a walled city ahead of them. From the ground it would have been impossible to see any details. From high above, however, where they were, they could see modest-looking homes that looked like something out of a medieval era. They were simple structures, no more than a story or two, with thatched roofs. There was what appeared to be a marketplace since there seemed to be booths and stores doing a brisk business and there was livestock being led around, probably for sale.

But what drew most of Mary's attention was the huge building that was squarely in the center of the town.

It looked like a castle, but unlike any that Mary had ever seen. To begin with, it was triangular. There were towers at each of the three points of the triangular castle, and each of the towers had a long metal rod extending from it with a flag fluttering in the breeze. The rods looked familiar to Mary for some reason, but she couldn't quite figure out why. There didn't seem to be any details on the flags. One flag appeared to be solid red, the second was yellow, and the third, blue.

"Why those three colors?" Purl wondered aloud.

"They all look gray to me," said Hunter, who apparently wasn't going to be of any help when it came to telling one color from another.

Then Mary realized. "We learned this in school," she said. "Those are the three primary colors. You can make any other color by combining two or more of them."

"All right. So what does that have to do with anything?"

"I have no idea," said Mary. "Do you think that's City Hall?"

Purl glanced behind them. "The Furies are heading straight for it. That makes it seem a fairly likely bet."

Suddenly Hunter's nostrils flared wide. "I smell something. It smells like...ozone. Like back in the volcano. Like you'd smell in the air after a—"

"Lightning strike?" said Purl.

"Yes."

Then they all saw where what Hunter smelled was coming from. The tops of the large rods from which the flags were flying were sizzling with electricity that was furiously dancing around the tops in ever-widening arcs.

"Well, *that* can't be good," said Mary, realizing exactly why the metal rods looked familiar. They were like the weapons that the Galoots had use at the top of the volcano, but much bigger and, she had to think, much more dangerous as well.

The man-made lightning leaped out from the top of the rods and came straight at the little vessel that was circling high above.

The three adventurers ducked so as they themselves would not be struck by the lightning. The lightning missed them, although it came so close that Mary felt her hair lifting out and standing up in all directions. But the *Argo* itself wasn't quite so lucky as the lightning slammed into the sturdy little ship. It was enough to send the airplane tumbling end over end. Not only that, but the sound of the thunder—well, you know how loud thunder can be when it's way, way overhead? Just imagine if you were smack in the middle of it. The lightning ripped apart the air, causing an explosion of thunder so loud that Mary might well have had her head stuck inside the muzzle of a cannon. It was like pure white noise blanking out her brain. Because of that, she lost her focus and couldn't think. That would have been less of a problem if the *Argo* had simply been a boat floating on a river, but an airplane soaring through the sky couldn't stay up if its pilot was stunned and confused.

So the airplane fell from the sky like a wounded bird. It entered what pilots call a Death Roll, meaning that usually there was no way that they could pull the plane up before it smashed nose first into the ground and killed everyone aboard.

The ground came at them terribly fast, and Mary—half-deaf from the thunder and flash blinded by the lightning—struggled with the control stick without having any idea whether it was doing any good. She yanked on the stick because that was what you were supposed to do, leaning as far back in the cockpit as she could, so much so that the back of her head clonked into the front of Purl's face. The princess let out a pained yelp. "*Sorry!*" shouted Mary, who truly was sorry but reasoned that, if they crashed and died, at least Purl wouldn't be hurting for too long.

She felt the plane's nose starting to come up and didn't know if it was going to be in time because everything was spinning wildly around her. Then the landing gear suddenly bang-banged against the ground, but the angle was wrong and the landing wheels snapped clean off. The *Argo* bounced into the air once more, then came down again, this time sideways onto the starboard wings. The wings crumbled like the cardboard that they were, even though her imagination had changed them into metal. The girls and Hunter covered their heads, not wanting to get their skulls crushed. Their seat belts held them securely in place, which is why you should always wear yours because you never know.

Then the plane rolled over and over, the other wings sheered off as well and the tail collapsing, the rudder shattering which was okay since they weren't going to be able to use it anyway. Finally, *finally*, the plane, or the remains of the plane, slid to a halt against the walls of City Hall. The front crumbled inward and the propeller was shoved right toward Mary. One end of the blade came to within an inch of Mary's eyes. Any closer and it would have gone right into her brain. She blinked at it several times.

Hunter saw that the broken propeller had nearly cut off the

top of Mary's head. "Are you all right!?" he cried out in alarm.

"Fine," said Mary with her usual cool. She didn't huff in relief over what a close call it had been. That wasn't her style. Instead she simply turned in her seat to the others and said, "And you?"

Purl's hair was sticking out thanks to the lightning the same way that Mary's was. She was doing her best to tamp it back into place. "That was a terrible landing."

"Any landing you can walk away from is a good one. You should feel relieved."

"Oh." Upon being told that, Purl pulled out her notes to scribble that down.

Mary didn't see the point. She didn't think Purl was going to be going up in a lot of airplanes, much less nearly dying in one. But once again it just didn't seem worth arguing about.

That was when low growling was heard all around them.

Mary, Purl and Hunter climbed out of the remains of the airplane and saw that Furry Furies were surrounding them from all sides. But then the Furies realized just who it was that was now in front of them. Hunter, smelling the fear from them, let out a low growl in his throat. This was enough to get the Furies to give them room by taking several steps back.

No one said anything for a long moment. Then, very loudly, and with the air of someone who wouldn't go away, Mary announced, "I am here searching for the runaway imagination of my friend, Anna. I have reason to believe that it's here."

"And I," said Purl, "am searching for my runaway parents and the people from my kingdom. I also have reason to believe they're here, or at least have been here, and so here is as good a place as any."

"And I," said Hunter, "am searching for no one, but know this: I will kill the first of you who tries to harm either of these girls."

This was enough to get the Furies to take a few more steps back.

Then they heard something. As one, they turned to see where it was coming from.

There was a very large door, ten feet high, inset into the wall. There was an array of oversized wheels on it with a bunch of interlocking cogs that at first seemed little more than decoration. But from inside there had been—and this was the sound they heard—a large clack, like a lever being shoved down or released. Immediately all the gears began turning, the teeth of the cogs smoothly moving against each other. This clackety clack went on for a good thirty seconds and then stopped. A few moments of silence followed and then, very slowly, there was the sound of a knob turning that was frankly a bit of a let down after all the noise of the wheels.

Then the door swung open to reveal a tall fellow who kind of looked like a walking corpse. Over six feet he was, and he wore a sizable top hat that added at least another foot to his height. He had a ruffled white shirt and long black coat that gave him the look of an undertaker. His white straggling hair stuck out from beneath the hat, and his lower jaw was twitching slightly, but no words were coming out at first. He was leaning on a cane that had the ornamental skull upon the top, cast in gold.

The oddest thing about him, though, was the way his head was tilted almost impossibly to one side. It seemed as if he were trying to look around Mary as if something behind her was more interesting. But however his head was positioned, his gaze remained locked upon her. Still, however strange his head's tilt seemed, to Mary it was familiar for some reason that she couldn't quite put her finger on.

Then she realized, for she had seen pictures of such things in some of the grimmer storybooks that she had read.

This fellow had been hanged. Even now, she could see the burn marks of the rope that had once been around his neck.

"My name is Mann," he said, and his voice was barely above a whisper. "Although naughty children such as yourselves sometimes call me the Boggy Man. Come. Enter freely and of your own will, and we shall see what can be done to take care of your needs."

Chapter 14

How Mary and Company Tried to Fight City Hall

Mary hadn't been sure what to expect upon entering City Hall, but what she found was a series of very long corridors, decorated with warm, classic-style furniture and many impressive statues lining the walls. There were no electric lights. Instead torches were mounted every few feet, providing a somewhat comforting glow as she, Purl and Hunter followed the Boggy Man.

His cane wasn't simply for decoration. He leaned on it when he walked, and the end tapped along the gleaming wooden floor. As they made their way along, he kept asking Mary questions about who she was and why she had come to this place. She answered them as briefly and honestly as she could. She saw no reason not to, for she had nothing to hide. Purl was quite silent, allowing Mary to do the talking for both of them.

Hunter, for his part, seemed as if he'd rather be anywhere than where they were. He had not forgotten the story that Mary had told and couldn't even stand to look directly at the Boggy Man, instead focusing his attention on furniture or torches or stray bits of dust that went rolling past.

"Are you some kind of ghost?" Mary asked at one point when the Boggy Man was between questions of his own.

"Are you afraid of ghosts?"

"No," which, as you know, she was not. "I'm just curious. I'd heard you had died, and you look rather like someone who was dead, but you don't look or seem like the ghosts I've met so far."

"I am neither here nor there," said the Boggy Man. "I live in the corners of children's greatest fears. I am he who hides in darkness, under their beds and in the shadows. I am never where you most expect me and always where you least expect me. Does that answer your question, little girl?"

"No."

"I'm not a ghost."

"Good."

"Why is that good?

"Because," said Mary as if it were the simplest thing in the world, "if you get in my way, it means you can be killed."

"Ah," said the Boggy Man, and if he was at all worried that that might happen, he certainly didn't show it.

He stopped in front of a room that was blocked by two huge double doors, with triangles carved dead center of both. The doors seemed to stretch up to forever. No matter how Mary squinted, she couldn't see to the top of them. Two Furry Furies—a leopard and a tiger—stood on either side, and glared at the new arrivals, but they made no move against them. Still, Mary kept her hand resting on the hilt of the sword that she had gotten from the Old Soldier.

The Boggy Man rapped on one of the doors and this casual

knock echoed on the other side. Shortly there was more grinding of gears from the other side of the door. Once they finished their seemingly endless clacking and shifting, the Boggy Man turned the knob and the door swung open.

"*They* are in there," said the Boggy Man.

Mary was suspicious. "What is the challenge?"

He looked at her blankly. "Excuse me?"

"There must be some manner of challenge to be met. A maze, perhaps? Or a series of death traps? That is how such things usually go. The Master Villain protects him or herself through a series of challenges."

"*Well!*" The Boggy Man actually seemed to take offense. "There is the problem, right there. That happens with Master Villains. *They* are not villains. *They* are your hosts. *They* are not fiends with some sort of evil plan up *Their* sleeves. *They* are above such things. Whatever challenges there are to be met, *They* have already met them. Whatever power there is to be had, *They* already have it. *They* have no interest in putting you through some series of tests to see if you're worthy or, even better, bring about your deaths. You have come here because you have a problem to be solved. So *They* will determine if *They* can solve it for you."

"In my case, *They* caused it," said Mary sharply. "So I would be asking *Them* to undo the mischief that *They* brought about in the first place."

"Then we shall see what *They* have to say about it," said the Boggy Man, not the least bit put out by the tone of her voice.

The double door pushed open upon the Boggy Man's touch, swinging on noiseless hinges, and the girls and lion entered expecting to see a vast throne room of some sort, with jets of flame bursting up, perhaps with tortured souls being dangled over them in cages begging for someone to let them out.

Instead what they saw was amazingly ordinary. Now it may seem that those two words don't go together, but in this case, they did. It was ordinary in that it looked like something pretty normal that you'd see in the real world. But it was amazing because of the scope of it.

What the travelers saw were three small wooden desks. One was painted red, the second yellow, the third blue, just like the flags outside. The desks were right up against each other. Above them was a skylight that was large and perfectly circular. It was stained glass, illustrated with a star field that had a sun and moon against it. It was actually quite pretty.

Three people were seated behind the desks: A man, a woman, and a man. The two men were identical to each other and the woman looked like one of the men, had one of them been a woman. All three of them were hairless as eggs, but had elaborate tattoos—thick lines that came together in confusing patterns—etched upon their skulls in inks that matched up with the colors of their desks: the men in blue and red, the woman in the middle with yellow.

What was creepy was that where their eyes should have been, there was just blankness. Overgrown skin instead of sockets. Yet they were "looking" straight at the travelers, as if not having any eyes was not really any problem for them.

They were each wearing gowns. Not evening gowns, but instead the large, shapeless things such as college students wear when they graduate.

Their office seemed to stretch on forever. Not upward since they could see the ceiling, but more like side-to-side. The endless walls were lined with file cabinets. The file cabinets were not red, blue and yellow but instead gun metal gray. There seemed to be hundreds of files drawers. None of the drawers were labeled with letters and such for easy filing, as was usually the case with file cabinets. Instead the ones to the left were labeled "Past," the ones toward the middle said "Present," and—as you can no doubt guess—the ones to the right were labeled "Future."

Slowly the three people behind the desks got to their feet, and that was when the travelers noticed something very odd.

They were joined at the hips. The red man's left hip was pressed up against the woman's right hip; her left hip was in turn shoved up against the blue man's right hip. There were slits in the sides of the gowns to allow for this, and thick pieces of skin were visible between each.

"This is *Them*," said Boggy Man with what sounded like a touch of pride, as if he were thrilled to be in *Their* presence. "This is Mr. Red, Miss Yellow, and Mr. Blue."

Mary, remembering her manners, curtsied. Purl stared at them stonily. Hunter gaped, not quite sure what to make of them.

Purl was the first one to speak: "What's wrong with them?"

"There is nothing wrong with us," they said together. Their voices blended to create perfect harmonies. "Have you never seen non-identical conjoined triplets before?"

"I don't believe such a thing is possible," said Mary.

"And yet here we are."

She couldn't really argue with that.

The woman, Miss Yellow, then spoke for herself. "Is this," and she gestured behind them, "yours?"

They turned to see that one of the Furies, a cheetah, was carrying in the *Argo*. Despite the disastrous way it had landed, it had changed back to its normal shape of refrigerator carton as if nothing terrible had happened. The Fury laid it on the floor, giving it one final angry glare before walking out again, closing the large double doors behind itself.

"Yes. That's mine," said Mary.

"You came here in that?"

"Yes."

"In an imaginary vehicle."

"It's what I had."

They looked at each other with what seemed to be a Very Thoughtful Gaze, at which point Mary said firmly, "We are here because—"

Red, Yellow and Blue put up their hands as one to silence her. Red said, "We know why you came here," and Yellow said, "And we know what will happen now," and Blue said, "And we know what is going to happen."

"I refuse to believe that," Mary said firmly. "I accept you know the past and present, but nobody can know the future. Not for sure."

"We do," *They* said.

"Then you don't know anything," Mary told *Them*.

They did not seem the least offended. Instead Red spoke up. "You came here because you are seeking the imagination of one who is your best friend. And you," he nodded toward Purl, "are seeking your parents and those who fled you."

"What about me?" said Hunter challengingly.

Red said nothing. Neither did Yellow or Blue. Mary found that odd, as did Purl. So did Hunter, who repeated himself but still got no answer, so he just sulked.

Deciding now wasn't the time to pursue questions on Hunter's behalf, Mary said, "Did you take Anna's imagination?"

"We did."

"And are my people and parents here?" said Purl.

"They are."

"All right, well...we want them back," said Mary.

"No. You cannot have them back."

"Then we will fight you," said Mary, pulling out the sword that she had gotten from the Old Soldier, "and we will defeat you, and make you do what we want."

And suddenly one of the file drawers above Miss Yellow leaped open, and a terrible wind whipped out of the drawer and seized Mary and Purl. Hunter leaped upon Mary, trying to drag her back down to the ground, but all he managed to do was wind up being dragged along with them. They were hauled high into the air, kicking and pushing against nothing at all, and suddenly blackness surrounded them. They were thrown about and something slammed shut all around them. It was as if they had been buried alive.

"That went well," said Purl drily.

They struggled fiercely to try and get out but they were unable to make any progress at all.

"Quiet down," came the sharp voice of Miss Yellow, "if you have any hope of getting out of there at all."

Seeing no other choice, they did as they were told, although it deeply wounded Mary's pride to have to give in to such a command.

So they waited. And waited. The only conversation was when Mary said to Purl: "Please don't ask me how you're supposed to feel like this."

"I wouldn't do that."

"Good."

"I couldn't see my list to write it down."

Mary sighed and they fell silent once more.

They had no idea how long they stayed that way, but finally the drawer was suddenly thrust open and the three of them thrown to the floor below, in front of the desks. The Boggy Man was right where they had left him, looking amused, which greatly annoyed Mary, but she had to focus on one thing at a time.

"You," *They* said, "cannot fight City Hall. However...we have had time to think about what you said. The question is: What will you give us in return? You don't get something for nothing. That is simply the way things are, which we know better than anyone, since we are the ones who made it that way."

"Why is that so?" said Purl. "Why did you get to make it that way? Who are you, that you are able to decide such things?"

"Since we are generous," *They* said, "we will tell you."

And they did.

Chapter 15

How They Came to Be

After the Seventh Day of Creation when the Lord was watching how the results of His efforts were coming along...

Or while the Great Earth Mother was resting from her labors of giving birth to the world...

Or the very first time that the Great Turtle walked out into the universe with our entire world sitting on its back...

Or whichever of many, many tales of creation you may believe in or have been taught or will be taught, but which we can all agree happened a very, very, very long time ago back when everything was new and while the Creator or creators were taking a breather...

The Sun, the Moon and the Stars got into an argument over which of them was more important to the humans that were already starting to spread over the world like rabbits.

Now you would think that being the Sun, the Moon and the

Stars would be impressive enough, but the truth is that all three of the celestial bodies were terribly insecure. The Sun and the Moon hated the idea that neither of them was able to be seen all the time, and they would argue over things that didn't mean much to anything except them. You could tell when they were really going at it because they would eclipse each other.

Meanwhile the Stars would look down and feel very left out since they were smaller and more distant and also constantly twinkled rather than being able to provide a steady light, and they also could only show up at night.

So when they saw the race of Man, they each wanted mankind to worship them, and they argued about it even as humanity turned its eyes to the heavens and speculated and wondered about the nature of what was above them. And each of the celestial bodies regularly boasted about how it was better than the other two.

"The people love me the most," said the Sun. "I give them warmth and light during the day. Without me, their plants and crops couldn't grow. Without me, they would be nothing, and I should control their destiny."

"No, the people love me the most," said the Moon. "For they do not fear the day, but oh, how they fear the darkness, and my light gives them comfort in the night. Without me, the tides would not roll in and out. Young lovers look to me and find me romantic, and poets and songwriters write hymns to my beauty. Without me, they would be nothing, and I should control their destiny."

"No, the people love me the most," said the Stars. "For at night the moon comes and goes while we remain permanent. Yes, the Moon causes the tides to roll in, but they use us to guide them across the oceans. Yes, the Sun gives them light, but there is but one Sun and many of us, so are we not many times greater? They see pictures in us they call constellations, and they try to predict their future by our movements. Without us, they would be nothing, and we should control their destiny."

And they argued and argued and continued to argue, and finally it became so tiresome that the Creator or creators of the universe stepped in, wanting to know what in all the universe could be so important that there had to be all this arguing?

So the Sun and Moon and Stars went before the Creator or creators and demanded to know who, of the three of them, should get to control the destiny of humanity.

Now truthfully, the Creator or creators did not care all that much, for if you must know, humanity was kind of an afterthought. Everyone involved in the actual creation of earth thought that whales and dolphins would be the main life form because the world was, after all, three quarters water. Humanity was simply something that the Creator or creators came up with at the last minute to just clean up after things and keep the world tidy and perhaps, at some point, get around to inventing peanut brittle, which mankind did eventually do, but not before inventing war and murder and air pollution. Honestly, if the Creator or creators had known about that ahead of time, they would likely have never gotten into the entire business of making humanity in the first place because, yes, peanut brittle was aces, as was also chocolate fudge, but it certainly wasn't worth people dying over. Not even stupid people.

The fact was that the Sun, the Moon and the Stars had a better sense of what humans could do—both good and bad—than the Creator or creators did.

Now if either the Sun or Moon or Stars had, at any point, thought to skip the whole business of fighting with one another and instead individually gone straight to the Creator or creators and asked for the job of being the controller of mankind's destiny—cutting the other two out of the loop entirely—it is quite possible that the Creator or creators would have said, "Certainly, absolutely, whatever you want, just go on about your business and leave me (or us) alone because I am (or we are) busy thinking about new challenges."

But the Sun, Moon and Stars didn't do that. Instead they argued until such time that the Creator or creators felt a need to step in and then had the need for a decision shoved in His or their collective faces and were asked to make an immediate ruling.

Now any child who has ever tried to force his or her parents into doing something will tell you that very rarely does this work out well for the child. Most of the time—we would say at least ninety percent, nine times out of ten—the parents will automatically say "No!" just because they're annoyed and feel the need to make a point.

This was one of those nine times out of ten.

"No!" said the Creator or creators. "No" to the Sun, "No" to the Moon, "No' to the Stars. "None of you gets to control Man's Destiny. Because all three of you are so annoying, Mankind will instead be given Free Will, allowed to make his own decisions and determine his own path. You will have nothing to do with it at all."

This made the Sun, the Moon and the Stars very angry and the decision brought them together for the first time. None of them wished to give up influence over Mankind to the others, but none of them wanted to be left out, either. And so after much discussion, they returned to the Creator or creators and said, "All right, we accept your decision, since we have no choice. But we must point out to you that free will without someone guiding them is just going to end in disaster. People will run off and do whatever they wish, going off in a billion directions at once. Mankind will need someone to keep things organized."

"What things?" said the Creator or creators.

"All the things. The things that you created but cannot be bothered to worry about because you need to focus on big, cosmic stuff. We, however, have plenty of time on our hands. So if it's okay with you, we will be happy to make certain that free will does not destroy mankind, which it very well may if they are left to take care of it."

"And how would you go about that?"

"Oh, you don't have to worry about it. That's part of the joy of leaving it to us. So you don't have to ask those sorts of questions."

And the Creator or creators decided that it seemed a pretty good idea, mostly because they didn't really give it all that much thought, and didn't have anyone around to tell them it was not a good notion at all. Had someone said something to them, let them know ahead of time, then maybe they would have thought better of it. But no one did, and so they didn't.

So it was that the Sun, the Moon and the Stars each created a single representative. Red was the color of the Sun, for that was the biggest and boldest, and because the rising and setting of the Sun often cast a haze of red upon the horizon. Yellow was the color of the Stars, twinkling and golden against the night sky. And blue was the color of the Moon, as you may well have guessed from the term, "Once in a blue moon."

And those representatives, or icons as they were called, came down to Earth and landed squarely in the mind of Mankind. The three became as one, which is why three is such a powerful number for humans. And they became the basis upon which other famous trios were formed, such as the Fates in Greek mythology, and other religious threesomes that we're sure you can name. Before any of those, there were the icons of the Sun, Moon and Stars. They also formed the basis for the primary colors, because together they could do anything.

But most importantly, they became *They*. You have heard of *Them* countless times. *They* didn't manage to get the snow plows out in time to clear the streets. *They* covered up the assassinations of famous world leaders. *They* know the truth about alien visitors.

They keep the trains running on time and *They* are the ones who cause the trains to break down at the worst possible moment. *They* are the ones who are behind everything that doesn't seem to make sense. *They* are the ones who decide what people will talk about. *They* are the ones who control all our fates. *They* are coming for you.

And there is absolutely nothing you can do about it.

Chapter 16

How Mary Agreed to a Deal That She Really Should Not Have

"Now then: to business," *They* said. Which member of *They?* It didn't matter, really. But *They* tended to speak as one more often than not. "You have come all this way because of your friend's runaway imagination, yes?"

"That's right," said Mary. "I don't understand. Why did you take it?"

"We require imaginations," *They* said. "Human imagination is part of what allows us to keep operating."

"People look to the Sun," said Mr. Red, "and they imagine a vast, unseen being drawing it across the sky with his chariot."

"People look to the Stars," said Miss Yellow, "and imagine what life on other worlds would be like."

"People look to the Moon," said Mr. Blue, "and imagine there is the face of a man staring down, or that it's made of green cheese."

"Without imagination, humans would be nothing. Without

humans, we would be nothing," *They* said. "We could not survive, and humanity would be on its own."

"Would that be such a terrible thing?"

"Yes. It would," *They* said with the air of individuals who are just supposed to know.

"What do you mean, you couldn't survive without them?"

"They are a resource. The details do not concern you. Ask something else or leave."

"But why did you take Anna's?" She knew the theories that she and Hunter had put forward, but she wanted to hear it from *They Themselves*.

"We have to take *someone's*," said Mr. Blue "And we are not uncaring. We don't want to take imaginations that we think are going to do great things. Those are the imaginations that look at bread mold and say, 'That might make a good medicine,' or look at birds in flight and say, 'People should be able to fly, too.' So we only take imaginations that we believe are not going to be put to any worthwhile use."

"You shouldn't get to decide that! Anna had a fine imagination!"

"Her imagination was nothing special."

"You're wrong," she said heatedly. "You are so wrong, and you didn't see her when her imagination was gone. It meant everything to her, and the only way I managed to calm her down was promising that I would bring it back to her. Well, actually, promising not to bring it back, but she knew the truth of it. And that's what I'm going to do, and you can stick me in a file drawer from now until doomsday, but sooner or later, I'll find a way to get out, and I will get her imagination back to her, even if I have to destroy you to do it."

The Boggy Man chuckled to hear her. "Such brave words from someone who knows so little about the way things work."

Purl pointed at him. "I am getting tired of you. Leave us."

He stopped chuckling. "Little princess," he said very softly, "you should not tempt my anger, for it is a terrible and far-reaching thing—"

"Leave us," said *They*.

Immediately he bowed. "As you wish," and he backed out of the door, pausing only long enough to cast one final, evil glance at Purl.

"You said we were to do business?" said Mary.

"That is correct. If you want something, something must be given in return. That is how it is done."

"Not always. What about her?" and Mary pointed to Purl. "Her parents came to you and asked for a child, and you gave them what they wanted. You didn't ask anything of them in return."

"There was no need," said Mr. Blue. "I knew what the outcome would be. I knew that Purl would be as unable to care as the stone from which she was carved. I knew that her people would wind up coming here, looking for somewhere to live."

"And where are they?" said Purl.

They smiled. Then *They* pointed at the files behind them.

"They're in...*there?*" Purl stared at the drawers. "You have them in your files? But...why?"

"We make use of them," *They* said. "It is not an easy thing, overseeing the affairs of mankind. We need to be able to send people out into the world to take care of things. Someone has to make sure elections turn out the way we want them to. Someone has to control what people see on television. Someone has to forget to send help to places that need it. Granted, we live in the minds of man, but we need hands and feet and faces to get things done. So we take people and scrub them clean, like laundry, of everything they were and are and ever will be, and make them over into what we need. That is how your parents and your people will now serve us. You, Purl, did what you were supposed to do. You drove your people to us. We took care of the rest. For that service, you have your life and your freedom, to use as you will."

"But..." Purl seemed puzzled. "That is not how a quest ends, with the people I'm looking for stuck in a file drawer."

"You wished to find them."

"Yes..."

"You have found them. You have done what you set out to do."

"But..." She was struggling for words. "I have things that must be said to them."

Miss Yellow actually seemed interested. "Really. Such as—?"

Purl hesitated. Mary immediately said, "Well, for starters..."

"Mary, you know better," Miss Yellow scolded her. "These sorts of things have to come from within or they mean nothing. Do not help her. You are, after all, merely her sidekick."

Mary fumed. "I am not her sidekick." Nevertheless, she said nothing more, because as much as she hated to admit it, Miss Yellow was right about one thing. If the person on the quest doesn't come to learn something by herself, then explaining it to her wouldn't mean a thing.

So Purl thought and thought and then, to Mary's dismay, admitted, "I don't know. I mean, I've had all this time to think about it, and I was sure that, when and if the situation presented itself, I would come up with something. But it hasn't. I wanted to ask how I should feel about their leaving me, so I could write it down and remember it and maybe make use of it, but now that I think about it, that goal doesn't seem big enough."

"Then," *They* said, "there's nothing more for us to say to one another. As for you," and *They* returned *Their* attentions to Mary, "a deal may yet be struck. You wish to take your friend's imagination. We want something in return."

"And what would that be?"

"We want your ship."

She blinked in confusion. "You want the *Argo?*"

"That is correct."

"But..." She was unsure of what to do. "But how would I get home?"

"Once you have found the imagination you are looking for, simply ride it back to its previous owner," *They* said. "The *Argo* will remain with us."

"But," Hunter said, "her imagination powers it. How will you operate it?"

They did not reply.

"This is getting odd," murmured Purl.

"My imagination powers it," Mary said. "How will you operate it?"

"In case you haven't noticed," Miss Yellow said sarcastically, "we have more than enough imagination at our disposal. We can use that."

"But why do you want it?"

"Think of it as a magnifying glass that focuses light and pinpoints it. It is basically the same idea. We will use it to focus the imaginations we have already gathered, and thus be able to do more than ever."

"What sort of more?" Mary said.

"All sorts of more. This is a busy time for us, after all. There are wars on and elections coming up, and we need to be managing them."

"You manage wars and elections? What do the two have to do with each other?"

"We control the elections," *They* said, "because the people who are elected are the ones who make the wars."

"Then shouldn't you want people elected who will get rid of wars?"

"Oh child," *They* sighed. "How little you understand. Wars are good for the economy. Wars help keep down the extra population. Without wars there would be too little money and too many people. Why do you think we keep wars going?"

"Wars are terrible!" Mary said. "They're destructive, they're awful!"

"We could argue about this all day, but it doesn't really matter. You are simply a little girl, and you cannot change the way of things. What matters to you is finishing your quest and helping your friend. Make your choice," *They* said, and then Mr. Blue added, "Although of course I know what you're going to say."

"I'm still not sure I believe you about that," said Mary. "It's easy to say you know the future, because then when it happens, you can just say, 'I knew that was going to happen.'"

Challenged by the tone of her voice, Mr. Blue said, "You are going to agree to our deal."

Now Mary felt stuck, and realized that she'd been outmaneuvered. If she refused the deal just to prove the point, then Anna would be left without her imagination and the quest would be a failure. But if she agreed to it, then Mr. Blue would be able to say, "I told you so," which would hurt her pride. And if there was one thing that Mary had a lot of, it was pride.

Still, there was nothing else for it. "I agree to your terms," she said.

"I told you so," said Mr. Blue.

Mary stuck her tongue out at him.

"I saw that," said Mr. Blue from behind his unseeing eyes.

Then, as one, *They* spoke: "Boggy Man, return to us."

Mr. Red then pushed a red button in front of him that caused the gears to start churning again, causing the door to unlock. Then it swung open and the Boggy Man stepped in. He waited to hear what they wanted.

"Take this young lady out to the corral," said Miss Yellow. "From there, it is entirely up to her to find the imagination of her friend."

He bowed slightly. "As you wish."

The Boggy Man then turned on his heel and walked out. Mary, Purl and Hunter followed him, with Purl pausing only long enough to look back at the file cabinets that contained, somewhere inside, her parents and subjects. Her face remained blank.

"Do you need me to tell you how you should feel?" said Mary.

"Actually," Purl said slowly, "for the first time...I don't wish to know how I should feel."

Mary was relieved since she wouldn't have known what to tell her. She was busy dealing with her own problems. The idea of leaving her ship behind was one she hated, especially since she was leaving it in *Their* hands. But it was in order to help another friend, and so she simply had to hope that the *Argo* would understand.

The three of them followed the Boggy Man out into the hallway, and then down a stairway that seemed to go on forever, followed by another longer hallway that smelled of mildew. Mary's nose wrinkled at it, as did Hunter's. Purl did not seem to notice it.

"Why do they keep ignoring me?" asked Hunter, looking for something to break the silence. "Why do they act as if I'm not there?"

"I couldn't say." The Boggy Man scratched the underside of his crooked chin. "It does seem rather odd. Then again, you're a talking winged lion cub, which is also rather odd, so I suppose it all evens out somehow."

They reached a large door at the end of the corridor, this one with no lock. The Boggy Man touched it once and the door swung open, almost as if it was eager to do so.

The travelers stepped out into bright sunlight and Mary had to shield her eyes against it.

"Here you are," said the Boggy Man. "The corral. Find what you're looking for, if you can."

What Mary then saw was, to her, the single most beautiful thing she had ever beheld.

The corral was exactly what it sounded like: a vast pen filled with animals. The fence stretched out in all directions, seemingly forever, and it was filled with many different animals. Not just horses, as Mary had thought it would be, but elephants, giraffes, tigers, pumas, dogs, all those and so many more, moving against each other, milling about, barking and roaring and hissing and making all the usual animal noises.

And they were all different colors: pale green, midnight blue, burgundy. There were colors that no animal had ever been since the dawn of time.

The Boggy Man was standing at the gate, his hand resting upon it. "In you go," and Mary headed in as did Hunter. But he quickly swung the door shut before Purl could enter. "This," he said, "does not involve you. This is not your quest; your quest is done. It is hers...and his, I suppose," and he waved toward Hunter. "But not yours."

Purl was still gripping the staff that she had been carrying with her since the jungle, and she looked ready to bring it crashing upon the Boggy Man's head.

"He's right," Mary said, and that pulled Purl's attention back to her. "This is my part now. You've done what you set out to do."

"But it's not over. How can it be over? I don't..."

"You don't what?"

"I don't...want it to be over," said Purl slowly. "You are the most annoying sidekick one could have, but I have become used to you, and am not ready to let you depart."

"It's not for you to let. It's for me to do. You're going to have to find someone else to tell you how to feel."

This angered Purl, who snapped, "I never really needed you to tell me how to feel. I simply told you that so you could feel useful. The truth is that I'm satisfied with the way I am."

Mary shook her head. "I will never understand you."

"And I do not have to explain myself to you."

"Well, then...I guess it all works out for the best, then."

"I guess it does."

Without further word, they turned away from each other. Purl proudly walked away, her head held high.

Mary tried to blank Purl from her mind, and found it extremely difficult. So instead she turned her focus to the matter at hand. "Hunter," she said, "you were able to get the scent of Anna's imagination from so far away. Can you do it when we're this close, even though there's all these animals here?"

"Of course. Follow me." Stretching his wings, Hunter lifted off and started moving through the air. Mary followed.

And as she passed each of the imaginations, they looked her in the eyes, and all she saw around her was misery. Deep, unspoken, misery. It struck her to the core of her soul.

She had known from the very beginning that Anna's case wasn't the only one. Where one imagination was stolen, there were sure to be others. And the other people who had lost their imaginations might well have been upset by their loss as Anna had been. Mary had not let herself think about the others because she had to worry about what Anna needed.

Now, though, seeing the misery of all these imaginations caged up by *Them*, she found she couldn't stand it. The juices in her stomach churned, first with upset and then with mounting anger.

The imaginations, thinking that they had somehow done something wrong, backed away from her because they could see the fury in her. Several times she stopped walking and just stood there, being angry, and Hunter had to return to her to get her to follow him.

She did so and finally found Anna's imagination.

It was a large purple Palomino, with a nub of a horn—like an infant unicorn—on the front of its head. Instead of a normal horse's tail, it had a lion's tail sweeping around on its backside. Hunter was a little jealous of it since it was so much more impressive than his own.

Upon seeing her, the beautiful creature clopped around, recognizing her instantly. It reared up on its hind legs and whinnied a joyous greeting.

"Did you find it?" It was the voice of the Boggy Man, calling to her from the gate. He sounded impatient, not to mention annoyed that he had had to shout; the Boggy Man preferred to speak in his spooky whisper.

"Yes," Mary said.

"Bring it here. Once I let it out of the gate, you'll be able to leave."

The Palomino had a bridle and reins. All of the imaginations were wearing some kind of restraint—reins, leashes, those sorts of things—and Mary's anger became even more fueled at seeing imaginations held back so. Of all things in this world, imaginations are the most deserving of being allowed to run free. Who were *They* to keep them penned up for *Their* exclusive use? And what exactly did *They* do with the imaginations, anyway? They were a resource? How were they a resource?

What was a resource, anyway? It was something that you made use of, like oil. Or it was something that helped you to live. But how could imaginations help *Them* to live? What could they possibly...?

Then a terrible notion occurred to her.

"Do *They* eat them?" she wondered aloud. "Or drain them of their strength like vampires drinking blood?"

Hunter immediately realized what she was talking about. "I don't know. I'm sure it's nothing pleasant, no matter what."

"And we're supposed to leave the others to *Them*?"

"That was the deal you made."

"Yes. Yes, it was. Hunter, get me up onto the horse's back."

Hunter wrapped his forelegs under Mary's arms and his wings fluttered with greater energy. Moments later he had landed her atop Anna's imagination. She gripped the reins firmly with her one hand. Her knapsack was weighing heavily upon her, as if urging her to put it to use.

She snapped the reins and Anna's imagination trotted forward. The others made way, looking at her sadly. "You can all follow me!" she called out, but none of them did. It might have been that the corral had some power over them, or perhaps they were simply afraid. Or perhaps it was exactly what *They* had told her. The imaginations that had been rounded up weren't all that remarkable, and so could not even imagine trying to get free.

As she drew nearer the gate, though, and as it got harder to urge Anna's imagination forward, she began to have a hint of what the problem was. The Palomino wasn't taking its eyes off the Boggy Man, and the more she tried to get the beast to go forward, the more it wanted to back up.

"It's afraid of you," said Mary.

"Of course it is," said the Boggy Man. "All imaginations are."

"Mine isn't," she said defiantly. "I'm not."

"Yet another reason why yours was not chosen for harvest," he almost purred. "Harvesting them is really no problem. I simply show up from out of the darkness or shadow, and say, 'Boo!,' and they run. And I continue to chase them, all the way to here, where they are locked up tight. They dare not leave knowing that I am here awaiting them." Seeing the Palomino's continued hesitation, he snapped, "You needn't prance about all frightened like. You have been given leave to go. Fly."

"It can fly?"

"Of course it can. All imaginations can. Have you never heard of flights of fancy? Or of an idea taking wing?"

"I suppose."

The Boggy Man waited until they stepped through and then closed the gate with a final click. Leaning on his cane, he said, "You are free to go. And do not think for a moment that you can somehow fool or betray *Them. They* see every living creature. *They* know all that is past, and present, and—"

"Wait." It was Hunter who had spoken. "Every living creature?"

"That is correct."

With growing excitement, Hunter—who had been hovering overhead—landed on the horse's rump. "They weren't ignoring me. They didn't know I was there. I was invisible to them because I'm not really living. I'm just a ghost wearing a stuffed toy, fired by your imagination. Which means—"

"We have something to use against them," Mary finished the thought.

The Boggy Man didn't like what he was hearing. Thus far he had been fairly calm and not all that threatening, but now he began to look and sound like something that terrified children just from the very mention of his name. His knuckles turned white as he squeezed the skull head of his cane, and in a tone oozing of danger, he said, "What are you going on about?"

"I need you to bring a message to *Them.*"

"I am not your messenger," he said with a growl. He took a step toward them, and the Palomino took two back. "But out of curiosity, what would you have me say to *Them?*"

"Tell them," and she raised her voice, "*that the deal's off! In fact, on second thought, I'll tell them myself!*"

She snapped the reins then and shouted, "*Yaaah*" because she'd seen enough movies to know that that was what you were supposed to do when you want a horse to take off really quickly.

The horse started to gallop and suddenly there was a hiss of steel and the Boggy Man had yanked out from his cane a dangerous looking sword. He moved to slash at the Palomino, and had he struck it, he might well have managed to slice open its stomach. There was no doubt in Mary's mind that the Boggy Man could easily kill Anna's imagination.

But he never got near enough, for Hunter leaped forward with a roar and slammed into the Boggy Man's face. He was blinded for a moment, his vision blocked by the winged cub, and it was just enough time for the Palomino to get up the speed to leap upward.

The Palomino galloped through the air. Interestingly, its hooves made "clack clack" noises even though there was no hard surface beneath it.

"Up! Up and around!" shouted Mary and the horse obeyed her, angling around City Hall. She wiggled around, reached into her knapsack, and pulled out the crowbar, with the rope still attached. "To the rooftop!" she cried out, and the Palomino descended. It landed on the slippery, angled roof but managed to hold its footing, and Mary threw the crowbar toward the skylight with all the strength she possessed.

The crowbar crashed into the stained glass window, shattering it. "Hunter! Get *Them*! Keep *Them* busy!" As she shouted that, she lashed the other end of the rope through the reins of the imagination and drew it tight, moving with amazing speed for a one-handed girl.

Hunter did not hesitate, hurling himself down and into the office of the Three Who Were One. *They* were looking up toward the shattered skylight, and *They* were shouting for *Their* guards to come at once. Hunter landed atop the desk, and he leaped directly into Miss Yellow, who was closest to him. He slammed into her with such force that it sent her stumbling backwards and, naturally, the siblings to whom she was joined on either side went down with her. With yelps of "What was that?" and "Who did that?" *They* crashed to the floor.

Gripping the rope with her hand and the stub of her right wrist, Mary slid down the rope. There was no time for delicacy; she went as fast as she could, and gritted her teeth against the pain as the rope tore at the inside of her palm.

Six feet from the bottom she released her hold and landed on the floor in a crouch. The glass crunched under her feet and she almost slid but regained her footing at the last moment.

The refrigerator box was still there, just as she had left it. It didn't surprise her. If it was as powerful as *They* claimed it to be, naturally *They'd* want to keep it close to *Them*.

"Where are you going to go?" Hunter called to her. He was still walking back and forth across the top of the desk, stopping only to growl at the confused figures on the floor. *They* were trying to get to *Their* feet, which was no easy task because, thanks to *Their* being joined at the hip, it was hard for *Them* to get up once they'd fallen.

"I only have one choice!" she said. "I have to go back to the beginning of time and convince the Creator or creators that putting *Them* in charge is going to be a very bad idea!"

When she said that, *They* let out an alarmed, even terrified cry, making it clear to Mary that her plan—as crazy as it sounded to Hunter and, very likely, you as well—might have some vague chance of working. With a unified screech of terror, *They* lurched to *Their* feet and Mr. Red hit the unlocking button.

The vast gears on the door began to turn. Within moments it would unlock and then the Furry Furies would come tearing in.

Mary reached into her knapsack and yanked out the monkey wrench. She threw it straight and true, and it landed squarely in the upper gears. The cogs caught, tried to grind forward, and couldn't.

"It's the permanent file for you—!" Miss Yellow screeched, and Mary felt a brief tug against which she was helpless to fight, but then just as suddenly it was gone. Hunter had struck again, and Miss Yellow was howling, because scratch marks were across her face, with blood welling up from them. She staggered, and Misters Red and Blue did so as well.

Mary started toward the refrigerator box...

...and stopped dead.

The Boggy Man was between her and it. "You thought to keep me out, child?" he said with a sneer. "I am the Boggy Man. I go into any room I will."

She glanced toward the doors but saw that they were still secure, although she heard the howling of the Furry Furies on the other side. They were trying to get in, but the lock was still holding them out.

Waving his sword in front of himself, any hint of pleasantness had vanished from him. He was as dark and fearsome as any description of him had ever been, and he snarled at Mary, "Keep back, child, or I will butcher you like cattle. Your little pet may be keeping *Them* at bay, but you'll have no such luck with me."

"*Then maybe I will!*" came a defiant voice from above.

Purl dropped down from on high, a dark angel as she landed squarely between the Boggy Man and Mary. "*Because a princess' quest isn't over until she say it's over!*"

She had her staff held crosswise across her body and now she whipped it around in a defensive position. The Boggy Man let out a snarl so horrifying that all across the world at that moment, children cried out in their sleep and didn't know why, and then he came straight at Purl.

Purl blocked the thrust of his sword, pushed it aside, and attacked faster than Mary would have thought possible. She could scarcely follow it. Hunter would have helped, but he was busy keeping *Them* busy, leaping upon *Them*, clawing and tearing at *Them* so that they couldn't pull themselves together and throw Mary and Purl back into a file drawer. Interestingly every time he ripped at *Their* skin, it would heal almost as quickly, but *They* could still feel pain and he was giving them plenty of it.

Purl shouted in annoyance at Mary, "Don't just stand there! Do what you're going to do!" as the Boggy Man attacked her with even more effort.

Mary scolded herself. She was usually more focused than that. She'd allowed herself to get distracted by Purl's battle with the Boggy Man. It wasn't the sort of mistake she could allow once more.

She scrambled into the refrigerator box and immediately commanded the *Argo* to transform itself into a time machine and take her back to the beginning of creation.

The *Argo* said no.

Chapter 17

How the Argo Said No

Very firmly is how the *Argo* said no. It did not speak aloud or in words such as you or we would understand. But it made it clear that it would not do what Mary wanted. That surprised Mary greatly because it never would have occurred to her that the *Argo* had that much of a mind of its own. Then again, she supposed she should not have been all that surprised since she usually left it to the *Argo* to decide what shape it should take for its surroundings.

Now, though, she was trying to push it into becoming something that it wasn't eager to be, and to do something it wasn't eager to do, and it was pushing back.

Or maybe it wasn't the ship at all. Maybe it was her very own imagination. She didn't know if hers was in the shape of a horse, like Anna's, or maybe some other type of beast. But it was certainly present within her, and it was making clear to her that this was not something she should be doing.

As we have said, they were not actual words that spoke within her mind, but instead feelings. It is impossible for us to tell you what that sounded like, and so we will settle for coming as near as we can to describing the internal struggle in words, even though no words were involved. If we try to do it any other way, it would take far too long, and it would just come back around to words anyway. So here is our best effort to put across what it felt like between Mary and either her ship or her own imagination arguing against what she wanted to do.

You know that all imaginations have limits, Mary. They have to, for the safety of the imaginer. It's why, when you're falling in a dream, you always wake up before you hit bottom, because no one should be allowed to imagine what it's like to die. It's the same thing here: you're imagining doing things that would affect the very make-up of the universe. It's been done, but never by one so young. It's too much for you.

"It's the only way."

Find another way. You saw what pushing your imagination too much did to you before. It will be worse this time. Far worse.

"So you're saying it can be done. It's just that there will be a cost."

Yes. Yes, I suppose I am.

"I will pay that cost," Mary said fearlessly. "I cannot leave those imaginations to suffer. I cannot let Anna down. I cannot leave these things as they are, and I will take whatever risk I have to."

You mustn't. Think about what you are doing, what you're asking. Think of the chance you're taking. Your parents, your brother will likely never see you again. Anna will have her imagination back, but she will never see you again either. You have so much you can do with your life, and to throw it away...

"I want," Mary said, with iron in her voice, "a time machine that can carry me back to the beginning of everything, so that I can speak to the Creator or creators."

There was a deathly silence, and then...

As you wish.

All of this happened very, very quickly—much less time than it took to tell—and just like that, the controls of a time machine appeared in front of her. The settings were fairly simple. There was a button that said, "Power On." And next to it was a lever with two settings. At the moment, the lever was settled into a space that read, "Now." It was set in a track and could be slid over into its other setting of, "Then."

Mary punched the "On" button and then she shouted, "Hunter! Purl! Come on!"

The box, which had been lying on its side, suddenly snapped upright, all on its own as energy surged through it. Then suddenly Purl tumbled headfirst into the *Argo*, as if she were rubbish being tossed away. She was unconscious. She had certainly boasted enough that she didn't feel things, but apparently she could be knocked cold as much as anyone else. Mary gasped. There was a bruise on Purl's forehead and a huge gash across her upper body, and blood was seeping from it. Mary didn't think it was fatal, but it was deep. Then the face of the Boggy Man appeared at the top of the refrigerator carton, and he snarled down at them and tried to reach for them, and once again sleeping children all over the world reacted, pulling away and crying out in their slumber and some even tumbling off their beds trying to get away.

Then the Boggy Man let out a roar, for Hunter was perched atop his shoulder and he was biting furiously on the Boggy Man's ear. Then Hunter twisted his head sharply and the Boggy Man screamed as one ear was torn loose from the side of his head, making a sound like ripping paper. Hunter spit it out and the Boggy Man grabbed at him, but Hunter leaped between his hands and landed next to Mary and atop Purl.

Without hesitation, since Hunter was no longer distracting *Them* and she didn't want to wind up inside a file drawer again, Mary slammed the lever from "Now" to "Then." Then she threw her body to the side, sending the box once more tumbling over the edge of reason.

This time it was completely different from any time before.

The *Argo* moved so quickly that Mary and Hunter felt as if gigantic fists were being pressed down on them. Purl was unconscious, so it was impossible to say how it felt to her.

Out the top of the box, which was open, it looked like they were inside some manner of tunnel that was swirling endlessly and dizzyingly around them. It was pure white light, and moving like water spinning down a drain, and as it spun it took them along with it.

And just as she had been warned, the demands she was making upon her imagination were beginning to affect her. Her head was pounding, as if gremlins had set up shop behind her ears and were slamming both sides with a hammer. Her vision was blurring, and she felt as if there was no longer enough fluid in her, like her entire body was beginning to dry out.

Even worse, the *Argo* was starting to shrink. She didn't know why, but it most definitely was.

Hunter was terrified. He had his eyes closed and his paws clamped over his eyes and his wings drawn over those.

And for the first time in all its travels, the *Argo* seemed in danger of coming apart.

Mary heard it creaking. The big brass staples that had always been so reliable in holding it together were starting to lose their grip.

"More imagination...I need more imagination," she whispered. She tasted something on her lips. It was blood. Her nose was bleeding again, much more than before. She wiped it away with her sleeve and then looked down at her hand.

You know the old saying, "I know something like the back of my hand"?

Mary didn't recognize her hand. The fingers were longer, her fingernails extended and cracked, and there were brown spots all over it.

Distracted as she was, the *Argo* began to slow, to lose its drive against the forces that were trying to push it back the way it had come. Realizing that she was in danger of being tossed back to "Now" without having reached her goal, Mary ignored what was happening to her and forced the sturdy vessel onward. She imagined it as being whole and not falling apart at all, and the *Argo* obeyed her and fixed itself.

As if she were shoving a full size automobile uphill with the power of her mind alone, Mary forced the *Argo* to go back, back, further back, back all the way. Her body was aching from head to toe, and it was all she could do not to moan aloud. *I can do this,* she thought, *I can do this, I am not afraid, I am not afraid!*

And suddenly the *Argo* stopped moving.

It didn't skid gently to a halt or even jolt them around inside. Instead one moment it was moving, and then the next, it wasn't. It was just sitting there and waiting.

Slowly Hunter lowered his paws and opened his eyes. Then he gasped when he saw Mary. He whispered her name in a strangled hush and then managed to say, "What happened to you?"

She looked down at herself and realized that the *Argo* had not shrunk at all. She had grown into an adult. A very old adult.

Mary started to push herself forward and heard creaking in her knees. She ignored it. All that mattered was doing what she had set out to do.

She shrugged off her knapsack as she did so, because it suddenly felt heavier than ever on her back and very tight in the shoulders. She also kicked off her shoes, which were pinching her feet since they had outgrown them. Some instinct, something that urged her not to leave herself without weapons, made her drag her sword with her even as she approached the open end of *Argo* so she could look out on the beginning of everything. She also pulled out a pen, because she had a feeling she was going to see something amazing and she wanted to scribble down a picture of it on the inside of the *Argo* so that she would remember it.

But when she finally saw it, she was so stunned that she was unable to do anything aside from drop the pen in her pocket. "Purl," she whispered. "Purl, you have to see this...it's...it's magnificent..."

Purl didn't reply. "She's still asleep," said Hunter. "That Boggy Man must've hurt her badly. She's still bleeding."

"Clean her up as best you can." Mary scarcely recognized her own voice. She sounded deeper and a bit broken. It didn't matter, though. Nothing mattered except for the splendor that she was seeing.

She floated in the depths of space and watched creation happening all around her. The sun was just starting to cool enough to allow the third planet away to support life. All around her was a vast, swirling mass of colors, as if a great, mad painter had thrown them about willy-nilly and yet somehow managed, through either genius or simply blind luck, to hit upon a design of staggering beauty. The stars were not twinkling, no, but instead were glowing steadily, as if they were inviting her to come visit them. Far, far below her, she saw what she was pretty sure was Earth, still in the midst of formation, the surface convulsing in volcanic upheaval, the oceans so newly formed that steam was still rising from them.

She felt wetness upon her cheeks. She was crying. It was just that beautiful.

I'm not supposed to be seeing this. This is beyond anything humans are supposed to see.

But she did not look away. Instead she gazed upon it, unafraid and determined, and then she called out loudly:

"Creator or creators? Are you there? Are you listening? It's me, Mary Dear. I won't be born for a very, very long time yet. Probably...I don't know...thousands of years from now, at least. But I need to warn you that you are going to put the Sun, the Moon and the Stars in charge of organizing mankind...and girl-kind, which would be me...and it's not going to be fair at all. *They* are going to pick and choose who gets to have an imagination and who doesn't, when that should be the right of all people! And *They* will keep wars going, and not serve your creations well at all! I mean, you want people to have free will! To be able to make their own decisions! How can that be happening if *They* are controlling everything?" She paused. "Is anyone hearing this?" She crawled forward, sticking her head out of the box and shouted, "*Is anybody there?!*"

"I am," a soft and sinister voice purred from above her.

A hand forcefully grabbed her by the hair and yanked her out of the time machine.

The Boggy Man was perched on the outside of the *Argo*, sneering his wicked sneer.

Chapter 18

How it All Came Around

The one thing that saved Mary from being stabbed to death by the Boggy Man just then was the fact that she was still clutching her sword. She whipped it around and sliced across his arm. The Boggy Man let out a startled yelp and released her, and she landed in a crouch atop the box, keeping the sword poised and ready.

"What's happening out there!" called Hunter.

"Stay inside!" she shouted back. "It's the Boggy Man! He hitched a ride on the outside of the *Argo!*"

"I'll help you...!"

"No," and her lips drew back in a snarl that equaled that of the Boggy Man himself. "He's *mine*."

"Such bravery from an old woman," said the Boggy Man. "Odd, isn't it? Old age usually brings wisdom, but not in your case. How little you know of anything."

"I know enough. Get off my ship."

"Do you truly think that *They*, those idiots, are the ones controlling everything? *They* haven't really been running things for quite some time." He waggled his sword in front of her. "I'm the one who has truly been overseeing things. I'm the one who makes the suggestions that *They* take. The fact is that mankind was making too many advances, too quickly. You were approaching a golden age. Someone had to step in to make sure that didn't happen."

"But why? Why wouldn't you want that for humanity?"

"Because, child...that would be no fun at all."

He came at her quickly, stabbing his sword forward, completely certain that he would run her through.

She blocked it. Deflected it quite easily, in fact.

"I think you're lying, because you are evil, and evil always lies," said Mary. "I think you're just a sad little thing that wants to believe it is way more important than it is. Do you see this?" and she raised her old woman voice. "Creator or creators? Do you see the type of evil creature that the Sun, Moon and Stars allow to serve them? What does that say about them, if they use someone like him? And if you allow it to happen...*what does that say about you?*"

The Boggy Man thrust again. This time she not only deflected it but answered with a parry of her own that came close to taking out one of the Boggy Man's eyes.

"You little idiot! Don't you know who you're dealing with?" he said, his voice rising. "I am the latest incarnation of an evil that goes back further than you can imagine!"

"You'd be amazed at what I can imagine," said Mary, and now she took the fight to him.

There was barely any room for either of them to move. A step back or side to side at most was what they could manage as they balanced atop a refrigerator carton hanging in the depths of space while creation happened all around them. Their blades came together and separated, brisk clashes of steel, sparks flying off as the swords struck and then separated, struck and separated, over and over. It's not like the sword fights you see in movies where they have these long, nonstop bouts of swordplay. These were quick and vicious and, without exception, potentially deadly. The slightest misstep would send one of them tumbling off the ship. If one of them reacted a split second too slowly, the result could well be a sword blade plunged into their heart.

Purl may have begun life as a slab of rock, but Mary was now displaying just as much emotion as one. Her elderly, wrinkled face was a mask of calm, and she beat back every thrust, knocked aside every attack, and responded to each one with one of her own.

Then she pinked the Boggy Man on the side of the face, and there was blood trickling down. It wasn't red; it was black, seeping like tar. With a roar the Boggy Man came at her again, and the blades went faster, and now Mary cut across his arm, deeper than before when she had simply cut through his sleeve. More of the black stuff welled up, and now the Boggy Man was howling in fury.

And Mary shouted defiantly, "*See, Creator or creators? See the result of your inattention? How can you be so blind? I'm an eight year old in an old woman's body, and I can see it!*"

Suddenly she spotted something over the shoulder of the Boggy Man. It was a meteor, some huge piece of rock unleashed during the explosive beginnings of the universe, and it was hurtling directly at the drifting *Argo*...a ship that was, at that moment, being held together almost entirely by what fragments of imaginary strength she had left.

It was just enough of a distraction for the Boggy Man to thrust forward with his sword. Mary realized at the last instant and she brought up her sword to deflect it, but it wasn't enough. The blade pierced her shoulder and came out the other side, running all the way through to the hilt, bringing her face to face with the Boggy Man. He cackled wildly, his foul breath washing over her, and the pain from the sword lodged in her shoulder was horrible.

And not for a moment did Mary hesitate, for she knew that if she did, all aboard the *Argo* would be lost, since the ship was drifting and the meteor was going to annihilate them. She released her hold on her sword, allowing it to fall away. The Boggy Man's glance went to the falling sword, and so he didn't see as she shoved her hand into her pocket, withdrew the pen, and jammed the point into the base of the Boggy Man's throat. He screamed, clutching at it, distracted.

"Hunter! Throw the switch back!"

"But you're outside!"

"Do it now!"

And just as she had first done on a playground so many years ago, or so many centuries from that point on, depending on how you look at it, Mary swung the arm around that ended in a stump and slugged the Boggy Man in the side of the head as hard as she could.

The Boggy Man staggered from the impact and lost his grip on the sword he had jammed into her. Mary then threw herself backwards, and the sword that had gone through her shoulder penetrated the hull of the *Argo*, or the side of the refrigerator carton, depending on how you saw it. As a result she was now flat on her back, pinned to the outside of the ship like a butterfly to a mounting board.

She heard the switch slam home from within, and the box lurched violently. The Boggy Man had been holding on with both hands and a vise-like grip when he had hitched a ride, but now he was standing and off balance, not to mention in pain from the pen in his throat. Mary swept a foot around, catching him in the back of the knees. The Boggy Man's legs went out from under him, and he fell onto his back, and even then he might still have managed to hang on except that the white vortex, the tunnel through time, leaped into existence around them and the *Argo* sprang forward with the force and speed of a cork from a champagne bottle, the meteor streaking right past where they had been an instant before and missing them. The Boggy Man bounced off the side and away from the ship, and his terrified scream echoed up and down the corridors of creation, embedding themselves forever into the deepest nightmares of all humanity to come as he tumbled away into the byways of time, never to be seen again, but only imagined, which might be rather worse when you think about it.

The *Argo* spun and spun, and it was a dizzying experience for Mary. She almost passed out several times but fought to keep herself together. There was swirling whiteness everywhere, and she caught glimpses along the way of the whole of human history. Everything was happening so fast that she couldn't single out any one moment. Instead it was an endless cycle of war and peace, death and destruction and rebirth and rebuilding and the names kept changing and even the reasons kept changing but the same things kept happening.

Hunter was shouting something from inside, but she couldn't hear him because there was so much pounding in her ears, and she was starting to feel weaker because of her wound.

Don't black out, don't black out, you might not make it all the way back if you black out, so don't black out, was the last thing she thought right before she blacked out.

The next thing she knew, something was licking her face.

She blinked and looked up, knowing what she would see. Sure

enough, it was Hunter. When he saw her opening her eyes, he sighed with relief.

"Are we back?" she managed to croak.

"We're back somewhere, but we're not back where we started," he said.

Slowly she sat up and that was when she realized that she was no longer stuck to the *Argo*. The hardy refrigerator carton was lying a short distance away, the sword having fallen to the side. There was a low moan from within the box; obviously Purl was starting to come around as well.

A sudden alarmed thought crossed her mind. "The sword didn't strike you or Purl when it went in, did it?"

"No, although it did just miss her. Where are we?" said Hunter, looking around.

She was as puzzled as he. They were in an alley filled with rubbish that had been lying there for who-knew-how-long. It appeared to be a sunny day, but the light was having trouble filtering down to where they were. They were not back in Afrasia, she was certain of that. From the front of the alley, she could hear what sounded like normal traffic noises. They were in a city somewhere. And since the passing comments she heard were in English, at least it was somewhere that she could understand what was going on.

Slowly she got to her feet and looked down at herself. Her clothing was stretched and in tatters because she had grown. There was a box of old clothes lying nearby that had been put out and marked for collection and she started to rummage around in them. She found a large gray, shapeless coat and a broad brimmed hat, which she put on because she didn't want people to look at her, since she felt self-conscious over how she looked. There was nothing that fit her feet, but they were fairly hardy, so she wasn't worried about remaining barefoot.

"I'm going to go look around," she said to Hunter.

"Should I come along? I'll come along!" He went ahead of her to the front of the alley and was now looking around with interest, while still trying to keep to the shadows. "I can keep my wings hidden so they don't attract attention."

"You're a lion cub in a city. Trust me, you'll attract attention." Her shoulder was aching, but the bleeding seemed to have stopped, so that was something. She heard Purl making noises such as, "Where am I? What happened?" from within the box. Mary said briskly, "Hunter! Stay here and keep an eye on Purl. Get away from the front of the alley before somebody sees you."

"Somebody already did. A little girl. She's very sweet looking. She kind of looks like you a little bit. Actually, more than a little bit. A lot."

And that was when she knew, and she whispered, "Oh no... oh, of course..."

"What is it?"

She turned to Hunter and said, "Stay here."

And then Mary sprinted from the alley, dashing toward exactly what she knew she was going to see and hearing what she knew she was going to hear: the loud, piercing scream of her mother as a little girl too fearless to know any better froze in the middle of an intersection and stared at a truck bearing down upon her.

Despite the age that had fallen upon her body, Mary moved as fast as any sprinter could have. She had a brief glimpse of the horrified expression of the trucker, and the grillwork loomed in front of her even as the brakes screeched, and then she had her hand on the little girl and flung her toward the outstretched arms of her mother, who stumbled backwards and fell onto the sidewalk.

And then Mary was in the air, realizing that the truck had struck her. She thrashed around and then hit the street only a few feet away. If the truck had hit her at full speed, she would have been killed instantly. As it was, she was badly injured.

The trucker was standing over her and the crowd was gathering around. "I'm sorry, lady! I'm so sorry!" the trucker, who was crouched over her, was saying. In the distance, she could hear the sound of sirens far, far away. Traffic had come to a halt in all directions.

She knew at that point the girl would be coming any moment. She rolled over in order to hide the handless arm because she didn't want the child to have the slightest idea of what was actually happening. She heard people muttering, "That's her. That's the little girl."

Then Mary's own, childish face looked down at her, and tears began to dribble down her face and over her mouth. "I'm so sorry," she whispered.

For a moment Mary wondered if her appeals to the Creator or creators had somehow changed things. That the world that she was in now was different from the one she had departed. There was one easy way to find out. "Is there still war?"

The little girl blinked in confusion. "Yes. There are wars."

"Oh well. I tried." She studied her younger self. "You're fearless."

"Yes." The child Mary paused and then said, "Sometimes I suck my thumb. I can't help myself."

She reached up with her good hand and grasped her younger self by the back of the head, pulling her close. "They will try to make you afraid. Because of this. And things to come. Mark me: *They* will try."

"Who's 'they?'"

"The great unseen *They*. The same *They* who does everything else that nobody likes, and people shake their heads over it and cluck and say, 'How could *They* let this happen?' *They* will want you..." She paused, steadying her voice. "*They* will want you to be afraid, because keeping people afraid is how *They* stay in charge. But you are fearless. To fight *Them*, you have to stay that way."

"I don't want to fight anyone," said the little girl.

Mary ignored her because she knew the truth of it. There was a warrior spirit in the girl that would love the challenges she was to meet. "If you take one lesson away from this moment, it is this: To be fearless does not mean to be reckless. The reckless person jumps off the cliff without hesitation. To hesitate is not to be fearful; it is wisdom. Be fearless but be wise. If you do this, you can defeat *Them*. Do you understand?"

"Yes."

Mary smiled, because she knew the child was just saying what she thought she was expected to say. "You do not. But you will when you're older."

"How much older?"

She looked herself in the eyes and loved what she saw.

"Eight, I should think," she said, and then she lay her head down on her arm. Her hand released its grip on the child as she saw final darkness sliding toward her.

And then she disappeared.

Chapter 19

How Prayers are Sometimes Answered

Hunter knew God.
 Well, not *the* God. But *a* god.
 He saw Mary lying on the ground a distance away, and he could smell that she was dying, for who better to know death than one who is already dead?
 Purl had emerged from the *Argo* and was now standing behind him. The wound she had taken was still dripping, although it was starting to slow. "What happened? Who is that old woman out there? Where's Mary?"
 "The old woman is Mary. Be quiet," and he pressed his paws together and closed his eyes. "I'm praying."
 "But how did she—?"
 "I said be quiet! I'm praying!"
 Purl would not have thought that Hunter would dare address her in such a manner. She promptly lapsed into silence.

And Hunter prayed.

He had no idea if he had ever done so before in his life, because he had little recollection of what his life had been and even less interest. But he understood the concept and he did so now. Mary had attempted to speak to the Creator or creators and it was impossible for him to tell if she had succeeded or not, but unlike Mary, Hunter had a name to call to, and names had power.

His lips moved, but he did not speak the words so much as think them with all the ferocity in his small body.

Hekate, help us. Please help us, oh glorious Hekate, and I will praise your name forever, I, your willing slave, your most humble admirer, please, Hekate, who sent me upon this journey. I have seen much and learned much, but I know this more than anything, and that is that it cannot end this way, there is too much to be done, too much left unanswered, and Mary may be fearless, but I am sore afraid, need your help, please, Hekate, please...

Suddenly he heard a scraping behind him, and then a rattling, and Hunter turned just in time to see that the *Argo* had risen up, entirely on its own. It was lying sideways, and then it was hurtling right toward them. Purl had been crouched next to Hunter and she saw it the same time he did. Faced with the opportunity to dodge it, instead—driven by instinct—Purl and Hunter leaped headlong into it. The refrigerator box spun and began to disappear even as it hurtled unseen through the crowd and scooped up the fallen Mary, leaving behind the ragged clothing she'd gotten from the alley.

"*What's happening!*" shouted Purl, who was starting to feel as if she was saying that a lot and never getting any truly good answers. "Are you making this happen?

"I'm not sure!" said Hunter. "I might be, because it responds to Mary's imagination and I have some of hers in me! But it might also be the answer to my prayers! I think we're...we're—!"

The *Argo* suddenly thudded against something, thumping and skidding as if it had just come in for a rough landing. They held on desperately and slowly the sturdy ship slid to a halt. Purl was gasping for breath; Mary seemed scarcely to be breathing at all.

Outside them was nothing but darkness.

And then there were whispers, a series of them, saying, "He's back!" "Hunter is back!" They sounded unearthly, which was natural since they were.

Hunter bounded from the refrigerator carton and Purl emerged moments later, cradling Mary's limp body in her arms. She looked around in confusion. "This is a graveyard," she said.

"Yes. It is."

Purl saw an elegant woman standing a short distance away, surrounded by shapeless ghosts and spirits moving around her. "Hunter," she said. "How prettily you prayed to me. So few people pray to me these days. How I've missed it."

Hunter knelt before her. "Help her, Hekate. Help Mary."

"I cannot," said Hekate. "I have helped you to bring her here, and that is the limit of my influence in this matter. Once she is dead, then naturally I will have say over where she goes and what she does, but not before."

"But I don't *want* her to die!"

"Since when does what someone wants, much less a dead someone, have any influence over matters of life and death?" Her voice was gentle but firm. "Nothing you can say will change what must happen, Hunter."

Purl crouched over Mary, cradling her head in her lap. Mary looked up at her wearily. "You're still bleeding," whispered Mary.

"And you are badly injured. It appears you are going to die."

"Does that matter to you?"

"I'm not sure. You tell me. Should it?"

Mary made a noise that sounded like distant laughter. "You'll never change."

"And what of you? Are you unchanging? You stand on the brink of death. At the last...are you unafraid? Are you still fearless?"

And Mary looked deeply into herself, deeper than she ever had before.

"No," she said, her voice so soft that Purl could scarcely hear her. "I...am afraid."

"Of dying?"

"No. But I am...I am afraid for so many other things. I am afraid of how my parents will suffer, not knowing whatever happened to me. I am afraid I have failed Anna, because I cannot be sure that her imagination will return. I am afraid that I failed in my mission, and that *They* are still in charge and will continue to steal people's imaginations, and feed on them, and do terrible things to mankind and people won't even know that that's what happening, but will instead just continue to complain about how *They* do this or that. And I am afraid that there really isn't any free will, because look what happened to me. I thought I was doing everything on my own, and making all my own decisions, and yet it all came back around to reliving something that happened years ago, so what difference did any of my adventure make if the end was already decided? That would be awful, if what we say and think and do doesn't matter one bit. And..." The eight year old trapped within the aged body began to sob, dusty tears rolling from her eyes. "And yes. I am afraid of death, as it turns out. Because I've so enjoyed my adventures, and I've no idea if, once I am gone, I will be able to have any more, and an existence without adventures is so sad...so...Purl...would you hold me close?"

And Purl lay down next to Mary, and held her close.

And Mary's tears fell upon the bloody gash on Purl's chest in a continuing stream, and they worked their way down, down into her system, into her heart, the water dripping steadily, steadily upon it, and as we all know and said before, but it bears repeating: water can wear down anything, even the hardest of stone.

Purl cried out, gasping, as if drawing breath for the first time, and she felt what seemed like a burning in her chest. She clutched at it, and then with passion in her voice and fire in her eyes, she grabbed at Mary's shoulders and said, "You can't die! You can't leave now! There are still things to do! You can save yourself! I know it!"

"Can't..." whispered Mary, for her long response to Purl had used up the very last of her strength.

"Yes, you can! Use your imagination! Imagine yourself to be better! Imagine yourself fully recovered! I know you can do that! People will themselves back to health all the time, and they don't have a fraction of the imagination you have!"

"No more left," said Mary. "I would love to...but...no strength... to imagine...no imagination...for strength...I'm all out...all used up..."

"Not all," came the firm voice of Hunter. "Not all of it is used up."

He was standing next to her and resting his paws upon her. "I took some of it from you, remember? And now...now I can return it to you. I can return it and more besides. I can give you of myself."

"I would not advise that, Hunter," Hekate spoke up sharply. "The imagination you would return her is not enough; her life force is fading, and if you do what I think you want to..."

"I want to give her everything she needs and more, because I have come to love her as I never had the chance to love anyone before, and never will again. And if some small part of me will live—*truly* live—within her, that is more than enough."

"Hunter, wait—" Mary managed to say.

But he did not wait. Instead he brought his head down to her and nuzzled her face, and then let go of everything that was within the confines of his lion body. He glowed with such a powerful light then that Purl had to shield her eyes lest she be blinded by it, and there was a noiseless explosion like air being sucked inward instead of blown outward, and when the noise and the glow faded, there was Mary, all of eight years old and very confused, looking down at herself, healed of all wounds.

Of Hunter, there was no sign, save for a small and somewhat battered looking plush toy of a winged lion.

She sat up, her clothes still tattered but now fitting her somewhat better since she had been restored to her previous size. "Hunter!" she called out, and she got hurriedly to her feet as she turned to face Hekate. "Where is he?"

"He is gone," Hekate said. "He gave up his afterlife so that you may live your actual life in full."

"Are you saying he's...he's haunting me? Possessing me?"

"No. But your spirit was fading. He has simply added the fuel of his spirit to yours, like the nourishment that food provides a starving body. For what it is worth, though, his strength and bravery will forever be a part of you, although I have to think you already had a good deal of your own."

"But..." Mary began to say.

Hekate silenced her with a single raised finger. "What has been done cannot be undone. He did what he did with no regrets. Obviously he would rather share a single lifetime with you than dwell many lifetimes here with me, as one of my favorites. Be flattered. It is not everyone who will choose a mortal girl over a goddess. He must have come to love you even more than he said."

"I...I never realized he felt that way," said Mary, and she felt ashamed.

"Now you know. Treasure his memory, as I will. Now off with the both of you," and she added with a hint of warning, "before I change my mind."

Chapter 20

How Things Ended

Since she had a fairly clear idea of where they needed to go, Mary was able to steer the *Argo* directly to the heart of City Hall, landing squarely in the office of *Them*. She was taking a bit of a chance, of course, because neither she nor Purl had the slightest idea what to expect upon their arrival.

When the *Argo* landed, the travelers heard startled gasps of shock, and voices saying, "What's that?" and "Where did that come from?" The voices did not sound at all like Mr. Red, Miss Yellow or Mr. Blue, so that was certainly a positive start. What surprised Mary was Purl's reaction of, "It can't be," apparently recognizing the voices that were speaking. Purl clambered out of the box first and let out, to Mary's surprise, a squeal of pure, unadulterated joy. When Mary emerged as well, she saw a stately-looking man and dignified woman behind two desks, and Purl was embracing them fiercely. They looked as astonished as Mary had been, and they were returning the embrace a bit uncertainly, as if thinking this might be some sort of big joke that was being played upon them.

Purl turned to face Mary then and said, "Mary...these are my parents. Mother, father...this is..." She paused and then said proudly, "This is my friend, Mary. I helped her in her quest, and she helped me. We helped each other."

"That's absolutely true," said Mary. "But...what are you two doing here?"

"It's the oddest thing," said Purl's father, who had a deep and commanding voice. "I seem to remember being someplace very dark and tight, with no way out. And suddenly..."

"We were here," said Purl's mother. "This place is our kingdom. We run it."

"But what about *Them?*" said Purl.

Her parents looked at each other in confusion. Then they looked back at the girls. "What *Them?*"

And no matter how much Mary and Purl tried to prompt them or their memories, Purl's parents absolutely could not recall anything between their being trapped in darkness and suddenly finding themselves installed in City Hall, apparently in charge of all Afrasia. Their subjects were likewise freed from their containment and were living in different parts of the city. All seemed to be as it should be, even though there was a vague awareness among all concerned that something wasn't quite right. Over time, however, such worries would fade away and life would return to normal.

(And just so you know, that type of thing happens more often than you would think. The world is not quite as solid or constant as you might believe it to be. There will be times where toys are not where you left them. There will be times where people who you absolutely thought were your friends one day suddenly say cruel things either behind your back or right to your face, and you wonder what you could possibly have done to bring about such a change. And then the following week, with no warning, they're back to being your best friends. The truth is that whenever someone has adventures in lands that are primarily based in imagination, there is a good chance that they will cause ripples throughout reality that can change things in ways both big and small. And one ripple touches another which touches another, and so on and so on, so that even though the adventure had nothing to do with you or anyone you know, it might cause a change to someone five ripples over whom you have never met and never will, but as the ripples move through reality, all of a sudden you're walking into a room and cannot remember why you came in there in the first place. It's not that you've forgotten; it's that the reason you went in there no longer exists. That, dear friends, is the truth of things, and if it seems that it makes the world frightening and uncertain, well, take heart in the fact that you're reading about it in something called a "novel" which generally means fiction which generally means made up. So you can just tell yourself that we're making all this up and the world isn't really as scarily fluid as all that. That should make you feel better. As for the rest of you who are willing to realize that everything we're saying makes perfect sense, be aware that you will probably wind up having to see a psychiatrist, if you're not already.)

"What about the imaginations?" said Mary with sudden urgency. "Where are they?"

"Imaginations?" chorused the parents.

Not wanting to take the time to explain matters, Mary saw the red button on the desk right where it had been. She slapped it and the great locking cogs started to turn. There was no sign of the wrench that she had thrown into it, which she found odd, but no odder than anything else she had run into in recent days. She thought to look up and saw that the skylight was repaired. It was simple clear glass now with sunlight coming through.

The doors swung open and it was only at that moment that she remembered the Furry Furies waiting on the other side to tear into them. Other things had changed, but what if they had not—?

Instead she was surprised, and yet somehow not surprised, to see several members of the Old Guard—including the sergeant—standing there, snapping to attention, saluting briskly. Unfortunately the captain was not among them. Mary had a depressing feeling that he would not be returning. "Do you require any assistance?" said the sergeant.

"No, we'll be fine. Purl...do you remember the way down to—?"

"Absolutely," said Purl. "I'll come with you. I want to make sure this all ends well."

"Thank you."

Mary picked up the now lifeless plush lion, stared at it for a moment, and then kissed it gently. Then she slid it into her knapsack and eased her arms through the loops, slinging it back on. She noticed that Purl's parents were staring at their daughter. "Problem?"

"I seem to remember her as being...very different," said her father.

"Yes, I'm sure you do," and Mary's jaw tightened. "And you abandoned the girl that she was. It was Purl's quest, and not my job to tell her differently, but I think what you did was terrible. I think it was evil. So she wasn't perfect. So she had problems. Lots of daughters do. You don't run away from them. You don't leave them on their own. The fact that she came chasing after you...it was more than you deserved. It was more than she should have had to do. It just proves what you should have known from the beginning:

that she was always able to care. She just had trouble getting to it. And you could have helped her, but you left her behind. And if she came all this way just to tell you how much she hates you for doing so, and to spit in your face, I wouldn't blame her in the least. And I think you better start being prepared to spend the rest of your lives making it up to her."

The king and queen were proud people, very proud, and were not accustomed to being spoken to in such a manner. But all they did was tilt their heads in acknowledgment of her words.

She then walked out of the room, Purl hurrying behind her. As they made their way down to the corral, Purl said, "You didn't have to say all that to them."

"Yes, I did. Because you were forgiving them far too quickly."

"It wasn't a matter of forgiving. Don't you remember? I wanted to find them so they could tell me how I should feel about it, so I could write it down here." She produced her list, flipped through it, then shrugged and tore it up. "Silly idea," she said, allowing the pieces of paper to flutter through her fingers.

"Still," said Mary, "It was unacceptable. You were too generous."

"Hunh. I didn't think I was capable of generosity," said Purl.

"Well, now you know."

"I thought you didn't like me."

"I thought you didn't like me."

"It wasn't a matter of not liking," said Purl. "I just didn't see the point of being friends with you. Or with anyone."

"And now you see the point?"

"I think it's because more can be accomplished with friends."

"That's a perfectly valid reason," said Mary. "And I guess...I guess it makes sense that everything came together when it did. Because whatever we look like on the outside..."

"Our blood and tears look exactly the same," said Purl.

"Yes. They do."

"But...just so you know...my blood is royal and yours isn't, so..."

Mary stopped, turned, stared at Purl...

...and then laughed and shook her head. "Okay. I give up. I *still* don't understand you."

"And I don't have to explain myself to you."

"And that's my problem, not yours."

"See!" said Purl triumphantly. "You *do* understand."

Still shaking her head, Mary pushed through the door and was hit with the same bright sunlight. And in front of her was the corral, just as they had left it. And standing just outside the corral, waiting for her as if it had been expecting her, was Anna's imagination.

"Not everything changed," said Purl.

"No. I guess this was something I had to take care of myself. Open the gate to the corral."

Purl did as Mary requested while Mary, with the Palomino's assistance, managed to clamber up onto its back. Standing in front of the open gate, Purl shouted in what Mary felt was a very queenly voice, "You are all free to depart. None will stop you. None will harass you. Return to those from whom you were untimely ripped and bring greatness to the world. Follow her," and she pointed at Mary, "and she will lead you truly." Then Purl turned to Mary and said, "What about the *Argo?*"

Mary didn't hesitate. "You keep it."

Purl was clearly stunned. "Truly?"

"I figure I have a better chance of finding another refrigerator box than you do. You can use it to come visit me if you wish."

Purl extended her hand and Mary gripped it firmly. "I was right. You asked me what I wanted, and I said I would know it when I saw it. I have finally realized. It is all this. My parents, a place in the world...and you in my life. I have that all, and I am content, for you...were a splendid sidekick."

Mary laughed. "So were you."

Then she snapped the reins of the Palomino and drove it forward. Immediately the rest of the imaginations followed.

It would later be said that the whole of Afrasia trembled under the beating of the feet or hooves or what have you of all those imaginations at once.

They thundered out of the great city.

They thundered across the plains, and through the mountains, and through the jungle, and every creature large and small scrambled to get out of their way. They thundered through the land of the Galoots, not to mention the land of the Yips, the land of the Nogoods, and the land of the Great Screaming Wazoos, none of which Mary had had occasion to visit before and none of which she really regretted not staying to see. They thundered to the very edge of Afrasia, where a great and vast ocean awaited them, and onto the surface of the ocean they ran, and then stormed across it. The waters churned beneath them, and the spray was in Mary's face, slicking down her hair, and she laughed in delight and petted the Palomino and urged it onward, ever onward.

And then she noticed that some of the imaginations were starting to fall away, the herd thinning out. They were heading off in various directions and she realized that, of course, naturally, they were not all destined for the same place. Instead they were galloping toward their respective owners, and perhaps there were a few living in the same country and city where Mary resided, but not all of them. And soon there was only one other animal alongside her, a sleek and beautiful lioness, sprinting alongside and keeping pace effortlessly. At one point the lioness looked squarely at Mary and then let out a beautiful, elegant roar, and Mary wondered why the lioness seemed like the most lovely animal she had ever seen. It even seemed vaguely familiar to her, although she couldn't fathom why. Part of her yearned for the lioness to be her very own, but she knew it belonged to someone else, who would doubtless be thrilled to have it back.

The Palomino continued to gallop, not slowing in the slightest. If anything, it appeared to be speeding up, gaining greater strength with every passing moment.

Amazingly, Mary found herself beginning to get tired. She shouldn't have been surprised; she had lost consciousness several times, but that was hardly the same as getting a proper sleep. But she was certain that this was not a good time to fall asleep. What if she slipped off the horse? Would it realize she had tumbled clear of it? Would it even hear the splash? Being stranded in a strange ocean with no hope of rescue wasn't exactly the way she wanted this adventure to end.

And yet the constant rocking of the horse was definitely lulling her.

She decided the best thing to do would be to rest her eyes, just for a few moments. Certainly the horse didn't require her to guide it; it knew precisely where it was going. She didn't have to see.

Mary closed her eyes.

The next thing she knew she was tumbling headfirst onto a carpeted floor.

She looked around in momentary confusion and then twisted around to see what had happened. She saw, lying on its side, a purple rocking horse that she now remembered was a fixture in Anna's room. Apparently it had just fallen over.

Anna was lying in bed and she sat up abruptly, jolted awake by the sound of Mary crashing to the floor. She stared at her friend, bewildered, caught in that strange place between sleeping and wakefulness when you first wake up but are trying to decide if you're still dreaming. The first light of dawn was beginning to encroach upon the horizon, visible through the eastern window in Anna's room. She saw that Anna was wearing the same bedclothes she had on when she'd last seen her, and realized that she'd been right. Time indeed did pass at a different rate in Afrasia. She had made it back before morning's light.

The thud was enough to bring Anna's parents running into the room. Her mother, Helen, and her father, whose name we still haven't remembered, gaped in astonishment. "Mary! What are you doing here? Why are you on the floor? What on earth happened to your clothes...?"

"*It's back!*" shrieked Anna so piercingly that her father grabbed at his ears and immediately complained that the child would simply not be satisfied until she deafened him. Anna ignored him, rolling out of bed onto the floor and crawling toward Mary. "It's back! It's back! I can feel it! Thank you, thank you, *thank you*, whatever you did, thank you!" and she covered Mary's face with kisses to the point where Mary was starting to get a little self-conscious about it.

Helen naturally called Mary's parents immediately, and by the time they made it over, the girls were happily engaged in a mutual game involving imagining all sorts of things that we will not describe to you now save to say that it was rather involved and only two girls with overactive imaginations could possibly have come up with it in the first place. Mary had changed into an old dress of Anna's to replace the torn clothing she had been wearing, and when Helen had asked what in the world had happened to her outfit, Mary had simply said, "I grew up very quickly," and Helen had sighed, "Yes, yes, children have a habit of doing that."

Colleen and Patrick thanked Anna's parents for calling them

so promptly, and Anna's parents, in turn, thanked them for whatever in the world Mary had done that had so completely turned Anna's spirits around. Mary tried to figure out just how upset her parents were as they led her to the automobile. She climbed into the back seat and they said nothing the entire drive home, and nothing as they led her into the house, and nothing as they brought her up to her room and then closed the door behind them.

And then, very softly, Colleen sank to her knees and began to sob.

It twisted up Mary's stomach to see this, because no child likes to see one of their parents crying, since only children are supposed to do that, not parents, and worst of all is when you're the one who made them cry. Then Colleen threw her arms wide and Mary ran right to her and hugged her tightly, and her mother rocked back and forth, saying her name over and over.

Patrick, all business, sat down on the floor to join them and said very simply, "Where did you go?"

"You wouldn't believe me," said Mary, whose face was slick with her mother's tears.

"Oh, you would be astounded what I would believe," said her father.

So she told them.

She told them everything, without leaving out a single detail, including how she nearly died and only the sacrifice of one childish ghost managed to save her. The entire time she spoke, she kept waiting for one or the other of them to interrupt her or stop her or tell her to stop making such things up.

And when she finally concluded, her father took her single hand in his and said, "Your intentions were good and worthy, Mary...but you must not run off like that again. There's only so many times that your poor mother and I can handle this sort of..."

"So many times?" Mary tilted her head at the way he said that. "What does that mean? I've never done this before."

Her father looked uncomfortably at her mother and then cleared his throat. "Actually...you may find this hard to believe, but something similar happened with your brother a long time ago. For that matter, you also have a rather odd uncle who has had a bit to do with magic and such. We never told you about it because, frankly, we didn't want to give you any ideas. But it appears the ideas show up whether we allow for them or not."

"I would very much like to hear about that," said Mary.

"I'll tell you about it some other time," said Patrick.

"Or..." Colleen said slowly, "I could tell it."

This drew strange looks from both Mary and her father, because they both knew full well that Patrick was the storyteller of the family and that Colleen, at best, merely put up with flights of fancy without ever getting involved herself in the slightest. "You, Mother?" said Mary, as if she were not sure that she had heard properly.

Even Colleen seemed surprised, as if someone else's voice was coming from her mouth. "Why...yes. I...I think I could. In fact, there are...there are so many stories I could tell!" and she spoke with increasing excitement. "Stories of...of pixies, and pirates battling great sea creatures, and far off lands of enchantment that you can only reach by walking on rainbows, and elves that live right next door wearing giant human suits, and selkies and mermaids and...my lord, Patrick!" and she looked to her husband in wonderment. "It's...it's as if I remembered things I did not even know I had forgotten! It just makes me want to...to..."

And Mary suddenly understood. "Roar?" she suggested.

"Yes!" Colleen cried out with delight, and she dropped to all fours and roared with the exact same voice used by the lioness that had been speeding alongside Mary on that long journey home. The lioness that had seemed ever so familiar to Mary, although she had not, for the life of her, been able to figure out why. Her mother's imagination, presumably stolen away from her so many, many years ago that she hadn't even recalled that it was gone, and was now delighting in its unexpected return.

And Mary Dear, laughing with more joy than she had ever known, went to all fours as well and, with the soul of a young lion within her, roared back.

About the Author

Peter David is a prolific author whose career, and continued popularity, spans nearly two decades. He has worked in every conceivable media: Television, film, books (fiction, non-fiction and audio), short stories, and comic books, and acquired followings in all of them.

In the literary field, Peter has had over seventy novels published, including numerous appearances on the *New York Times* Bestsellers List. His novels include *Tigerheart*, *Darkness of the Light*, *Sir Apropos of Nothing* and the sequel *The Woad to Wuin*, *Knight Life*, *Howling Mad*, and the Psi-Man adventure series. He is the co-creator and author of the bestselling *Star Trek: New Frontier* series for Pocket Books, and has also written such Trek novels as *Q-Squared*, *The Siege*, *Q-in-Law*, *Vendetta*, *I, Q* (with John deLancie), *A Rock and a Hard Place* and *Imzadi*. He produced the three *Babylon 5* Centauri Prime novels, and has also had his short fiction published in such collections as *Shock Rock*, *Shock Rock II*, and *Otherwere*, as well as *Isaac Asimov's Science Fiction Magazine* and *The Magazine of Fantasy and Science Fiction*.

Peter's comic book resume includes an award-winning twelve-year run on *The Incredible Hulk*, and he has also worked on such varied and popular titles as *Supergirl, Young Justice, Soulsearchers and Company, Aquaman, Spider-Man, Spider-Man 2099, X-Factor, Star Trek, Wolverine, The Phantom, Sachs & Violens, The Dark Tower*, and many others. He has also written comic book related novels, such as *The Incredible Hulk: What Savage Beast*, and co-edited *The Ultimate Hulk* short story collection. Furthermore, his opinion column, "But I Digress . . . ," has been running in the industry trade newspaper *The Comic Buyers's Guide* for nearly a decade, and in that time has been the paper's consistently most popular feature and was also collected into a trade paperback edition.

Peter is also the writer for two popular video games: *Shadow Complex* and *Spider-Man: Edge of Time*.

Peter is the co-creator, with popular science fiction icon Bill Mumy (of *Lost in Space* and *Babylon 5* fame) of the Cable Ace Award-nominated science fiction series *Space Cases*, which ran for two seasons on Nickelodeon. He has written several scripts for the Hugo Award winning TV series *Babylon 5*, and the sequel series, *Crusade*. He has also written several films for Full Moon Entertainment and co-produced two of them, including two installments in the popular *Trancers* series, as well as the science fiction western spoof *Oblivion*, which won the Gold Award at the 1994 Houston International Film Festival for best Theatrical Feature Film, Fantasy/Horror category.

Peter's awards and citations include: the Haxtur Award 1996 (Spain), Best Comic script; OZCon 1995 award (Australia), Favorite International Writer; Comic Buyers Guide 1995 Fan Awards, Favorite writer; Wizard Fan Award Winner 1993; Golden Duck Award for Young Adult Series (Starfleet Academy), 1994; UK Comic Art Award, 1993; Will Eisner Comic Industry Award, 1993. He lives in New York with his wife, Kathleen, and their daughter, Caroline.

Inside the old House called Tanglewood are the Doors: too numerous to count, made of the wood from the Norse World Tree Yggdrasil, leading to every time and place that ever was—or ever could be. A few rare children have the ability to step through such Doors. They are the Latchkeys, the Wardens, the protectors of Tanglewood and its Doors. But now many of the Doors have gone missing. And many have splintered. Those missing pieces must be restored for the Doors to be returned. And Splinters can be anywhere and assume any form. Almost like they don't want to be found. Read all about the Latchkeys and their exciting, thrilling, spooky adventures to places that were, places that might have been, and places that almost could be!

You thought you knew about King Arthur and his knights? Guess again!

Learn here, for the first time, the down-and-dirty royal secrets that plagued Camelot as told by someone who was actually there, and adapted by acclaimed *New York Times* bestseller Peter David. Full of sensationalism, startling secrets and astounding revelations, *The Camelot Papers* is to the realm of Arthur what the *Pentagon Papers* is to the military: something that all those concerned would rather you didn't see. What are you waiting for?

DuckBob Spinowitz has a problem. It isn't the fact that he has the head of a duck—the abduction was years ago and he's learned to live with it. But now those same aliens are back, and they claim they need his help! Can a man whose only talents are bird calls and bad jokes be expected to save the universe?

No Small Bills is the hilarious science fiction novel from award-winning, bestselling author Aaron Rosenberg. See why the NOOK Blog called it "an absurdly brilliant romp"—buy a copy and start laughing your tail feathers off today!

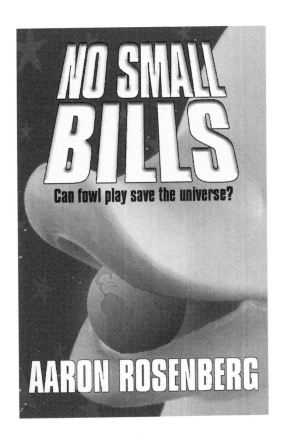

At the age of thirty-eight, Zeno Aristos has quit the NYPD and is trying to figure out what to do with his life. Then someone close to him is kidnapped by dark and cryptic forces. The deeper Zeno digs, the more he realizes he's dealing not with a mere earthly adversary but with an entity steeped in the deepest and most malevolent of ancient mysteries.

In *Fight the Gods*, Michael Jan Friedman takes a major creative step beyond the *Star Trek* novels, comic books, and television scripts with which his name has become synonymous, and braves the sinister rooftops and mystical back alleys of urban fantasy. Whatever you think you know of him or of his work...you ain't seen nothin' yet.

London, 1593. Christopher Marlowe, playwright, spy, and renowned womanizer, is desperately working on what could be his greatest play. But inspiration eludes him, until a chance encounter with a dark temptress rekindles his passion and the words start to flow with that famous passion.

But forces are arrayed against Marlowe. Something doesn't want him finishing, and Marlowe suspects there is a foul, unnatural agency at work. Can the incandescent playwright stop the chaos before it overwhelms the entire city?

This new occult thriller from bestselling authors Aaron Rosenberg and Steven Savile combines Elizabethan theatre, ancient mythology, and ageless seduction to create a dark, gripping tale that is both as old as time itself and wholly original.

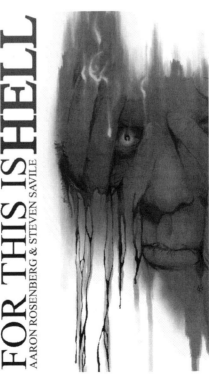

On the Damned World, it's every man for himself. Only it's not just mankind who inhabits this crumbling, desolate world. Twelve very different species, creatures out of Earth's mythology that live on the land, in the sea, and underground, vie for survival in a hostile land. Humanity is nearly extinct. But now the Twelve Races have discovered that their own fortunes are inextricably linked with the remnants of the human race.

As a result, a young slave girl named Jepp may hold the key to the future of the world. But can she and her new companions survive long enough to save everyone . . . or will they damn the world instead?

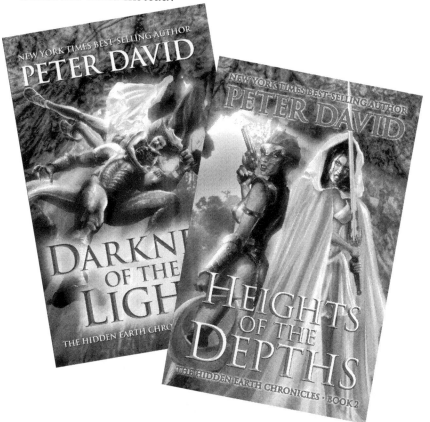

It's 2012. Maxtla Colhua is an Investigator for the Empire—an Aztec Empire that successfully repelled Hernan Cortes in 1603 and now stretches from one end of what we call the Americas to the other. But now it is the Last Sun, and someone has decided to punctuate it with a series of grisly murders reminiscent of the pagan sacrifices of ancient times. Can Maxtla find the killer before his city is ripped apart? Then he has to locate the missing star of a burtal Aztec ball game, the idol of millions. But to do that Maxtla will have to challenge the most powerful men and women in the Empire—or see the streets run red with blood.

Aztlan is a pair of murder mysteries set in an exciting world that never was but could have been!

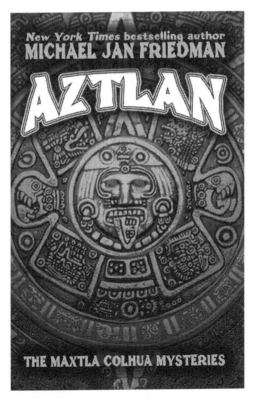

Meet Vince Hammond. He has a secret that, if his mother finds out, she will absolutely kill him.

No, he's not dating a girl she'd hate. No, he's not gay.

He's a vampire. And Mom is a vampire hunter. And all of his friends are vampire hunters. And his fiancee is a vampire hunter, and so are his future in-laws.

Need an antidote to every other vampire novel out there? Then you're going to want to be *Pulling Up Stakes*. After putting a silver bullet in werewolves in his classic *Howling Mad*, *New York Times* Bestseller Peter David now sinks his teeth into vampire lore, with bloody good results.

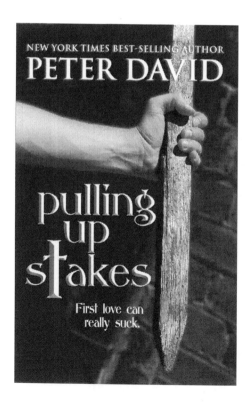

Hotdog pilot Marcus Powell has been selected to test Taurus Enterprises' *Crossline* and its newly developed warp thrusters, which, if successful, will revolutionize space travel as we know it. But during his psychedelic jaunt across the stars, Powell is forced into a parallel universe, where he finds himself at the center of a civil war he may have been destined for all along!

Teamed up with a gorgeous, trigger-happy rebel leader, a pot-smoking Shaman, a crafty pie maker, and a weary soldier who hates his guts, Powell must survive a cross-country rescue mission and his own trippy vision quests long enough for his wife and young daughter to outsmart Taurus' reclusive CEO, whose own secrets may prevent Powell from ever making it back to Earth.

From author Russ Colchamiro, *Crossline* is a hallucinogenic, action-packed romp across time, space, and dimension that asks the question: once you cross the line, can you ever really go back?

Made in the USA
Lexington, KY
13 September 2013